I0771998

RED LINE

Chicago Horror Stories

edited by

Michael W. Phillips Jr.

Red Line: Chicago Horror Stories © 2025 by Agita Publishing
Agita edition, June 2026
All stories © 2025 by their respective authors.
Cover art © 2025 by Daimon Hampton
Print book and ebook design and layout by Michael W. Phillips Jr.

Published by
Agita Publishing (formerly From Beyond Press) | Chicago, IL
agitapublishing.com
mike@agitapublishing.com
Instagram @agita.publishing, Bluesky @agitapublishing.bsky.social

ISBN: 979-8-9875743-9-3
Library of Congress Control Number: 2025941291

CONTENTS

★ ★ ★ ★

EDITOR'S NOTE

Michael W. Phillips Jr.

'**ve lived in Chicago for half my life. It's my home, more than any other place I've ever lived. I couldn't dream of living anywhere else.

It was important to me that this be a book about Chicago, by Chicagoans. Twelve of the authors in this book live in the city; two were born and raised here but now live elsewhere; five are from the suburbs, but their knowledge and love of this city is apparent on every page.

It was also important to me that this book reflect the gorgeous patchwork quilt of ethnicities and gender identifications that make up my beautiful city. I was not entirely successful—despite my best efforts, there are no stories here by writers of East Asian descent. That is my fault and does not reflect on the talents of those communities. I should have tried harder. Next time.

I hope that Chicagoans who read this book see their city reflected accurately, and that people in other parts of the country get a sense of the immense talent of Chicago writers.

This book would not have been possible without our Kickstarter backers, especially the top-level backers: Kenny Endlich, Eriksen, Suzette Pierson, Ian Chung, Clifford Clark, Adgee "Horror Is My Special Interest" Harville, Michael H Turner, Mason Ritter, Elizabeth Aspbury, Sir Ogelthorpe Jigglepants, Teresa B. Ardrey, Brit, Alan Lastufka, Coyote Jack Wilson, AJ Rumpelstiltskin, Senior Chief Schilling, Alejandro L. Alvarez, and the person who wished to be credited as "Delay, Deny, Depose. Take the power back." Hear, hear.

From Beyond Press is donating 10% of sales to Brave Space Alliance, a south side Chicago center that provides services, programs, and an affirming space where trans and LGBQ+ people are centered. Learn more about them at bravespacealliance.org.

PREFACE: SAINT MAKER

Cynthia Pelayo

We go looking for saints sometimes in this town, or sometimes they go looking for us in the form of devils.

Let's first talk about these saints. There's Julia Buccola Petta, buried in Mt. Carmel Cemetery. She died in childbirth and was buried in her wedding dress with her stillborn son. For years after her death, her mother had nightmares of Julia in that grave in which Julia pleaded to be dug out.

It took six years, but they finally exhumed her. What they found was her fully preserved body. Her son had completely decomposed, but not Julia: she looked just like she did the day she was buried, a woman asleep.

Her mother quickly snapped a picture, and in 1927 a new tomb was raised, a sculpture of Julia in her wedding dress. On the front of the new tomb there are two pictures of Julia: one of her the day she married and the other of her in her coffin when her mother finally dug her out. You could say that maybe she hadn't decomposed because of the soil, or something, but then explain her son? Believe what you will, but her mother believed in "The Italian Bride," that her physical preservation was proof of her incorruptibleness, her saintliness.

I visited Julia in my own wedding dress, late one day before the cemetery gates closed. I stood barefoot at her grave wondering if the close proximity to her saintliness would cleanse me of my sins, but when I looked down a pistol was still strapped to my waist. The skirt of my dress was still speckled in blood.

In Chicago we do what we must, and as we do, sometimes a prayer rests on our lips.

Then there's little Mary Alice Quinn, buried at Holy Sepulcher, "Chicago's Miracle Child," another unofficial saint. Mary died in 1935, but was said to always be whispering little prayers to St. Therese of Liseaux. Mary claimed to hear voices, experience visions, and before her death at fourteen from a chronic illness, she told her parents that she would return to heal people. Many Chicagoans, and people from across the globe, claim that she has healed them. Sometimes Mary is seen walking along the cemetery. Her gravesite is dotted with flowers and lined with toys. Visitors say she's granted them miracles and soothed them of their ailments after visiting with her, and after being overcome by the smell of roses around her grave.

Believing little Mary is a healer, I rushed to her one day myself, a deep gash in my shoulder. It stung so bad the blade hit bone, but no matter how much I screamed as I pulled out the knife, I kept reminding myself that the person who dealt this regretful blow would never get an aim at me again. I left him slumped over on Lower Wacker Drive. He'd surely decompose there before anyone checked on him.

In thinking about bones, I went looking for bones.

There are quite a few at the nearby Shrine of All Saints in Morton Grove. A fingerbone of St. Martha of Bethany. A part of the jaw and two teeth of St. Christina, a Virgin and a Martyr. The skull and the fibula of St. Rema. A lock of hair of St. Therese of Lisieux, little Mary Alice Quinn's favored saint. The shrine also claims to display a piece of the Holy Shroud of Turin, and a part of the veil of the Most Blessed Virgin Mary.

It's a bit of a ramshackle of a place, the second largest collection of relics in the country, after one in Pittsburgh. It's like Chicagoans want to believe in the supernatural, in more. Here, there are statues and paintings and prints, and various body parts in varying brass and gold and silver receptacles displayed on wooden shelves affixed to a cinderblock wall. It's just a cold room with faded purple cushion office chairs. I wound up here after some guy returned fire on the Eisenhower. When you see a car spin out and crash out like that, all there is to do is to keep driving, with prayers to anything and anyone that you'll get away.

If you're looking for a shrine in the city, then there's The National Shrine of Cabrini, named for America's first saint, who lived, worked, and died in Chicago. It was in 1905 when Mother Cabrini founded Columbus Hospital in Chicago. She spent a lot of time in a small chapel built there. Over a hundred years later Columbus Hospital closed and in Chicago fashion, condos were set to be built in its place. The hospital was demolished but the shrine was maintained and preserved. It's these little miracles that reminds me that Chicagoans sure are blessed with a supernatural sort of perseverance.

If you'd like to visit the room where Cabrini died, or one of her relics—a femur—you can.

I didn't hurt anyone before visiting Mother Cabrini. I've got a little bit more respect than you might think.

There are shrines on our street corners and intersections: white crosses, yellow plastic flowers, deflated mylar balloons, novena candles, and teddy bears for those shot and killed or struck by a driver. There are white painted bicycles, ghost bikes, serving as both memorials of those killed in fatal cycling accidents and haunting reminders to motorists to be mindful and share the road.

In Chicago, anything can become a shrine. Sometimes we'll allow ourselves to go all out and build a little shrine of La Virgen de Guadalupe in front of our houses. There's Our Lady of the Underpass where many set tables and flowers and pinned their petitions to the concrete walls.

There are then ladies who weep and whimper, linked arm and arm in protest—a moving holy site, yet all they demand is for the killing to stop. We bury our dead and raise our dead. We construct sculptures, ship in bones for veneration, work around demolished people, and leave trinkets out in the rain, all to acknowledge that at one time someone existed connected to this thing, and perhaps in being at this place and time, in leaving an offering, or merely being in the presence of a strip of their remains connects us to them. And maybe we hope somehow that in establishing that connection to something saintly, we can wash away the killing.

There are also the saints of the slaughtered men of St. Valentine's Day. Each one lined up against a brick wall and at once sprayed with machine gun fire. That building we tore down, but each time I walk by it, or drive past it, I make sure to place my hand over my heart, just a small gesture, it's all in kind, a gangster to a gangster.

Parts of Chicago no longer exist, the neighborhood's name nearly fading into the pages of history books—The Levee. Here saints sang and danced and drank and more, and shortly after the son of a wealthy man died in a brothel the neighborhood was razed and all evidence that any of its saloons, brothels, or madams ever existed was erased.

We do that around here too, make things disappear.

We're a little vindictive in parts: we'll stamp you out and try to make it seem as though you were never real, like a man named H.H. Holmes, he built a castle on the south side that many women entered and never left. There's also Adolph Luetgert, the once "sausage king" of Chicago, who dissolved his wife Luisa in a vat of lye at his sausage factory. Let's not forget the mobsters who went missing, a candy heiress too. A sad patch of land remains where the Dunning Asylum once stood. Lots of kids were told "Act right or you'll get sent off to Dunning." To this day when there's construction in the area crews still dig up bodies from the asylum's mass graves.

Still, ghosts rise up and saints and sinners haunt our bloodlines.

Chicago has devils too.

One story goes that a religious Italian girl married an atheist. When she tried to hang up a Catholic image in her house he tore it down and said that he'd rather have the Devil in his home than these superstitions, and well, that's what he got. When she gave birth, it was said to be a monstrosity, the devil himself. The woman brought the baby to Hull House and rumors soon spread, and lines quickly formed outside of people wanting to see the devil baby. No devil baby was ever produced for the crowds, but people say to this day two red eyes can be seen peering out from the attic windows.

That's what people say, but I know what I saw that night, one night, a long time ago.

There are stories of a man who killed nurses in their home. There are stories of another man who buried young men beneath his floorboards. There are stories of a group of men who drove around town dragging women into their van where they'd be ripped and torn to pieces. A lot of devils live here, so maybe that's why we need all of these relics and saints in hope to strike some sort of balance, or at least to not tip the scales.

A winged devil has appeared to some on the West and South Sides of the city. The Chicago Mothman some say. I call the idea cute. A creature with wings, standing about six to ten feet with a wingspan of ten feet. People said it looks like a massive owl, or bat. Its eyes are red or green or yellow or orange. Some have observed it screeching or screaming, flying across Lake Michigan, disappearing and reappearing. It's been seen at Northerly Island, in Fulton Market, West Town, and more. This one I haven't seen yet, but I'd like to. They call this one ominous, an omen, and I don't know what you can possibly warn Chicago about that we haven't already been through or seen ourselves.

Chicago is heaven and hell. We are above and we are below. A town that spins gold and bullet holes. A city that shut down for the funeral processions of hundreds killed in our river, in America's largest maritime disaster. A city where gangbangers have stormed funeral services of their rivals and dragged the corpse into the street, as they throw just one more series of blows.

There's a thread of viciousness that runs through our parts, yet there's a glimmer of holiness to it too.

LUCKY CHARMS

Sandra Jackson-Opoku

Nobody was running, nobody gunning. No one was halfway trying.

Sun spread down the darkening sky like butter in a skillet. A tepid lake breeze blew in from a mile away, but it was still too hot to be out bricking in the schoolyard. The boys shot a lazy hoop here and there, but their hearts weren't in the game.

The two of them did more trash-talking than one-on-one anyway. One insulted his partner's clumsy lay-up. That other boy, in turn, signified on the amorous misadventures of his best friend's mother.

Both were known by different names than those they'd been given. The one called Trey thought it sounded cooler than Tremaine. The other felt answering to a dead boy's name would make anyone look weak. If he'd been there back in the day, you best believe he'd have murked that Florida cracker before the man had a chance to murk him.

The boys didn't notice or chose to ignore the meeting point of their nicknames. There was the *Trey*, and then the *Von*. Like lynched Jesus in the tomb, the dead one was resurrected.

Von paused mid-shot, wiping his sweaty forehead against a bare arm. He aimed and let fly. The ball circled the rim and bounced back out. He rebounded and missed again.

"Gonna give it a rest, Von-Von?" Trey taunted, though he was three points behind. "I know you ain't ready for all this smoke. Take your ball and run home to Mama."

The beat-up basketball, in fact, belonged to Trey's older brother who knew him neither as Trey nor Tremaine. La Marcus called his brother Wreck for what it meant, or reckless, which was much the same.

Clumps of people began drifting over from the 47th Street L station. They didn't seem like the usual folks dragging home from a long day's work. These people moved in small, tight groups, picket signs against their shoulders. They appeared tired but happy. No, not happy. Energized.

"*George Floyd's life mattered.*" Von made out one of the signs. "You ain't even got to tell me."

The boys raised fists in solidarity, chanting along with passersby. "*No justice, no peace! No racist police!*"

"Man, we should have gone to that Black Lives Matter march," Trey complained. "I don't know why I even hang with you. You make me miss everything."

"They rerouted buses, the L train wasn't coming, and downtown is too far to walk. That's why."

"Just tell the truth, Von. Your mama wouldn't let you go."

They spotted a scrawny figure in the distance, shuffling across Wabash Avenue. Like a scarecrow on the move, it hunched over a broken hockey stick, leaning on it like a cane.

The man came closer, revealing a face so dirty you'd think he was a brother if not for that flaming auburn hair standing on end. A crooked *A* was splotched across his ragged shirt, a letter to match his hair color, unlike the matted beard and whiskers. Those might have belonged to a whole other person, so much lighter were they than the shade of red on his head.

The man trudged in their direction, oozing sweat and seething menace. He didn't match the mood of the marchers they'd just seen. Von Matthews felt an uneasy prickling at the back of his neck.

"Hey, Trey." He pointed. "Does old dude look like someone to you?"

"Yeah, he looks like a bum."

"But doesn't he remind you of that red-headed monster from the old horror movie?"

"What red-headed monster?"

"Aw, you know the one." Von wrinkled his forehead in thought, then snapped his fingers. "*Leprechaun in the Hood.*"

"Leprechaun, like Frosted Lucky Charms?"

"No, like 'I'm gonna murk you and take back all my gold.'"

Von didn't care to divulge his phobia. It would have made him look weak. He wasn't just afraid of leprechauns but any miniature monster—Chucky, Bride of Chucky, gremlins, that gruesome Annabelle doll.

Vampires or zombies, you saw them coming and could try to get out of their way. But little things that lurked in corners or hid under beds? Those were spooky as hell. Von was traumatized as a kid by the Snuggle Bear TV commercials. He wasn't even feeling Santa's little elves.

As the red-haired man came abreast of them, they could see he wasn't that old. Maybe he was homeless or high or hurt. Maybe he was just plain crazy.

The man shambled past the school sign, then stopped to look back at it. He didn't seem to be reading the words but frowning at the image of a Black man's head in profile.

"What place be this?" he demanded in a strange, creaky accent. "Who is such a naygur to have his face up on a broadside? Has he stolen someone's horse?"

"Can't you read? That's DuSable, it says so right there." Von didn't know what *naygur* meant but didn't like the sound of it.

"Aye? And where has he hidden the fur skins?"

"Oh, snap. The Leprechaun lost his treasure!" Trey laughed. "'Always after me Lucky Charms. The frosted oat cereal with sweet surprises.'"

"Hush up," Von muttered. "You see he ain't right in the head."

Ignoring him, Trey broke into song. "'Frosted Lucky Charms, they're magically delicious.'"

The man leaned so close they could see bloodshot streaks in his bleary green eyes.

"What place be this?" he repeated. "Where are the fur skins hidden?"

Von thought he sounded like that murderous movie monster who tore out people's guts with clawlike fingernails. He hugged the basketball to his belly and took two careful steps backward.

Trey hadn't seen *Leprechaun in the Hood*, so he didn't have the sense to be scared. Though, to tell the honest truth not much seemed to frighten that boy.

"'What place be this?' Man, you can't even talk straight. You better come correct when you speak to us. This is Chicago, not Po' White Trashistan."

Von snickered around the edge of his apprehension. "White Trashistan. You got jokes."

Though they turned up regularly at DuSable's school grounds, neither boy played high school basketball. They were still at the tail end of seventh grade. Trey knew the Panthers' fight song, though. "Go back, go back, go back to the woods. Your team ain't nothing, and your coach is no good."

"Watch yourself, Trey," Von warned again. "Don't be riling up no crazy person."

The man raised his broken stick. "You dare mock a White man? I have a mind to give you both a good thrashing and clap you in the stocks."

"Nigga, I wish you would." Trey could surely recognize a White man, even one covered in grime. But Tremaine Dickerson didn't give a damn. He'd call anyone nigga, regardless.

Nay-gur. Von rolled the word around his mind.

Wait, what had old boy been saying? Oh, hell no! It was one thing for Trey to call out the word. It was another for some rag-gedy-ass Leprechaun-looking vagrant to fling it at them with the hardest "r" he'd ever heard. Like he was a danged pirate or so.

Rage overcame Von's reticence. "You better watch your mouth, or I'll take that hockey stick and shove it where the sun don't shine."

If Trey and Von didn't think he was crazy before, they certainly knew it now. The man dropped to his knees in front of old DuSable High. Kneeling beneath the school sign, he pounded the sidewalk with his fists, swinging his shaggy head back and forth.

"'Tis a dream, tis only a dream," he growled. "Soon I shall awaken and put things back to rights."

Trey smirked into the palm of his hand. "Can you believe this shit?"

Von stared in nameless dread at the grown man in full tantrum mode. He wasn't sure why this scared him. It wasn't like old dude was going to jump somebody, right? Von could probably take him, and Trey would fight anybody. With two against one, no contest.

Leprechauns were vicious little assholes, though, hoarding their pots of gold. Maybe Von would have been angry too, with folks trying to steal his shit. He remembered the hideous green movie monster doffing his top hat to show a bristling thatch of red. Von could almost hear the menacing sneer: *I'm a leprechaun, me dear.*

Von's palms began to sweat, and the basketball slipped from his hands. It bounced twice, then rolled over to the kneeling, howling redhead.

Trey Dickerson crept forward to retrieve his brother's ball. Von Matthews turned and took off down Wabash, quick enough to create distance but not enough to seem weak.

The hem of her linsey-woolsey dress dragged in the dust, but Suzanne did not notice.

Summer had come early to Shikaakwa Village. It was too warm to light a parlor fire, so the grate stayed cold all day. Suzanne squatted on the hearthstone, tracing images in ashes. So absorbed was she in the task that she barely heard the knocking. It was only when her mother went to the door that she looked up to see who was there.

A brisk lake breeze seemed to usher three men through the door. Well, in truth, they were two men and one tall boy. They had all removed their boots and left them out on the doorstep. Papa and François entered the foyer, followed by Suzanne's brother. Like his father, the boy's given name was Jean, but everyone called him Cadet.

"Maman, the deer is skinned and butchered, hung in the curing shed," he proudly announced. "We found a nice fat buck, full of meat."

When Maman flicked a spot of mud from the boy's cheek, Cadet shied away. Since he'd turned twelve, her brother pretended to hate being touched.

"I am not a baby, Maman," he whined, sounding exactly like a baby. Cadet hung his coat on a peg and climbed the ladder to his room in the overhead loft.

"That deer did lead us on a merry chase," Jean Sr. joked, hanging François's frock coat beside his own. "He seemed headed straight to Michilimackinac before he tired of the chase. Any further, he'd have led us to your front door."

"That place was once your home too, my friend."

Papa flinched in remembered pain. "Please, François. Do not remind me."

Jean Baptiste Pointe du Sable rarely hunted anymore since their trading post and larder were always well stocked. They harvested nearby waters, taking bass and sunfish from the river, trout and smelt from the lake.

Hogs grunted in the pigsty. Chickens pecked about the yard and lay eggs in the henhouse. A herd of cows gave them milk and meat, and a mill ground their wheat and corn. Horses grazed in pasture, though these weren't eaten unless a pack of wolves were prowling or a coyote tried to take down a foal.

Yet their mother, Kitihawa, at times yearned for the taste of wild game—venison, raccoon, rabbit, turkey. Buffalo, when they could find it. That morning father and son took bows and tomahawks and led their visitor out beyond the marshlands that skirted the village.

François Thiam had come down from Mackinac, Jean having encouraged him to gather his family and resettle in Shikaakwa. François was there to visit and seemed to like what he saw.

Kitihawa smiled at Jean Sr. ever so faintly. One blink, and it might have been missed. She touched Papa's arm in welcome and returned to the kitchen. Suzanne knew her mother worried whenever her husband and son were away. Their village was safe enough, but trouble stirred in the outskirts.

Jean Sr. and François entered the parlor. Both men were handsome in their ways. Jean Baptiste Pointe du Sable was sand-colored and wiry, François Thiam earth-dark and barrel-chested.

François looked around as he always did, clicking his tongue in admiration—the gleaming pine-planked floors, thick woolen carpets, the sturdy Directoire furniture. Oil-painted portraits and landscapes hung on the walls. The beechwood piano Papa had shipped from St. Louis held pride of place against the far corner.

"Well done, my friend, well done. You are living like a White," François Thiam murmured. Then he turned and waved to Suzanne. "Bonjour, mademoiselle la professeure. Je te vois."

Whenever he called her "Miss Professor," and said to her, "I see you," Suzanne knew M. Thiam wished to hear her speaking English.

Most people in Shikaakwa used various forms of French, smoothing over differences so they understood one another. Muskrat French, Illinois Country, Creole, or the joual of Québec, New France. Others spoke the Potawatomi of Kitihawa's people or Native languages like Ojibwe and Odawa. Only a few spoke English, though their numbers were growing. François thought it clever that such a small child could master this difficult tongue.

English came easily to Suzanne. When their father managed a British trading post on the banks of the Pine River in Michigan Territory, she and Cadet took lessons with an itinerant Jesuit. Even when the family came to settle at Shikaakwa, their father encouraged them to keep their English, "for one cannot have too many tongues in one's mouth." Jean himself had several, including smatterings of Native dialects. He said Shikaakwa meant "stink onions."

"A pleasant good evening to you, Oncle François." Suzanne scrambled to her feet and dipped into a curtsy. She always called him "uncle," though they were unrelated by blood. Suzanne was reaching to offer the firm handshake her father had taught her when Maman came rushing from the kitchen, wiping fingers on her apron.

"Suzanne du Sable, mind your hands!" Kitihawa turned to their visitor. "Please forgive her, François. Always playing in the dust, this one."

"Sorry, Maman," Suzanne dipped her head in embarrassment. "Sorry, Oncle François."

"No need for apology," François reassured her, "for artists aren't known to be tidy. I should know. I married one."

"Artist?" Maman scoffed. "Will art finish this one's chores or bring her a husband when time is ready? Better she should learn something practical."

Maman thought every Potawatomi female should know how to embroider with porcupine quill, weave baskets from sweetgrass, and string purple and white wampum beads. Women and girls made things to use, not to hang on walls and decorate shelves.

"Art takes many forms, Kitihawa." Jean Baptiste crouched to examine the images stirred in ash. "Are these rabbits, Suzanne?"

"Mais oui," she nodded proudly, then remembered to speak English. "Why, yes, Papa. A family of rabbits, they are mother, father, and two little kits."

"Finger drawing is a place to begin, but a serious artist needs tools." François removed a buckskin pouch from his pocket. "Madame Thiam has crafted you a paintbrush, charcoals, and palette of colors."

"C'est vrai?" Suzanne exclaimed. "What a very kind auntie she is. What are they made from?"

"Berries, fruit skins, tea leaves, charcoal . . ."

". . . charmed with African magic, no doubt." Papa winked.

"Magic!" François laughed. "Ah, non. Pas du tout. My dear wife would shudder to hear such a thing."

Before François Thiam purchased her freedom, Delphine served a Québec City order of Augustine nuns. With their cloister of enslaved postulants, they supported the convent by stringing castor seeds on silk thread for rosaries, hand painting prayer cards of Jesus, Mary, and the saints, and boiling sap in large copper pots for maple walnut penuche.

Unlike François, who prayed to Allah, his wife was a strict Roman Catholic. She barely tolerated his practice of Islam and flinched at any talk of witchcraft.

"By your leave, François." Jean smiled. "I am known to be a tease. I can see this is no witch's wand but boar's bristle tied to a twig for a child's paintbrush. I will shave some sheets of birchbark for Suzanne's practice work. In the next parcel from St. Louis, perhaps there'll be proper paints and canvases."

"M. Thiam, your family is much too kind," Kitihawa said, then turned to face her daughter. "Thank uncle for the gifts, and offer your regards to Madame Thiam. Then leave the parlor so your father can visit with his guest."

The horsehair settee and wooden bureau were grouped around the unlit fireplace opposite the kitchen. While her mother prepared the meal, Suzanne crouched behind the settee, unpacking her art supplies and eavesdropping on the men's talk.

"You are ready for the Kokomo trading expedition?" her father asked. "We leave first light of day."

"Since when did the Miami camp so far from their hunting grounds?"

"Ah, but Kokomo was once a Miami village before the warring Yankees, British, and Odawa came. Among them all, it is the Yankee that I fear."

Suzanne had heard of wars that raged among different kinds of Whites and some of the Native tribes. A group of English had already settled in their village. Suzanne didn't know if they were British or Yankee, for all English speakers seemed the same to her. Yet, as wealthy and powerful as Jean Baptiste Pointe du Sable was, she wondered why her father should fear any man.

He seemed to answer the unspoken question in her head. "They do not respect me though I am headman here. They look at a Black man and only see a slave."

"And don't forget, a spy."

"C'est vrai, François. The British did denounce me as a Yankee sympathizer."

"Ah! Just imagine." François had heard this all before but was ready to hear it again.

"My wife's people were loyal to the crown. The Potawatomi fought right alongside King George's army. Sometimes, they even fought *for* them. Yet, the British came to seize my property at Rivière du Chemin, pack me off to Fort Michilimackinac, and hold me captive four long years. You know this all too well, François, for it is how we met."

François shook his head sadly. "Some treachery knows no bounds. But why do you fear the Yankees when the British misused you so?"

"Écoute-moi bien! Mark my words. Now that war is won, Americans are moving steadily westward. Shikaakwa is in their sights. Michilimackinac will not be far behind."

"What do they want from us?"

"Whatever there is for the taking. Land, fur skins, power. Maybe our livestock and weapons. Maybe even our women and children. However grasping and acquisitive, the Yankees are an enterprising lot. They have built great cities, yes? Boston, New York, Philadelphia. Surely you know of them."

"None finer than Québec City," François insisted, proud of the place that once held him captive.

"Ah, so much grander. Huge stone buildings. Fancy carriages driving paved brick roads. Gas lights that make the night seem like day. In time, they'll arrive in great numbers, bringing with them all their greed and enterprise."

"Shikaakwa will become a much different place, Michilimackinac also. Will we be the better or worse for it, I wonder?"

"Only time will tell, my friend."

Kitihawa called Suzanne to help set the table. With the clinking of cutlery and clack of crockery, Suzanne could no longer overhear the men's conversation.

"When will Papa and Cadet return?" Suzanne yawned. Two days had passed since the men and boy left for Kokomo.

"Do not worry. They will be back before you know it." Maman tucked the coverlet around her daughter. "Now sleep, mon enfant."

As soon as her mother left her, Suzanne threw off the covers. She didn't need the bedclothes. The May weather was still summery. She took a charcoal stick from the buckskin pouch she had brought into bed with her. By the crescent moonlight slanting through the curtains, she sketched onto the wall the figure of a deer nibbling a bough of flowering dogwood.

Suzanne flinched at a noise outside the cabin, perhaps a cone falling from the pine tree. Then, a sudden flash of green light obscured the waxing moonlight. She giggled with delight to see her charcoal drawing come to life. The deer wiggled its nose and twitched its tail before scampering across the wall. The image seemed to draw her toward it like a sinkhole. Suzanne was reaching out to touch it when a furious pounding rattled the cabin walls.

"Open, I say," an English voice demanded, "or I'll break this door apart."

Maman rushed to her daughter's bedside, a lighted candle in her hand. "Dépêche toi, Suzanne! Hurry to the secret place and stay until I call you. Do not make a sound."

With the pouch clasped to her chest, Suzanne scampered into the parlor. There was no light at that end of the room, so she felt her way across the beadboard wall. Finding a loose panel, she pulled it aside, eased herself into a space behind it, and slid it shut. Hidden in the secret place, she heard the noise of bursting wood, boots thundering across the floor, her mother's shriek, a man's shout.

Susan wanted to yell from her hiding place. *We do not wear our boots in the house!* Yet Maman had told her to remain quiet.

"Where are the fur skins? Your man is a storekeeper, I know you have them."

Suzanne recognized the voice. It belonged to one of the English speakers she knew as Thomason Cutler, the night watchman.

"S'il vous plaît," Kitihawa pleaded. "Je ne parle pas anglais, monsieur."

It was true. Despite their years among the English, her mother learned not a smattering of that language. She knew it as the tongue of her husband's captors and accordingly despised it. Her mother had no way of knowing what Thomason Cutler demanded of her.

Sobbing into her left fist, Suzanne fished out a charcoal stick with her right. If only she could send herself somewhere far away.

She began to sketch a scene she had heard described. *Huge, stone buildings. Fancy carriages driving paved roads. Gas lights that make the night seem like day.*

Furiously, impetuously, she drew. She heard something shatter on the other side of the partition, a teacup or a plate perhaps. Footsteps pounded closer. The image on the floor shimmered, and Suzanne reached to touch it. A flashing green light seemed to pull her inward.

The ground beneath her was hard and solid, like so many fused gray pebbles.

Suzanne found herself in a paved courtyard surrounded by mountain-sized buildings. Who could have made such houses? How did they remain standing? She saw no horses, no fine carriages on the wide, empty road that fronted the courtyard.

What she did see were words carved onto buildings and printed on signs. She sounded them out like the Jesuit friar had taught her. *Pioneer Court. Chicago Tribune. Equitable Life Insurance.* Behind a wall of glass, the image of an apple with a bite taken out was lit up like the moon.

In the shadows of the courtyard, Suzanne saw something that frightened her—a tall man perched on one thick leg. He didn't seem to be moving, so curiosity edged her closer. Suzanne saw that it wasn't a man but a bust set atop a stone column. She read the sign beneath it.

Jean Baptiste Pointe DuSable, 1745-1818, founder of Chicago
African-Caribbean, born in St. Marc, Haiti

It looked like the bust had been doused in black. Motionless drops stood on its face like war paint or petrified tears. Suzanne wondered who had defaced the image, the Yankees or the British. She stared at the head frozen in bronze. The man did not look much like Papa. Her father's cheekbones were sharper, his forehead higher, and eyes narrower.

And how could he have died in 1818 when this was only the year of our Lord, 1781? Was *Chicago* the same as Shikaakwa? And why did this say he was born in a place called Haiti? Suzanne suddenly realized how little she knew about her father. She wondered if he, like M. Thiam had once been enslaved and had to buy his freedom.

"I bested the White man by working ten times as hard," François was known to boast. He had hired out his own labor as a blacksmith, paying a slaveholder the lion's share of his wages and keeping a pittance for himself.

It had taken him twelve years to earn enough to buy his wife's freedom, for he wanted any children from their union to be born free. Another eight years later, he finally purchased his own. He and his wife were nearly grandparent-aged, yet still with small children underfoot.

A rumbling noise tore her attention from the du Sable bust. It was like a roll of thunder echoing in the distance, growing louder as it advanced. Yet this was a thunder with voices in it.

A group of people came marching toward a bridge and down the middle of a road whose sign read "Michigan Avenue." They were oddly dressed, some of the women wearing trousers like the men. They shouted loud words Suzanne could barely decipher. Yet she could read the signs they carried. *No justice, no peace!...I can't breathe... George Floyd's Life Mattered.*

She sounded out the words and struggled to make meaning of them. Could these be the Yankees her father warned would be arriving en masse? The crowd she saw was mostly young Black people, though some were older and a few were White.

On the edges of that group of Black and Whites, another set of men wove and darted, shaking their fists and hooting. She could see they were taunting the young marchers.

Suzanne heard a rumble from the other direction, the stomp of marching feet. She turned to see a group from the opposite end of the road approaching in military formation. They were men and women in identical blue clothing carrying weapons and see-through shields.

One voice was magnified by the large cone he carried. "This is an illegal gathering. You are not allowed to advance beyond this point. You must disperse. I repeat, you must disperse."

Suzanne could differentiate the groups by what they carried— their signs, their weapons, their manner of movement. Could these be the Yankees and British at war once again? Suzanne watched, frightened and fascinated, as the groups drew closer. It seemed to her a horrible war dance would soon explode in bloodshed.

A woman came hurrying from one of the buildings. She passed Suzanne crouched at the foot of DuSable's bust. "What you doing out here, child? It's not safe in these streets tonight."

"I know," Suzanne told her, "but home is not safe also."

"It can't be worse than here." The woman touched the girl's forehead like she was testing for a fever or giving benediction. Then she shook her head, clicked her teeth, and walked away. "Ain't no time for all this. Got my own kids at home to worry about."

Suzanne took a charcoal stick from the pouch and drew on the hard ground beneath her.

"Hey, look at that one." One ruffian in a Tartan plaid shirt pointed her out. "Defacing public property."

His companion grabbed his arm. "Forget it, man. That's a kid."

"Put 'em in their place when they're young, you won't have to worry when they're grown. That little nigger needs a lesson." The man in plaid broke away from his friend. "And I'm just the one to teach it."

Suzanne finished her sketch as the man raced toward her. In a flash of green light the mountainous buildings, the hard gray ground, and the man loping toward her were gone.

Back inside the secret place, the nightmare hadn't ended. Suzanne still heard sounds of shouting and crying, of things being broken. She covered her eyes and wept anew. Then she saw through her fingers that her charcoal drawing on the floor still pulsed with green light. She quickly rubbed it out and drew another.

Suzanne crept into the kitchen, where her mother sat cowering in a chair. Bent, gaunt, red-haired Thomason Cutler used a long, wooden lacrosse stick to ransack their home. He yanked up rugs and knocked things off shelves, prised up floorboards, and rummaged through bureau drawers.

Maman half stood in her seat and mouthed the word, retourner! but Suzanne shook her head. She would not hide behind a wall to cower in fear. *No justice, no peace!*

"Pardon me, please," she spoke in careful English. She approached the man from behind, tugging at his sleeve. Thomason whirled around to face her. His wild red hair stood on end, his lacrosse stick upraised.

"We have many furs," Suzanne pointed across the room, "in the secret place."

The man grabbed her arm and dragged her to the wall. "Show me at once. God help you if you're lying."

When Suzanne pointed at the panel, he frowned at it suspiciously.

"Everything is all inside," Suzanne promised. "I've seen it myself."

"What, behind this wall?"

"It's our special hiding spot. You see?" Suanne swung the panel open.

The man elbowed her aside, dropped to his knees, and thrust his upper body into the crawl space. If he'd been a larger man, he never would have fit. Suzanne heard wood splinter as he forced his way inside.

"I do not see any . . . What in God's name!" A mist of green light leaked from the space, diffused by Thomason's body. Then he was sucked into the secret place, splinters from the lacrosse stick flying back into the room. The cracked beadboard panel swung crookedly back into place.

Suzanne rushed over to her mother, assuring her the man was gone.

"Es-tu sûre?" Maman whispered, wiping tears with the sleeve of her nightdress. "What if he returns?"

Suzanne went back to the secret space, crept inside, and rubbed away the image she had drawn on the floor. Then she called across the room.

"He will not return, Maman. I am sure of it."

Thomason Cutler stood stunned within a valley of tall, gray buildings. He gazed around at the bright streetlights, the broad boulevard, the crowds of milling people.

A man in a plaid shirt dashed past him, slapping a long wooden club against his palm. A short distance away, people gathered around a body lying prone on the ground.

"What happened?" a woman asked. "Who did this to you?"

"Baseball bat." The young man groaned weakly. "He hit me and ran off."

The crowd's eyes turned toward Thomason. People slowly converged upon him.

"Coward!" one of them shouted. "Attacking an unarmed man."

Thomason's cracked lacrosse stick dragged the ground as he backed away. "No, not me. Please, I am innocent. I swear it!"

"Don't touch him!" someone shouted. "There's CCTV all around here."

"Well, somebody get his ass on video at least."

People whipped out objects that shone bright lights on his face.

"I don't give a shit about CCTV, he gets a scarlet letter." A woman took a canister from her knapsack and sprayed red paint across his shirt. "That's an 'A' for assholery, asshole."

Thomason turned and plunged into the bleak landscape. He ran and ran, the streets, buildings, and strange carriages blurring as he passed them. Still imagining the crowds roaring behind him, he came upon a set of stairs leading down into yawning darkness.

Had he been able to read it, he'd know the sign above spelled out: *Chicago Transit Authority, Red Line Station.* Thomason scrambled down, behind a group of people holding sticks with lettered broadsides attached.

He thought he'd descended into a nightmare but worried it might be Hell.

NOTES FROM THE DUNNING ASYLUM

Aleco Julius

Wilbur Wright College Library, Chicago, Ill.
Chicago Regional History Special Collections.
Dunning Neighborhood Historical Society.

Item Description: *Rectangular tin box. Rusted and discolored, with brown spots of decay. Dented on one side. Lid is bent, but closes. 8 X 10 inches, 3 inches deep. Two light gray envelopes inside, stuffed with folded, loose sheets of paper.*

Both envelopes are labeled in dark pencil; one reads "Smyth," and the other "Prendergast." There are notes and letters inside, also written in pencil. Smyth's penmanship is legible and smooth, while Prendergast's is erratic with deep impressions made by the pencil point. Another loose sheet inside, typewritten, mottled with stains of unknown origin.

Collection: Discovered July 17th, 1985 by the McNichols Construction Company. Submitted to the Dunning Historical Society later that month by demolition supervisor of the west building of Wilbur Wright College and the new construction in that same location. Excavated approximately 4 feet underground.

April 17, 1893

The absolute first thing I notice upon entering the Cook County Insane Asylum is its insufferable stench. I believe it is a mixture of hundreds of unwashed bodies, mixed with soot, rat droppings, and human waste. Among these odors are the traces of other substances such as rotting food and the sharp sting of chloroform as well as other various chemicals.

Dr. Kennison has graciously allowed me access to patient P.E.J. Prendergast, who was brought into the asylum by police mere days ago. I had read the brief announcement in the *Inter Ocean* newspaper that a man exhibiting exceedingly bizarre behavior in Humboldt Park was committed, and I telegraphed Kennison directly for the chance of studying the man.

Prendergast was observed walking in circles, face to the sky, hat pulled over his eyes. He was apparently scaring the children who were out playing on that Saturday morning. A local milkman called the police, and, against his will, Prendergast was delivered north to this asylum for the insane. He was literally "taken to Dunning," a threatening phrase each Chicago child has heard from a parent when they choose to act naughty. Strangely enough, a bit of research I did yesterday tells me that Prendergast was once employed by the selfsame paper.

Upon my inaugural visit, Kennison led me to the second level. As we walked the low-ceilinged, poorly lit corridor, I heard the lonesome howls and manic shrieks of patients throughout the building, as well as some disturbing laughter, like that of a dying dog. One might have thought we had entered Pandemonium itself.

At the base of the wooden staircase we found a listless group of men and women of various ages. Some were sitting on the floor and staring into their laps. Others stood and stared at us while muttering incomprehensible gibberish to themselves. A toothless man kicked some dust in our direction and guffawed crudely as the powder engulfed my shined shoes.

Prendergast's room, or rather cell, was furnished with one wooden chair. Set on the chair was a stack of papers and a pencil. A few tattered books lay on the floor. His bed was a lumpy heap in the corner covered by a tangled blanket. There was a high window slit with iron bars embedded in the crumbling brick wall.

Prendergast himself greeted me with a hesitant handshake. I hadn't known what to expect, but the patient was polite. I guessed he was in his mid to late twenties, with dark, longish hair and protruding ears (somewhat like my own, I must confess).

I asked why he believed he was here, but if he remembered anything about being in Humboldt Park, he did not admit it. He appeared thoroughly unhappy, frowning all the time. I thought I detected the slightest Irish accent in his speech. I asked if I could visit him again soon, a notion which he tepidly welcomed. I did not broach any serious topics, electing instead to first gain the trust of the patient.

Dr. Alistair H. Smyth.

4-17-93

The new doctor came for a nice chat. He told me his name was Smith. We both bade each other good day, and it was quite a good little visit, especially because I have not had a visitor since the day I arrived at this castle of misery. He said he may come back soon.

I think I will comb my hair nice for the occasion. That will look more presentable, and he will listen to my words more carefully, hear how I have been wronged by Harrison and by the damned police.

We had carrots and potatoes for dinner again, in a rank stew. I barely managed to swallow a few spoonfuls before feeling queasy. The tin cup of water they left me was yellow and smelled musty.

They will still not let me out of here, which is a terrible injustice. Today I heard the wind push its way through the leaves on trees outside, and I imagined myself in their shade, free to feel the breeze. I also heard the distant laughter of children at play. But THEY will not allow me to join.

Perhaps tonight I will sleep without the bad dreams.

P.E.J.

April 18, 1893

After signing into the lobby's book of visitor records, I walked around a group of old women on my way to the staircase. Their faces were cracked and wan, their hair twisted. Probably melancholics. At arm's length, I was alarmed to realize they were much younger than I had first gathered.

Prendergast had shaved his facial hair, although I wasn't exactly sure how he could have done it without a razor, for a tool like that was not allowed in the hands of the inmates. Perhaps a guard did it for him. I asked him about it, and he said that "a man like me can be quite resourceful." In any case, he is now clean shaven like myself. He also had combed his hair like mine, with a neat part and to the side, though my own hair is of a slightly darker shade.

His initial conversation centered on the deplorable conditions of the asylum, especially the food. He then discussed how he had been betrayed by a man named Harrison. Judging from his story, I asked him if meant the Mayor, to which he replied, "certainly he." I could not fathom why he believed our Mayor would have wanted him committed. Apparently, he believed that the Mayor owed him for "broken promises."

I fear he suffers from a type of delusional insanity, perhaps circular. I expect the next visit will be fruitful for my study.

On my way out of the asylum I barely escaped the incidental blows of two scrawny men grappling like animals in the corridor nearest the exit. One man had the others' fingers between his teeth before the guards struggled to separate them.

Dr. Alistair H. Smyth.

4-19-93

Beans and onions for breakfast. Beans and onions for lunchtime. Beans and onions for dinner. I fed much of it to a couple of brown rats that scuttled into my room from a crack in the wall.

Yesterday the doctor came for another little visit. I was pleased that he noticed my new facial hair style. (I shaved it to look like him.)

I wanted to see his spectacles, but I got a fine look at them when he cleaned the lenses during our conversation. Cannot deduce why he is here, but as other-wise there is no variety in my days, his visits are a respite in my world of unfair confinement.

Have not been let out for exercise. The guards look at me and point and laugh. I suspect it is Harrison who is keeping me here. He locks me up so that the city does not learn what kind of a man he truly is—a man who breaks his promises. But one day they will know, if I have anything to say about it. Perhaps I should announce it to a crowd of thousands at the great Fair, when it finally does open to the public.

Heard a man wail like a wild beast early this morning. It was still dark out. His cries of No! slowly faded as they took him away to God knows where.

It has been raining all day, which means a humid night of sleep. I sweep away a congregation of weevil bugs from my bedsheets. Oh—if only my night terrors would cease.

P-Gast

April 20, 1893

This morning I had a pleasant brunch with Mrs. Smyth out on the veranda. Fresh boiled eggs and buttered bread with wild strawberry preserves prepared by Eula. There was a coolness in the air after yesterday's torrential rain. I was in such a fine mood that I gave Eula the afternoon off, to which she was very grateful.

My good mood quickly dissipated shortly thereafter, however, back inside the foreboding asylum. The stuffiness of the dank corridors lent the wretched place an oppressive weight to match the sufferings of the confined. I covered my nostrils with my sleeve so as not to breathe in the sickening miasma, which now seemed worse after the rains.

When I got to his room, Prendergast was stripped down to his undershirt. He profusely apologized and insisted on putting on one of his two unwashed shirts, while combing back his hair with his fingers.

In a placid spirit, he talked of the upcoming World's Columbian Exposition. He inquired whether I would be taking my wife and children to the fair. I was taken aback that he knew these personal details, but in hindsight I realized he must have merely taken a guess. I regret not immediately denying these facts, but I do not see the harm anyhow. He then told me that he desires to be like me, but will never get the chance because Mayor Harrison has sought to destroy his life.

Interestingly, Prendergast asked if I have ever heard of Joseph Merrick, otherwise known as the Elephant Man, a deformed British curiosity. He had read news of his death a few years ago, and since then has been fascinated by him. "He was monstrous on the outside, yet gentle and cultivated on the inside," Prendergast said.

Yes, I told him, of course I knew of Merrick. It was part and parcel of my field, I continued, to study the opposite: gentle and cultivated on the outside, yet monstrous on the inside. "Quite like you, Mr. Prendergast," I said.

His face darkened when I spoke these words, his lips twisting into a scowl. Finally, a noteworthy response.

I continue to be intrigued by Prendergast. I feel quite like a pioneer in this new field of psychiatry as I endeavor to discern the exciting causes of this disturbed individual.

Dr. Alistair H. Smyth.

4-21-93

Yesterday I acquired a pair of spectacles. They finally let me out of my room for a time, so I had the chance to interact with the other patients.

In the halls, I met a tiny, white-haired woman who was kind enough to let me borrow hers for a while, a patient who does not need them anymore. This will bring me closer to being like Dr. Smith. I don't understand why Dr. Smith has been unkind in his words, whereas I have been a perfectly genial host.

He suggested that I was hiding a monster inside of me, when in fact anyone in my position would feel the same. When you have been wronged like I have, the fog of vengeance rises up from Perdition and invades your brain. The thought of such flagrant betrayal overwhelms one's mind.

When outside my room, I saw a naked man brought in from the outside who was covered in dirt. I heard him shout that he was digging for something that he lost long ago but was trying to find.

I saw a young lady being carried by two stewards. She appeared to be asleep or dead. A doctor visited a little while later and said she was dead, and that she had poisoned herself with laudanum. The doctor was angry that she had been unsupervised and permitted to break into the drug closet. They didn't realize that I was listening to their words.

They found me and took me back to my room earlier than they said they would. It was still light outside, and I could see through the windows. I was unhappy but did not complain. They left me some bread with fuzzy green mold on it, and a hard piece of cheese, which tasted foul.

In my nighttime terrors, I am perpetually being chased by someone I can't see. So that is why I choose to instead sit awake and write by the dim light of the yellow moon.

PRETENDER-gast

April 21, 1893

When I arrived at the asylum this morning, there was a commotion near the entrance. Two horses were tied to a post there, along with a covered cart. Staff appeared to be on edge, worriedly moving to and fro, in and out of the building.

Peering from the corridor windows of the second story were a host of flat, hopeless faces. Their faraway gazes registered no discernable emotion.

I learned from Dr. Kennison that the body of an elderly woman had been discovered in a small storage room on the ground level, located some ways off the main corridors. Judging from the deep, purple mark across her throat, Kennison said, the lady was presumably strangled to death. I caught a glimpse of the corpse's white hair under the shroud as the stretcher was carried through the foyer and outside toward the wagon. Unfortunately, no one present was able to identify her by name.

At that time, I wished Kennison Godspeed, for he was on his way out to the East coast for a month-long conference on diseases of the brain.

Upon reaching Prendergast's room I was rather surprised to see him wearing a pair of spectacles. His appearance truly resembled mine more with each visit. It occurred to me that he was just about my height, as well. I also noticed that his hair was now darker complexioned, comparable to mine. He said he had smeared on some black oil that he found somewhere in the building. How did he get into a supply closet, I wondered? I have read about patients who become deeply besotted with their doctors, so I ought to take heed and keep my distance.

This idea was made more difficult when Prendergast told me that there was something in my manner that reminded him of his home Isle of Inishbofin. It is true that I am of Irish descent, and there was a moment of weakness when I felt pity for him. But it quickly passed.

We discussed his foray into the other parts of the building, where some of those patients with lesser manias are allowed to cavort. Prendergast said he met some "nice people." He positively must be delusional. I will never get accustomed to the ghostly echoes of these men and women who are already dead inside, their flesh and bones like withered, empty vessels.

I observed that Prendergast had made his bed for the first time, and I pointed it out to him. It now looks like your bed at home, he said to me. I was unsettled by that particular comment.

He proceeded to ask, "How are your children, doctor?" I told him I never admitted to having children. He replied that he could tell I had children from the start, because only those without children deny they have children, and I did not do that. I left his relatively sunlit room and escaped into the gloomy corridors.

Overall, this was a most productive visit, I feel. There is valuable material to examine and eventually write about, perhaps to publish.

Dr. Alistair H. Smyth.

4-22-93

Farewell! I take my leave of this mausoleum for the living.

I would like to thank Dr. Smith for his recent visits, which truly were my salvation in this godforsaken prison. He has thankfully declared me cured and fully sane. I am obliged, as well, for his waistcoat, jacket, trousers, and shoes. It is an honor to borrow and wear them.

Perhaps I can meet Harrison in this fine clothing and commend him on his Mayorship, which I can claim much credit for, having worked tirelessly to get him elected. Oh—the hundreds of cards and letters I painstakingly wrote out to garner him support among the citizens of Chicago. Perhaps I might visit him at his home, where he will have the opportunity to apologize to me in person.

Dr. Kennison, when you are returned from your trip, you will no doubt be proud of my rehabilitation, though you never took an interest in me.

The anguished legion of voices that reverberate through this building had become the perverse chorus of my confinement, but tonight I will have no night terrors. For I am the terror in the night.

Yours somewhat truly,

Mr. Patrick Eugene Joseph Prendergast

April 23??? 24???

I APPEAR TO BE STUCK INSIDE OF A NIGHTMARE.

I have yelled for 2 hours or more but to no avail. My throat is hoarse. Finally, a steward came to the door and threatened to have me beaten or worse. "Prendergast," he began. But I screamed, "I am not Prendergast! I am Dr. Smyth!" To which he laughed heartily and ambled away down the corridor. I heard his footsteps diminish one by one until they were gone in the gloom.

Please— someone— find DR. ELBERT KENNISON (in NY, I believe) and report that he must return to this facility at once. It is of the utmost urgency. Kennison ought to be found posthaste. Also!— immediately contact Mrs. Hannah Smyth of Dunning. She is my wife, and shall surely help sort out this nasty business to which I am victim. I fear that she and the children are in danger.

Prendergast dealt me a nasty blow on the back of the head as I was leaving, and there is dried blood in my hair. I have been rather nauseous since coming to, and fear I have suffered a concussion. A chunk of the brick wall is lying nearby, which I believe he used as a bludgeon. Now I am wearing only my underclothes, for Prendergast has taken my suit, and placed his own clothing under his bed blanket.

Help me! Whoever reads this letter, please use your cognitive faculties and ask yourself: Can this letter have been written by a madman? Send someone, anyone, to this cell so I can talk to them myself!

In dire need,

DOCTOR ALISTAIR H. SMYTH.

Entry Report from Assistant Patient Records Administrator of the Cook County Insane Asylum.

Date: Wednesday, April 27th, 1893

Patient: J.E.P. Prendergast, diagnosed with acute delusional insanity.

Description: Believes he is someone else, a doctor who has "switched places" with him, along with his clothing and spectacles. Mania grows worse by the day.

Note: Records show that a Dr. Smith did indeed sign out on the afternoon of April 22, further substantiating the patient's delusion, or attempt at criminal deception. Furthermore, no family or friends of the doctor have come to this asylum to inquire about anything suspicious whatsoever.

Treatment: Staff doctors have recommended a heavy dosage of laudanum, which was begun yesterday. Patient's limbs were strapped down by stewards onto a gurney, with tranquilizing elixir regrettably forced by mouth. Prendergast will be rendered comatose with drugs for a period of 45 days, after which observation and diagnosis will continue as necessary.

Location: A vacant bed for him was found among the incurable.

THE PAPERGIRL

RL Gehringer

January, 1966

I was fourteen when Dalk showed me his basement. We met at the doorway with no door, on a six-degree night.

"You girl. Not scared?" Dalk said.

"Nope."

"Why not?"

"Just ain't."

"Frankie Fazzolari—is Italian?"

"Half Irish," I said.

"Irish-Italian. Tough. Short sentences, too. Not like Woody."

Woody bounced foot to foot, trying to stay warm.

"Tell her about the staircase, Dalk," Woody said. "The steps are rotten the whole thing's ready to collapse last week I was almost killed when—"

"Shush," Dalk interrupted. "You talk her out from job."

That wasn't going to happen. Woody and I had a deal. We were swapping paper routes. And for reasons he didn't know, I wanted his sinister building and creepy landlord. I also wanted the basement tour at night. We ran early morning routes, delivering in darkness half the year and collecting payments after dinner, also in darkness. Why see an evil basement in daylight?

To arrive at the doorway with no door, we'd entered through the alley gate. It was so cold the metal latch was frozen shut, and the fence itself was breaking apart.

"Dummies used pine for an outdoor fence," Woody laughed.

He chomped two chunks of pink Bazooka bubblegum while jiggling the frozen latch. When it opened, he blew a tight bubble, then snapped it, loud as a firecracker.

"Letting Dalk know we're here," he grinned.

We stepped into the gangway and I looked up at the building that had induced Woody to swap routes after only sixteen days on the job. Three stories high, four city lots wide, open back porches. No yard, no coach house, no garage. Just dirty brown bricks and worn wooden porches from sidewalk in front to alley in back.

"Why not toss the papers onto the porches?" I said.

"Too many interior apartments and furnished rooms," Woody said.

"So, no porches. Just fire escapes."

"Yup. It's a chop-job, totally illegal. And wait 'til you meet the weirdos in the furnished rooms—whoa, Nellie. Hope you're ready for this, Frankie, 'cause a deal's a deal," Woody said. And spat for emphasis.

"I'm ready," I said.

We followed the gangway to a flight of concrete steps that dropped us below the sidewalk and into a long, low tunnel that ended snugly ensconced within the building's brick façade. Dalk waited at the other end, neck bent flat to fit under the tunnel's low ceiling. He was all angles—as thin as he was tall, with black hair and eyes—his face a map of Eastern Europe.

Now, the black eyes sized me up.

"Come," he said, leading me through the doorway with no door.

Woody stayed up in the tunnel. "I ain't *never* going down there again," he said.

On the rotting staircase, Dalk shined a flashlight on the best places to step. Once at the bottom, we were eight feet below the tunnel and fourteen feet below the sidewalk. The air was dank, the temperature like a jelly jar lifted from the fridge.

Dalk ran his flashlight along the ceiling to a naked bulb mounted on a porcelain base with a short metal keychain. A foot-long string extended the keychain. The bulb popped on, and I looked around, then wished I hadn't. Centipedes. The floor was a swirling hundred-leg hell.

"March feet op down. Bogs get on shoes, under pantlegs," Dalk advised.

He pointed to a stairwell midway across the room. "Op to hallway," he said and started walking. I followed, through a winding path of crates and boxes, worn sofas and chairs, lopsided tables and dressers, even a small piano—spent relics from a century of human migration.

We went up the staircase and into the hall. Dalk walked me through every hallway on all three floors, pointing out the doors where my newspapers would go.

Back in the tunnel, Woody griped. "Where'd you go, Siberia? I'm freezing my ass off."

Dalk flattened his neck and explained the missing door. "Own building seven years."

"Four score and eighty-four paperboys ago," Woody quipped.

Dalk resumed talking. "Two years, I give paperboys keys—" Woody blew a bubble and snapped it, grinning with satisfaction. This was payback for Dalk's earlier shush. I figured they were even and hoped that was the end of it.

Dalk began again. "Two years, they lose every key. Who ring doorbell six in morning? Is paperboys. Ring every bell in building for buzz inside. Upset tenants."

Dalk had tried to find a tenant to buzz the paperboys in each morning, but he didn't get a single volunteer. Frustrated, he removed the tunnel door and routed the paperboys through the basement. That was five years ago. It was also when the paperboys started quitting.

Dalk thought the sheltered location would protect the staircase. But five years of Chicago weather blowing down a tunnel and in through an open hole had ravaged the wood.

"Outside staircase fine. Inside kaput," he said.

"Your outside staircases are oak. Your shit staircase is poplar," Woody said.

He blew another bubble that I popped in his face. The warm gum stuck to my cold finger, forcing Woody to suck the long pink string back into his mouth like a lizard's tongue.

Dalk's laugh was immediate. Slavic. Loud.

I knew the next answer. And it didn't matter, because I wanted Dalk's building at any cost. But I asked anyway. "So, give me one key—just one—the key to the foyer. I won't lose it. Let me drop the newspapers in the foyer."

"No foyer. Tenant want paper in hallway. You go through basement. I fix steps soon."

Six months later, the steps still weren't fixed. I couldn't hold it against Dalk. The man had health issues. Some nights, he looked normal. Some nights, he looked like death.

July, 1966

With twelve flat newspapers balanced on my forearm and pinned under my chin, I test each step before giving it weight. The metal hoop of Route Address Cards, including the red card for NEW CUSTOMER, hangs like a bracelet below my left wrist. My right hand grips a banister of dry, cracked wood covered in chipped paint. I hold tight, despite the risk of slivers, in case today's the day the staircase finally gives out. That would be bad for me, worse for Gerald, the cart bum who sleeps under the steps.

"You took the job; you *do* the job." Dad's words from when I delivered fliers for Matthews Roofing Company and wanted to quit after some punks spooked me in a hallway. Dad was right. I stuck with it and discovered my courage.

Two months later, Dad was gone.

But I still talk to him.

Each morning, I tell him how I'm doing. And then I do my job, descending this rotten staircase with a rusty box cutter in my back pocket, ready to slice any creep who gets friendly.

Who I am is Frankie Fazzolari, 15, Irish/Italian, daughter of a slain Chicago cop.

What I am is anybody's guess.

People put labels on girls like me. But in my heart, I'm a protector like my dad. And in my gut, I'm a fighter. I can punch your Adam's apple into the back of your throat, bite off a hunk of your ear, and send your orbs to outer space. There are days I pray some shit-bird steps from the shadows. Being tough doesn't mean I don't get scared. Some days, the tension in my chest makes my breath come in shallow jets. Some days, I count my newspapers three times.

It's July, so I don't need a flashlight to find the overhead bulb and weave through the graveyard of broken possessions. I get to the top step of the midway staircase and take a breath. The blonde banister, "live oak," according to Woody, cools my sweaty palm. The hallway door is heavy. "Mahogany," I've been told. I swing it just enough to slip through.

In the hallway, I balance the papers between forearm and chin again, using my free hand to quietly close the door. Silence is why I never plop a paper. I lay them gently. Because my worst days are when I've woken a night owl, and now he's following, whispering.

Silence is my ally as I walk the narrow passageways of the nineteenth-century tenement where H.H. Holmes came calling, where Louise Vermilya served arsenic tea, and William George Heirens's lipstick scribbles appear on bathroom mirrors at midnight. Where paperboys see vampires entering hidden rooms, and where the madman who last night murdered eight is waiting on me, The Papergirl.

The first floor is mere degenerates.

Jelinek, a hopeless drunk and skin-popper, gets the first paper.

The Potee family is next. White gang bangers, violent, quick to anger.

Mr. Bonadonna, AKA Carmine "The Neck" Bonadonna, lives down the hall.

Cherry and Rose, the women Carmine employs, come next. They're nice and tip well. I've got a little crush on Rose. Who wouldn't? Olive skin that tans caramel in summer, big inquisitive eyes, and a thick black mane that sways when she walks.

I save the Plichtas for last. They're a normal family who've lived in the building twenty years. The small crush on Rose makes room for the big one on Johnny Plichta. Brylcreem hair slicked back with that floating wave up top. Sharkskin slacks and silk summer shirts. I tap lightly. We share the closeness of a doorway, touch while talking.

I climb the staircase to the second floor.

Welcome to *Murderer's Row*.

Paul Tombs gets the first paper. Paul's on parole for liking children. Technically, Paul's not a murderer. "I murder souls," he likes to say.

Mrs. O'Brien's a fun gal. Poisoned her first husband with antifreeze. Poisoned her second with insulin.

Chester Augustine had a farm in southern Indiana that he left in a hurry when bones were discovered under the barn.

People ask how I know so much about my customers. That's easy—I listen. I ask good questions, and then I listen. It's not a gift; it's a skill my father taught me.

But it's not *all* skill. I also have a gift. And that gift makes some want to label me. They ask if I'm a seer. I don't know. I only know that I possess insight into people, situations, and events. And I know when those I care about and I are in the presence of evil.

Third floor. Here are the infamous killers, the ones everyone *thinks* are in jail.

A squeak in the floorboard as I bend to place the morning edition at Jack Marvin's door. The door swings open, and Jack stands above me. "Good work, Frankie," he says.

Laszlo Kiraly is next. Johnny Plichta told me Kiraly's a former Hungarian general who executed thousands before the Uprising of 1956. He fled to the United States, choosing Chicago for its large Hungarian population.

Dalk gets the next paper. If Dalk's an infamous killer, he's got me fooled.

Last week, he gave me a thank-you card and a $10.00 gift certificate for Rose Records on Wabash. "No paperboy good as papergirl," he said and hugged me. I didn't mind Dalk's touch. He's weird in that old country way, but he's not a monster.

Any other day and I'd be done. But today, I have a new customer. Room #308, a rent-by-the-week furnished room that comes before Kiraly's. Why did I pass this door earlier with my head down? Because there are eight dead women on the front page, and the man inside killed them, that's why.

I knew he'd be here. I'd felt it back at Chuck's garage, where each morning we stuff and roll our newspapers. Where this morning's front page flipped my stomach like a giant spatula.

Mornings at Chuck's are loud. Guys shucking and punching, singing the latest Beatles or Stones song. But this morning was quiet as a math class. Chuck with his head in his hands, body turning slow circles like a leaky boat. And every paperboy sitting cross-legged on the cardboard-covered floor where we stuffed and rolled.

Chins on palms. Eyes on the headline.

I spied the front page and fell to my knees.

They were students, not much older than a papergirl. Away from home for the first time, studying to be nurses. There were nine. He killed eight. The lone survivor hid under a bed. Fueled by booze and methamphetamine, the killer lost count. Hours later, she managed to untie herself and run to the open window.

"They're all dead! All of my friends are dead!" Corazon Amaurao wailed to a sleeping city.

I'd read a lot of crime stories while stuffing and rolling newspapers, but nothing like this: a front page on fire in a city already ablaze in race riots, teenage gang crime, and Outfit killings.

The canvas bag slung over my handlebars didn't feel any heavier, but there was an extra paper and a NEW CUSTOMER delivery card. That's when I knew I'd soon be meeting the man the newspapers called a "subhuman." The animal said to be "on the loose in our city."

Eight kills in four hours.

Of course, a room would be ready for whoever did that.

I wanted to fake sick, go home, and crawl under the covers. But that would be a betrayal of everything Dad taught me.

You can't hide from evil, Frankie. You have to defeat it. Dad again.

He was shot responding to a domestic disturbance. I'd felt his death two hours before it happened. Yet, in some ways, I'd always felt his impending death. That's not a gift; it's a curse. And it's not special. Every cop's kid knows the feeling.

My gift starts as heat. A hot nugget in the palm of my right hand. If the situation grows serious, the heat jumps to my throat and chest. From there, it spreads to the belly and trunk. Two hours before Dad was rushed to St. Elizabeth's, I was burning nose to toes. The older I get, the hotter the heat, the further it spreads, and the deeper it drills.

I'm working to turn my gift into power. I want to help people with it, maybe save a life someday. It starts by learning to control myself when the heat appears.

This building is my university.

Room #308, the door's ajar. I *feel* his impatience. He wants to read about his big night and I'm the only thing standing between him and the front page. My palm is burning. Printer's ink smears my hand. The newspaper's spine feels like it'll catch fire.

I bend to place the paper, and he's there.

"You're late," the new man says, towering over me.

"Sorry," I say from my knees.

Heat spreading, I rise to an impossible face. Striking ice-blue eyes set over the grayest, most pockmarked cheeks I've ever seen. The slacks are wrinkled. The blue work shirt has long sleeves buttoned at the wrists. My hand feels light and I realize why. I failed to grab this man's newspaper off the hallway floor. I look down. The dead women's faces pulse back up at me. Sixteen pleading eyes like a string of warning lights. *Run!* They're telling me, *Run!*

"I saw you pass by earlier," he says.

"I wasn't sure who got this paper."

He rips the metal hoop from my hand and flips to the red card.

"Says right here: Sheppard, #308."

"I guess I—"

"Dalk tells me you're reliable. Are you reliable, Papergirl?"

I back away, eyes on his knees to detect motion.

His top lip curls, a row of rotten teeth emerge. Faces imploring me, *Run!* I envision them struggling against him, thrashing for life, punching, pulling, kicking—surrendering.

"Bend down and get my paper," he says.

I bend without taking my eyes off his knees.

He grabs the paper and backhands the metal hoop at my face. I flinch and throw up an arm. My wrist deflects the hoop and it bounces off my breastbone. I catch it on the bounce.

He turns and slams the door.

Back at Chuck's, every paperboy has a story about last night's killer. Woody saw the madman ducking down a gangway. Some weirdo in a blue Mustang told Tommy Falaren he had a nurse in the trunk. Eddie knows where the killer's hiding. I'm straddling the banana seat of my Schwinn Stingray, empty canvas bag tied to angel wing handlebars. *Was the guy in #308 just another braggadocio?*

We ride home together, all thirteen of us. Excited, scared, seeking comfort, reluctantly splitting off as our houses and apartment buildings come into view.

Mom and Grandma are up in their rooms, so I grab a towel and fresh clothes and head down to the basement for a shower. The houses on our block were built by German immigrants in the 1870s. The bathrooms have tubs but no showers. Dad put a shower in the basement. It's nice in summertime; too cold the rest of the year.

Warm water soothes my leftover tension. I let my soapy hands trace the contours of my body, lingering in places, imagining Johnny and then Rose. I like my emerging femininity, and I'm not embarrassed by my attraction to both sexes.

Growing up, the adults called me "tomboy." Dad said wear it with pride, and I did.

Then I struck out their sons from forty-six feet.

I was a different type of kid; it's only natural I'm a different type of teenager. Out of respect for Mom, I keep my attraction to girls private. She would never understand, just as I'll never grasp why we have to choose.

These are the times I miss Dad most. He could talk about anything.

The kitchen radio's playing WLS. Tommy James's baby is doing the Hanky Panky, while Mom and Grandma are stubbing butts into hollowed-out grapefruit halves.

"Grapefruit, it's a fruit, it's an ashtray!"

I've cracked that joke too many times. Nobody even looks up anymore.

"We're reading about those poor girls," Mom says. "Have you seen this, Frankie?" She holds up the paper.

"Seen it, read it, delivered it."

"Hope they chop his balls off," Grandma says.

"Gotta catch him first, Gram," I say, snatching the Sports section. There are no baseball updates due to the All-Star break.

The We Five song, "You Were on My Mind," comes on.

"Oh my God, it's that heroin song again," Mom says, shaking her head.

"Mom, it's a love song."

"It most certainly is not. Just listen to those lyrics, Frankie."

We've been having this debate for a year.

I deal Sports across the table like a poker card and push back my chair. "I'm heading out. Need me to pick up anything?"

Grandma's digging in her frock when the phone rings.

"Hello," I say.

"Frankie, my God, did you hear about those nurses?" It's Julie.

"Yeah. I can't believe it. You doing anything?"

Grandma presses a dollar and a quarter in my palm. "Two Salems for me and two Kools for your mother."

Julie and I went shopping along Milwaukee Avenue. She found a cute fall sweater and I bought caramel corn to share. We stopped at the schoolyard on the way home.

The girls were sitting in the cubbies, recessed cement window-sills the size of a car interior, listening to transistor radios while the guys played Fast Pitch. I found Johnny in a cubby with his greaser crew, smoking cigs and waiting to bat.

"Little Red Riding Hood," by Sam the Sham and the Pharaohs was blasting.

"Hey Julie," Johnny said. "And oh, wow—HELLOOOOOOOO Frankie!"

What a goof. He'd revved up his crew, so of course he kept go-ing. "Damn, Frankie, where you been hiding that bod? Nice to see you in something besides jeans and t-shirts."

I was in mint green culottes and a sleeveless white summer blouse. Johnny started doing Sam the Sham wolf howls. I laughed and told him to knock it off. Things grew quiet, so I asked Johnny if he had a minute. That was an unfortunate choice of words. Johnny's buddies were merciless. "A minute's more than enough, Frankie," and, "Give her two minutes, JP, make it your personal best." It was Johnny's turn to laugh it off, and he did, which was why I liked him.

We walked to an open cubby.

"What's up?" Johnny said.

"Sheppard."

"Who?"

"The new guy in 308. He killed those nurses."

"Come on!"

"I'm serious."

"You call the cops?" Johnny's head dropped as he remembered my dad. "Sorry, Frankie, I forgot."

"It's okay. Anyway, no. Not yet. But I know he did it."

"Who else have you told?"

"Just Julie. She thinks I'm crazy."

"Hah!"

"I want him out of the building."

"What? Why?"

"I just told you why. Will you help me?"

"You want me to drive a guy out of his home based on a hunch?"

"It's more than a hunch."

"Is it? How? And don't say your *gift*."

We weren't getting anywhere, so I dropped it.

We sat in the cubby until it was Johnny's turn to bat. He didn't try to kiss me. Because his crew would have hooted? Or did he think I was too young? I was a little disappointed but also a little relieved. I didn't want our first kiss to be in a schoolyard.

I wasn't mad at Johnny for not helping with Sheppard. I'd asked too much. After all, the guy hadn't done anything to Johnny. He hadn't done anything to me either, except act like a jerk. Maybe Julie was right. Maybe the headlines were making me crazy.

That night, Julie and I hung out at her house, listening to records and talking about the boys we liked. I left at 11:30 p.m. I'd planned to go home, but my feet had other plans.

Soon, I was standing at the doorway with no door.

It's a menacing basement at midnight.

I don't have my flashlight, and the length of string tied to the keychain is impossible to locate. It keeps tapping the back of my hand and floating away, like gnats at a picnic. Finally, I spin the string around my fingers. The light pops on, and I'm slicing through the maze of boxes and discarded furniture.

I reach the midway staircase and dash to the top.

Beyond the staircase is a dire wilderness I've never dared to enter, but from my perch I can see what it holds. Tricycles with bent wheels and broken spokes, abandoned dolls with their eyes plucked, lone items of children's clothing. A single mitten snapped to the wrist of a little girl's spent winter coat hangs over a wooden crate, the coal-smudged faux-fur collar boasting black handprints. I try not to look at the dolls, but they lock my gaze anyway. And now they're beckoning... *Oh, papergirl... Oh, papergirl... Come hear our stories...*

Near the back of the building, a half dozen oil tanks the size of Cadillacs crouch along the southern wall, while a massive boiler rumbles six feet away. Woody swears Dalk sleeps back there. "In an African blackwood coffin, Frankie. Behind a door that disappears."

I use a shortstop's sidestep to quietly enter the hall. I tiptoe to the Plichta's door and listen.

"Who's there?" Oh God, it's Johnny. *What the hell am I doing?*

"Who's at the door?" He doesn't want any part of this. *Get out!*

I run to the staircase, taking the steps two at a time.

Again, the door to #308 is ajar. But Sheppard's not in the room. I bury my fear and slip inside. Evil, like a bad smell. And now the heat. Burning, traveling, soon it's everywhere. I turn just as he's stepping into the room.

"Papergirl," he says and closes the door.

Sheppard's long freaky legs hustle across the floor. Arms reaching. He grabs my wrist and there's the evidence: Sheppard in a grimy short-sleeved t-shirt, *Born To Raise Hell* tattooed on his left forearm. Exactly as described to police by Corazon Amaurao.

Sheppard yanks my arm high up behind my shoulder, and the jolt of pain surging from wrist to neck is otherworldly. It's my right arm, the one I use for the box cutter in my right back pocket. The pain unites with the heat of my burn and I shriek, loud as a cat in a trap. I stomp on Sheppard's foot and slip out of his grip. The arm drops like a weight, hanging limp and useless at my side. Cradling my right arm in the left like a sling, I juke and watch Sheppard roll an ankle.

I get the door open with my left hand and scamper into the hallway.

"Hey, asshole, I'm calling the cops!"

"What?" Sheppard says, struggling to rise on his bad ankle.

"You heard me, Sheppard. Shit bird."

He's limping. But coming . . .

I hit the steps, flying down two stories in three seconds, bolting through the first-floor hallway. The front door is too far; the fire escapes too complicated with only one arm. I yank the mahogany door. When I reach the basement, it's a horror show—the staircase has collapsed!

It had to be Gerald. I hope he's okay.

I spin and head to the back of the basement, scoot inside the boiler room, and make myself small. My right arm is dead. I can't reach the box cutter with my left arm.

Sheppard limps into the room and finds me crouched behind the boiler.

"Know why you're afraid?" He hovers above me.

"I'm not afraid."

"Because I know what you are, Papergirl."

"What am I?"

"You're the *worst* kind of woman."

I scramble back, but there's nowhere to go. He yanks me from the floor. His lips quiver like a cornered dog, eyes roll back, a country preacher handling copperheads.

Sheppard grabs my throat and chokes me while lifting me straight up above his head. "Show me, Papergirl," he bellows. "Show me the wounded daughter of a slain Chicago pig!"

I want to take this guy apart. But my legs are below his groin and I'm suffocating. I pump air, a train without a track.

"Sheppard. Shit bird!" I poke down with my left hand and get both eyeballs and finally, a foot lands square on his nuts.

He throws me down like a bag of trash. I crash to the floor and crab-scoot back to the wall.

Still holding my arm, I jump to my feet. But oil tanks and a boiler leave little room to squeeze past. And his arms are so long . . . Sheppard clamps both thumbs on my throat. I struggle and thrash, kick and fight. But he's too big, too strong—too much evil.

There's a low, breathy bounce of laughter. And satisfaction in Sheppard's glacial eyes. "Time for you to die," he says.

A slow descent. The puppy tumbling down a grassy knoll. The day spent reading under ancient oaks. The warm bath after a morning shoveling snow out on open streets.

It's quiet. I'm comfortable here.

A rumble rises from Sheppard's chest. It enters me, rolling and spreading like an avalanche. It's jungle laughter and it's voodoo. It's predatory contempt, and it's driving deep down into my bones. It wants to obliterate me, the worst kind of woman.

I'm burning up, my skeleton vibrating like the whole spinning, shaking, trembling planet is witness to the darkness nesting inside me.

This baleful, venomous man is shutting out my light.

No! No!

My right arm comes alive. I snatch the box cutter from my back pocket and slash Sheppard's forearm. The blood flows down his forearm to his fingers. Striking hard, I bury the rusty blade in his bicep.

And then it falls. I've dropped the box cutter. And my arm is worse than ever.

Sheppard's arm is painted in blood. And yet, somehow, he tightens his grip, crushing my windpipe, driving me to my knees. My left hand pats the floor for the box cutter, but it's nowhere.

I punch at Sheppard's groin with my left hand. He blocks it by turning, laughs as my fist bounces impotently off his thigh.

That's when I hear the wolf. There's a wolf somewhere, and it's howling.

A door opens. Black peasant shoes on a basement floor.

The wolf again.

A fist crashes down on Sheppard's temple. It's Johnny, barefoot in boxers and dago-tee, soup can biceps and snaking, sinewy muscle. He hits Sheppard again and again. The killer crumbles.

Johnny yanks Sheppard to his feet, puts him in a full-nelson, and holds him for me. "Do him, Frankie. Do him for those girls. Do him for your dad."

And I do. With my left hand, I pulverize Sheppard's Adam's apple. My right leg sends his balls to the moon.

"Enough." I hear from behind me.

What happened next, I can't say. It's jumbled.

Same for Johnny. "Just a swirl of images, Frankie, nothing solid."

This, I can say: Dalk emerged from a room that was no room. Through a door that wasn't.

He wore dark sharovary and shuba that blended seamlessly with brick, oil tank, and boiler. He was stone and he was iron, and he hovered over Sheppard like the moon.

And the moon came down.

In the flickering light of the boiler, Dalk engulfed Sheppard in his shuba.

There was blood. Johnny and I both remember blood.

And screams. Sheppard pleading as they disappeared inside the wall.

Johnny found my box cutter, and we left.

I was still shaky in Johnny's living room. "Oh God, what *was* that, Johnny?"

"I don't want to know."

And we laughed like criminals.

"Frankie, you need to know something," Johnny said.

"Okay."

"I enlisted in the Marines."

"You what? You're only 17."

"My parents signed the waiver."

"Johnny, Vietnam. It's bad."

"I want to do my part."

"Oh God, Johnny, don't. I'm begging you, don't. It's bad there."

"I have to."

"Johnny, why?"

"Why do you do what you do?"

I had no answer for that.

"I report in five days. My parents are throwing me a Ship Out Party tomorrow night. I'd like you to be there."

"Of course."

"I'll invite Dalk," he grinned.

Julie and I went to Johnny's party, along with the neighborhood greasers and every lunatic in the building. Looking dapper and healthy, Dalk was vivacious. As the party progressed, he presented Johnny with a gorgeous replica of a seventeenth-century Claymore sword.

Sheppard was found alive on Skid Row. We figured Dalk dumped him there before the party.

Late that night, Sheppard attempted suicide. On Sunday morning, we learned his real name: Richard Speck. That was the best newspaper I ever delivered.

The staircase got replaced. Gerald and a lady friend had tried to drag their shopping carts down the steps. They were more shaken than injured, but the incident motivated Dalk to install a tunnel door with a deadbolt lock. While the new staircase was being built, Dalk gave me keys to the building, and I never went down into the basement again.

I returned the keys on my seventeenth birthday, after landing a job bagging groceries at Jewels. As a favor to Dalk, I trained my replacement, a sweet thirteen-year-old boy named Sonny. Dalk transferred my keys to Sonny, and the young man did a fine job for many years.

It was the next summer when Johnny met Dad. He had five days left on his tour.

In 1978, I moved to California. Grandma had died from lung cancer, which scared the cigarette habit out of Mom, so I took her along. She lived thirty years in the Golden State. I spread her ashes in a redwood grove.

My powers are strong. I use them when it matters. Like the time I bumped into Woody talking to a rotund man in Paske's Bakery. The more I watched this man, the more I envisioned him in a clown suit. The guy was pressing Woody to go somewhere with him, and I was burning like a wildfire. I got the creep's attention and read the fear in his eyes. I gave him the index finger windshield wiper and nodded him out the door.

He knew what I was.

And he knew I saw the monster.

THE LAST GRAVEYARD SHIFT
AT THE ENGLEWOOD BRANCH

Tara Betts

Apparently, everyone knew but me. At least that's what I hear now. At first, they thought I just left, but the old heads knew exactly what happened. The person who was training me didn't think about where I was and what happened here before we were all here, before this post office was even built.

I was a new sorter on the job working the night shift. There's always good work at the post office, they say. Since I lived in Englewood, a job near Kennedy-King College on 63rd Street sounded like a good deal. I didn't need to take a bus and a train to work, and I'd have benefits. I could afford to take my girl out two or three times a month, and the bills are paid. The supervisor told me that they had high turnover rates, and I figured it was because no one really wants to work a night shift where you're moving around bags of letters and packages. At least the machines read the numbers that ran into a blur of ink in less than a few hours.

Bryce was the brother leading me through my training. He had a big barrel chest and the sharpest lines for a shape-up I'd ever seen. I suspect he had some of that spray-on hair that the barber shops offer now because his hair was exactly polished coal black. He showed me where the incoming mail went and how to input each piece into the machines that sorted local mail and mail headed out of state. Bryce had a low hum of Motown classics and 90s R&B gently flowing through the open work space. "The music helps keep you awake sometimes." I wonder now if Bryce was unaware of how much the music was drowning out other noises.

Aside from the music, Bryce made sure I met all the folks at the gig, when to take a break, and I knew where the best corner to smoke was on the eastern side of the building facing a small open lot of grass with a tall tree. The smokers kept a small garbage can to stub out the butts on its side. They'd toss the used-up cigarettes in the trash with chip bags and water bottles. Sometimes, you just wanted to breathe, so some folks would take a break when the smokers were done. Humans need to be outside.

My last night here was when Bryce had me scheduled to work solo for a few hours. The trucks had all pulled in for the night, and it was only sorters working from 11PM to 7AM, a graveyard shift. Bryce was calling people to work the shift with me, but no one would take it. I overheard Bryce talking to one of the old heads who'd been there for over 25 years.

"Now, Bryce, you know I never work the graveyard shift during the full moon, not never. You shoulda told that young brother to call in sick and lock up for the night."

I didn't know that they would just shut down for the night sometimes, but it would explain why mail got to people's houses slower on the South Side in general.

"I know, I know. The higher-ups been stressing the hell outta me about complaints and low numbers, so I thought it might be okay. It's all superstition anyway, right?"

The old head didn't say anything for a beat before saying, "You better do right by that new sorter, Bryce."

"Okay, man, we're good. I'll holla at you later."

Bryce was acting like it wasn't no thing, but I should've been suspicious then. Bryce was putting on his coat when he saw me around the corner.

"Hey man, I'm going to handle some business but someone should be coming through to help for a couple of hours around 4 or 5. You good?" Bryce said.

"Yeah, I guess. I'm doing the same ol thing I've been doing. Anything I should know?" I asked.

Bryce paused and said "Look, the superstitious stories about the Murder Castle started in the late 1800s during the World's Fair. H.H. Holmes was a real deal serial killer. They still don't know how many people died in that hotel he built. No one wanted to build a house here, but a post office isn't really haunted. I meant to tell you about it, but I feel like it's just some whatever-whatever. I've worked with a couple of folks on these graveyard shifts during the full moon. People say the last person died during a full moon, and they hear things. Some people claim folks still disappear. Just stay away from the east corner lot with the tree."

"Damn, so no smokes tonight."

"Nope. Maybe it's time to quit."

"You right, you right, so I'll see you tomorrow night."

"Bet."

I didn't know that would be my last words to another human being.

Besides, I'm still in this damn post office, and they don't hear me anyway. Occasionally, I manage to push something off a shelf, but no one notices, or they pretend not to notice.

What I do remember is wishing I had some nicotine patches or a piece of candy. I had three more big bags to load into the sorter and a form to fill out. It was probably turning midnight when I figured a Moon Pie would calm down my cigarette fix. I was turned around and not sure which side of the building I was heading toward. I was walking east.

Behind the counter where you buy stamps and drop off packages, there's usually a wall between us and the public. In that enclosed area, we sometimes joked, laughed, and did what we could to get through a tedious shift. I knew no one else was in the building. It was locked up tight. Most people aren't even out on the streets at that time of night so it's pretty chill. Post offices are made of brick, marble, and steel. The parking area full of trucks is well-lit and fenced, so no one can just walk into the area where I was walking to the vending machine and thinking about a cup of coffee to keep me awake. I wasn't worried about a slightly dim, quiet hallway walk.

I could see the vending machine with Moon Pies, Snickers, pretzels, trail mix, and chips. The light in the vending machine flickered a bit. I was digging into my pocket for change and about to hit M6 for a selection when I heard a rumbling. Nothing was visibly shaking. I figured it might be a semi-truck nearby, but it didn't quite feel like that. I dropped my coins into the machine and watched the silver coil slowly unwind the Moon Pie as it tilted toward the vending machine opening. Then I heard rock cracking and a sharp keening pitched to a scream. My ears stung. I left the Moon Pie in the machine and started running before it hit the bottom.

Sheer sheets of gray and red silk rushed past me and surrounded me. The seemingly soft fabric began to lick at my skin and nick my arms and face with tiny cuts. The marble floors softened into a sticky muck. My shoes sunk into the muddy floor. It smelled like I was sinking into rotting flesh.

I was hoping to make it to the back door, but I wasn't in the well-lit area where the bags and paperwork waited for me. Not even close. I couldn't see the clock, but I knew no one was there so soon after midnight. I still screamed for help anyway.

When the overtime sorter came in at 5:30 AM, he saw my keys on the counter. The radio was still playing. The sun had just peeked its orange head over Lake Michigan. I'm sure he didn't hear me yelling for help. He didn't hear me or the mutilated ghosts trapped here since the World's Fair groaning in confusion and anger.

The next shift of postal workers grumbled about the leftover bags and chalked me up to being one of the people who quit the night shift again. They didn't know I was stuck there, an invisible ether whipping around while seeing and hearing everything in the post office deep within the foundation, a haunting deep in the walls and earth below. It wasn't just a humble post office where you can't even get a passport.

I'm never leaving, trapped like all the victims of H.H. Holmes. I thought some dark, shadowy version of Holmes himself would appear to me, but I never see him, even now. It's like he's dead and gone and he left a sinkhole full of hungry soles who snatch fools like me into their personal hell. They were lost long ago in the walls of his murder castle, underneath trap doors, in secret rooms. They lingered as nightmares in various states of dissection and decay. Some tried to wag tongues that weren't even there.

The only solace I had was knowing that Bryce simply didn't believe that danger he exposed me to was real. He left me alone during a full moon graveyard shift. He should've just locked the doors and said "Let's go get some pancakes at the 24-hour spot downtown."

When Bryce realized I was gone, he knew I was still trapped here. He saw my cigarettes, an unopened pack of Newports, sitting in the unopened plastic wrap. He looked around. I think he felt me staring at him. Bryce said, "Hey Youngblood, I'm sorry. I thought it was just a story. I shoulda been 100 with you and locked up. If you still here, I'm sorry," Bryce said.

I wanted to reach through the invisible barrier between us and shake the hell out of Bryce. The best I could do was raise the cigarettes in the air for a few seconds, then slam them to the floor. Bryce looked around and picked up the pack of cigarettes. He knew now. When they started training my replacement, they made a point to say this branch is always closed during the full moon graveyard shift. Everybody who works there stays home on those nights. Bryce insists that he prays for me, and the old heads cluck their tongues.

PEDAL TO THE FLOOR INTO DARKNESS

K.A. Roy

The first thing you need to know is that my sister died when I was fifteen and she was nineteen. Story goes that Lisa was driving too fast through the bendy part of Lake Shore Drive, you know the one, smack dab between Grand and LaSalle. She took that s-curve doing seventy, like she was running from something in her rearview mirror. Spun out. Hit the median like a spinning top, front passenger bumper crumpling like a stomped pop can. It was past eleven, which if you've ever driven down LSD at night, with all the lights and the trees and city on one side, the lake on the other, is something you never forget.

It was the last thing she ever saw.

I say she died, but the truth is more like she disappeared. Left a shattered windshield with a human-sized hole over the driver's seat. Don't ask me why she wasn't wearing a seatbelt. It makes no sense to me, either. She was the oldest sister; responsibility was ingrained in her very bones.

I've heard people saw her flying. High up over the cars going south, through the sparse trees along the road, right into the city like she was being called home.

No one ever found her body. I like to think she got up and walked away with the scraped knees of a kid who fell off their bike. It doesn't do me any good to sit in this idea of her, so torn to ribbons that she disappeared in a spray of red mist somewhere between the lanes of traffic and the highrises. That passersby clicked their windshield wipers on and washed Lisa away with the drizzle that had taken up not fifteen minutes before the crash.

No, I don't like that idea at all. I believe she's alive somewhere. That she got away from the thing she was running from, or maybe she went with it.

Everything reminds me of Lisa, a creation of my own design. I set my feet in the prints she left behind. Lisa went to Columbia College, so I enrolled, too. Her first apartment was in Logan Square, so I found some college kids on Craigslist needing a roommate and now I pay a third of the rent to live on the top floor of a brownstone in the very same neighborhood. On the very same street, even, but not the same block.

I like that I can walk around, chain smoking cigs from the corner gas station that no one ever fills their tank in, and feel the echo of her existence in every step. I look over my shoulder, hoping one day she'll be standing right there. Watching.

I'll never give up the search. Moving here, going to her school, it all felt like I was that much closer to finding her. I spent an inordinate amount of time at the school library, perusing the shelves, hoping to one day shift some aside and find her green eyes peeking through from the other side.

It's been three years and I'm too close to graduating, but I'm no closer to Lisa.

My sister hated clowns. She had a real, honest to god fear of them. I think of her every time I climb out of my street-facing bedroom window to sit on the slanting roof. Lighting a joint in the night, the neighborhood washed in yellow streetlights, I can look to my left and see the Little Clown Pizza that divides my side of Central Park Ave. from where Lisa lived. Shadows move beyond the windows. Sometimes, as smoke billows thickly around me, the shadows pause, lingering in place. Like whoever stands there is watching, their eyes set on me, seeing how I pull my knees to my chest. How I rest my chin on top of the bones. It makes me shiver, even on a humid night.

I wonder if Lisa ever got the creeps having to turn the corner in front of the shop just to get home. Whether the smiling clown tossing a pizza in the air was a threat to her nervous system, or maybe the shadows within turned and watched as she passed by.

Well, I know she did. She's my sister. My blood. Every time a chill ran down her back, I'm sure it echoed over mine, no matter our distance. We were tied together like that. Not twins, but might as well have been.

We were bound by loss.

Our family has a history of disappearing.

Shortly after I turned one, which made Lisa around kindergarten age, our dad left us. Well, that's the story, anyway. My first memory goes something like this:

Mom, skinny as a rail, sitting cross-legged on the hardwood floor of our family room. All the lights were on in every room, even though it was morning, like she was keeping something out. Her blonde hair shone golden in the warm glow. Arms outstretched, palms up, fingers beckoning. Me, standing, swaying, before high-tailing it across the narrow room and into her arms.

"Lisa!" Mom called, hugging me against her gray sweatshirt. It was damp against my cheek. "Lisa, your sister just took her first steps!"

Lisa's pattering feet entered the room from the kitchen, a red popsicle trickling juice down her hand.

"Sophia walked?" she asked, licking her skin clean.

"She did!" Mom pushed me back to standing and said, "Soph, walk to your sister."

I took a few teetering steps and stopped halfway between them, mouth opening and closing like a fish out of water. The popsicle had caught my attention.

"Dad's gonna be sorry he missed it."

"Dad's gone." Mom got to her feet, brushed off her jeans, and scooped me up on her way to the kitchen. That was it. No fanfare. No explanation. She set me on the floor next to the fridge. "I think you deserve a popsicle."

Mine was purple.

The memory isn't mine, not really. It was given to me by Lisa, one day when we were older, sitting on the porch of our north Chicago bungalow steps, melting in the summer sun. I said to her, sipping ice cold Kool-Aid, "I don't know why, but grape flavor always makes me think of Dad."

Now, my memory is tied to too many things. Driving. The sounds of the city. Lake Michigan and nighttime and clowns and this brownstone I live in and taking the stairs at school because the elevators in the old as fuck building are always too small and too packed to bother. It's everything she's done or was doing when she left, but I wish it was as infrequent, and avoidable, as the taste of artificial grape.

Lisa confessed to me, not long after our porch convo, that she often felt watched.

"It's cus you're pretty," I said.

"Not like that."

"Like how?"

We were in the parking lot of a White Hen, propping our bikes between our thighs as we ate Snickers we'd just bought. Our Slurpees balanced precariously on the trashcan lid beside us; she preferred cherry, and I took a long pull from my icy Coke as I waited for her answer. Preoccupied, Lisa kept casting glances over her shoulder to the alley. A group of teenage boys about her age stood there smoking, fucking around doing ollies on skateboards. They weren't paying a lick of attention to either of us.

"Like, creepy," she said, and shuddered. I shuddered, too. It was the Slurpee, I told myself. But I think I knew, even then, that it was something more.

"Scaredy-cat."

"I'm serious, Soph." She polished off her chocolate bar and wouldn't meet my eye.

"Okay. Sorry. Creepy how?"

Lisa looked at me sharply then, her green eyes glinting in the scorching sun.

"Like something's watching me, waiting to snatch me up."

"That's not gonna happen. I'm always with you."

It wasn't a lie. Mom had us stick together whenever we left the house, and when we were home, we were together already anyway. We were often alone together, because Mom had to work. Back then wasn't like now. Kids went without supervision younger, and for longer, than they do these days.

"Sure," Lisa said back then, crumbling up her wrapper after licking the melted chocolate out of it. And that was the end of it. We got on our bikes, awkwardly kicking off. One-handedly, we rode through the city, sucking away at our Slurpees to combat the summer heatwave.

I noticed the way she turned her head at alleys and gangways, almost like a tic. I tried to see what she saw, but there was never anything but brick and stretching darkness, chain-link fences and junkyard dogs.

She didn't tell me until much later, when she got into Columbia College and was moving to Logan Square, that it never stopped. I should have known from the purple circles around her eyes, from the paranoia and the unwillingness to leave her apartment after dark. If wishes came true, I'd wish that I had taken her seriously back then, but I was only a kid. And honestly, what could I have done?

I understand now. It took a few years to happen to me, just like it did for her after Dad left. On a random spring day, I woke up with a feeling. One of being watched, observed. I'd fallen asleep in Lisa's bed, something I did a lot in the years before I, too, entered adulthood. It was the feeling that woke me. I peeled my eyes open one at a time, but not fully. My heart thumped in my chest, anxiety pumping through my veins.

"Mom?"

I can't say I called out for her. I was too scared. My voice caught in my throat, came out in a whisper. The clock on Lisa's nightstand read 4:58. The sun hadn't come out yet and the bedroom was bathed in grays, with the exception of the digital clock which cast a bright glow over the wood beneath. A minute ticked over.

I heard a breath. An exhale followed by a sharp inhale.

"Lisa?"

I don't know why I thought it was her. Maybe the sound of the breath, or because I was in her room, or I wasn't fully awake or something.

The next sound was more of a chuckle than a breath. I froze halfway to sitting, my elbow digging into the mattress. Trembling so hard, the duvet shook. I lowered back down and pulled the blanket over my head. Can't explain how, even after all this time, but whatever was watching stayed watching until the clatter and clank of Mom in the bathroom gave me the courage to fling off the cover, sprint from the room.

We nearly collided in the hallway.

"Soph? You okay?"

Her hands on mine, squeezing. My eyes wild, searching. I could still hear breathing, somewhere behind me. In the depths of the hall. In the linen closet, slightly ajar.

I remember looking over my shoulder. Mom tugging my hands, asking for my attention.

"No," she said.

"Huh?"

She shook her head. Her golden hair had lost its luster, weighted by the grease of grief.

"Not you."

Shaking, baffled, I said nothing.

She pulled me into her, wrapped herself around me in a way she hadn't since Lisa disappeared.

"Not you, too," she whispered, muffled, into my hair.

It's been three years since that day. Six have passed since Lisa flew through the Chicago night, never to be seen again.

At first, I tried to ignore the feeling. When I realized it wasn't letting up, when I truly understood why Lisa had jumped at every turn and checked every shadow, I tried something new. What did I have to lose? Mom understood, so nonchalant about Dad's leaving—less so about Lisa, though a daughter is a different breed—that I thought for a while she felt it, too. But the longer the feeling clung to me, wove into my every day, the more I saw that she didn't understand. She only accepted it as a coping mechanism, a way to stay afloat.

I get that.

I wanted to stay afloat, too.

So I started to chase after it. In alleys between buildings, I'd turn and sprint, trying to catch the watchers unaware. Determined, eyes narrowed, fists pumping. Always, I'd stumble out onto the other side of the dark. Into the sunshine of people's yards, of parking lots, of back-alley dumpsters. Smashing out a joint on shingles, I'd double back through my bedroom window, fly through my apartment and out onto the street. Skin slapping on pavement, on rocks, sometimes shards of glass, I ran to the corner, barely waiting for cars flying down Diversey to stop. But when I got to the storefront glass, cupping my hands around my eyes to peer in, I'd find only staff staring back, surprised. After a while, I stopped that habit. The workers probably thought me deranged.

I was deranged.

I've grown crazy with it. The feeling is forever nipping at my heels. Lisa slept with the light on to chase the shadows away, but I do the opposite. I turn them all off. Welcome the dark. Give the watchers an opportunity to loom, to lurk, to snatch me up and take me away.

Dad left. Lisa ran, pedal to the floor, accelerating toward the end.

Or maybe she didn't run.

As I pull onto Lake Shore Drive, I wonder. Was she running? Or did she, like me, finally transition from haunted to pursuer? Did she know that night, six years ago, was the one when she'd succeed?

My window is down. I blow a funnel of smoke out of it, caught in the whipping wind. To my right is the lake; I can smell it, fresh today, the perfect lake smell. To my left is the city, noisy and robust, brimming with people who may be running—or chasing down—their own watchers. The lights are bright against the darkness, but that only means there are plenty of shadows. I squint against them, eyes stinging from the wind and the blown-back smoke.

Did Lisa feel it, too? The draw?

The bend is ahead, the turn where she spun out. An urge washes over me, one I don't fight. Incrementally, I press my foot against the pedal.

Maybe I'll atomize, rain down across the road and the people, disappear into thin air. Maybe that's all this ever was, daughters of a father destined to vanish, called by the darkness that surrounds us.

My foot falls harder. I can feel it, that what's been following me is up ahead. That we'll collide if I push a little faster, if I go a little farther.

When the game is over, I'll finally find where she is.

She's been waiting.

I feel it in my bones.

LOWEST WACKER

Christopher Hawkins

She stood on the sidewalk near the river and watched the snow fall. Unhurried, it drifted down among the glass and steel towers in fat flakes as wide as dimes to settle on a blanket of white so pure and unblemished that it would have been at home in a display window at Marshall Field's. How long had it been since she'd seen a snowfall like this? Not since she was a child, she was sure. And how long ago had that been? Enough years that she'd lost count and still so few that it seemed like only yesterday. There was a hush over the city that only this kind of snow could bring, a hush that muted the shouting voices and kept them from echoing up the skyscrapers, a hush that turned the sound of passing cars into the rumble of a distant lullaby.

She'd forgotten her coat. That wasn't like her at all, or at least she didn't think it was. She looked up at the building with its arches and high balconies and thought about going back inside, but the people on the sidewalk were crowding in closer now and the door seemed so far away. A cab pulled up to the curb and she dove for it without checking to see if the fare light was lit.

"It's really coming down out there," the driver said. "Hell of a night to be out in it."

She said nothing. Outside the window, the people moved like pigeons, darting back and forth as if the snow had panicked them somehow and left them running in circles. The cab slid away from the curb and left them behind, and though she turned her head to watch them, they were soon lost behind a curtain of white.

"Haven't seen a storm like this since the one in 2018," the driver said. "Remember that one? Drifts three feet high. People just leaving their cars on Lake Shore Drive? Hell of a mess. Whole city was shut down for a week."

She wasn't sure if she did remember. Her head was all swimmy from the booze. Or was it just the booze? She remembered little piles of powder scraped into tidy lines, like piles of snow at the edge of a sidewalk.

"Won't be anything like that this time," the driver said. "Should stop by midnight and the plows will do their thing. Come morning, it'll be like a whole different place."

He was wearing sunglasses, though it was already dark outside, and he had long sideburns that ran down his rounded cheeks. She thought that perhaps she'd seen him somewhere before but couldn't think of where. She thought to check for his name and license, but realized then that she didn't have her purse or her phone. She searched for her pockets, but found she didn't have those either. She was wearing her black cocktail dress, the one with the high neckline that made her look like Audrey Hepburn. She'd left her shoes behind, along with her coat, and wondered how she'd managed to make it this far.

"Course, it's not the snow you have to worry about. It's the other drivers. First snowfall of the year and everyone forgets how to drive. Don't worry about it, though. I know a shortcut."

"But I haven't told you where I'm going yet." She hadn't thought about that herself yet either. She'd only known that she had to get away and that she'd taken the first chance she saw. The driver hadn't seemed to hear her though. He was busy with the radio, one of those old-style types with two knobs, the speakers full of static until they found a station with a driving harmonica backed by a rollicking piano and high, brassy horns.

Come on now baby don't you make me late. Come on now baby don't you tell me no lies . . .

"Junior Wells and Buddy Guy," the driver said. "Man, that takes me back. You know 'em?"

He didn't give her a chance to answer before the cab slid into a quick turn that pressed her body against the door.

"Nobody played the blues harp like Junior. They say he stole a harmonica when he was twelve years old, but when the judge heard him play, he paid for it out of his own pocket. I don't know if that's true, but I believe it."

The cab took another turn that sent her listing across the vinyl seat. There was a sensation of moving downward and suddenly the sky outside the windows went dark. Rows of metal columns passed them by, rising up to meet the steel decking of the roadway above.

"Is this Lower Wacker?" she asked.

The driver had a cigarette dangling from his mouth as one hand fiddled with the lighter in the dashboard. "Michigan."

"What?"

He pressed the tip of the lighter to the end of the cigarette until it grew red, then he tossed the lighter out the open window. "Lower Michigan. See, that's the Billy Goat Tavern." He inclined his head toward a row of windows set into a brick wall, neon signs glowing like a beacon in the perpetual darkness. "Saturday Night Live, remember? 'Cheeseburger, cheeseburger'?"

"No Coke. Pepsi," she said absently, the memory clearer than anything she could recall from the past few hours. A little man with close-set eyes in a trenchcoat and a too-small hat stood smoking a cigar on the sidewalk with a notebook in one hand. He watched her as she passed by, and she turned her head to watch him back, and kept watching until he slid out of sight.

"This whole place is like a maze," the driver said. "Every part of the Loop from one end to the other, it's all connected down here, from the post office all the way to Lake Shore Drive."

"Why'd you bring me down here?"

He shrugged. "This is the quickest way to where we're going. No snow. No traffic up top. Easy."

"But I never told you where we're going."

The driver smiled. It was a charming smile, and she felt herself being charmed by it. "Don't worry," he said. "I know this city like the back of my hand. Just leave it all to me."

She thought about where she might want to go. Not back home, certainly. There'd been a party. She remembered that now. She must have been drunk or high or both, because she could barely recall who'd been there, or when she'd left. She remembered Richard, though, his hand on the small of her back, guiding her. She hated when he did that, moving her the way he wanted her moved, like she was some kind of pampered pet that he only wanted to show off. He'd whispered something in her ear. She didn't remember what it was, but she remembered that she hadn't liked it. No, she wasn't going back home. Even down here in the dark was better than that.

The car swerved, and metal columns gave way to concrete pillars. A loading dock slid past, a row of makeshift tents and cardboard boxes lining the cinderblock wall. Hunched shadows moved among them with scruffy beards and threadbare coats, bodies huddled around trashcan fires, searching for warmth.

"This is definitely Lower Wacker Drive," he said. "You live in this town long enough, sooner or later you find your way down here, one way or another. They filmed that Batman movie here, remember? Heath Ledger? Went way too young. They always do. Drugs, they said. It's always drugs, isn't it? I know a thing or two about that, myself. Used to really know how to party back in the day."

He tapped a finger against the side of his nose. She remembered lines of powder on a little glass coaster, an itch deep in her sinuses, then nothing at all.

"Could you take the next exit?" she said. "I'd like to get out, please."

The driver shook his head. "On a night like this? You don't even have a coat."

"All the same, It's imperative that you let me out at the next exit, please."

"All right. There's no call to use big words."

The cab lurched again and she felt almost weightless as they hurtled down a narrow ramp and jolted so hard at the bottom that the chassis sent up sparks. "Why are we going down?" she asked once she'd righted herself. "We need to go up."

"I told you, this is a shortcut."

The space they were in was cavernous, with wide lanes and large parking lots arranged on either side. Garbage trucks rusted in the shadowed corners, hunched like sleeping bison next to leaning stacks of wooden pallets and rows of unused barricades.

"Shortcut to where? I've never even been down here. What is this place?"

"This is *lower* Lower Wacker. The Emerald City. They call it that because the lights down here used to be green before they changed them all."

"But the lights are green now."

The driver nodded, as if surprised. "Well, what do you know?"

The glow of the lights gave the place an unworldly tinge, as if the cab were gliding into some other where, or some other when.

"Most people don't get down this way unless they need to get a car out of lock-up," the driver said. "They used to run illegal street races down here at night. Got to where you could hear the noise from the engines all the way in the fancy apartments up top."

"What do you mean 'used to'? They're right there."

They slid past one of the parking lots where a muscular-looking black car spun, tires squealing as it laid down dark circles on the pavement. Young people were arranged all around it, leaning on the bumpers of their own cars, arms around each other's shoulders, the sleeves of their jackets rolled up to the elbows as they downed their beers and smoked their cigarettes. Engines growled and rose as smoke filled the air with the thick smell of burning rubber. The driver gave two friendly honks of the horn as they passed, and a few heads turned their way and regarded them with narrowed eyes until they were finally out of sight.

"Where are you taking me?" she asked.

"I'm a cab driver. I take you where you *need* to go."

"But I didn't tell you where I want to go."

"It ain't about want, lady. It's about *need*."

"Then what I need is for you to pull over so that I can get out of the car, please."

The driver shook his head. "You don't want to get out here."

"And why is that?"

The driver turned and regarded her over his shoulder, one eyebrow raised behind dark glasses. "Because it's not your stop yet."

The car dived again, no ramp this time, but darkness all around. She felt her rear end leave the seat, and she had to grab onto the door handle to keep from flying up into the cab's roof. She tried the latch, but it would not open. She tried the handle for the window, but it would not roll down.

"There's a whole network of tunnels down here that flooded back in the nineties." The driver's face glowed red, lit only by the bobbing tip of his cigarette as he inhaled. "Fish in the basement of the Merchandise Mart, if you can believe that. Way after my time, though."

Light flared, so bright that she had to squint until her eyes adjusted. When they did, she could see the decking of the roadway above them as it sped past. Outside, the snow was gone and the sun was shining. The side of the road opened up onto a view of the river. Across it, she could see people crowded shoulder to shoulder, dancing in the street. Some carried flags, some wore jerseys, but nearly all of them were dressed in red and black. Or was it orange and navy blue?

"Those were the days, weren't they? Felt like the whole city was one big party." The driver had the windows rolled up, but she could hear the sounds of celebration filtering in through the stereo's speakers. "There was this optimism in the air, like anything was possible. Hasn't been anything like it since."

She watched the revelers as they danced, and felt her heart grow lighter as it filled with their energy. When was the last time she'd had that feeling? Never with Richard. Not since the beginning, anyway. Who had fallen out of love first, she wondered. There had been so much of it between them in those early days. Where had it all gone?

"Of course, it didn't last," the driver said. "There hasn't been a championship in twenty years. Feels like those days are over now, like there's no point in even getting your hopes up sometimes."

She remembered leaning out over the railing, the snow falling below her, converging on a point in the darkness like a tunnel to nowhere. She blinked the thought away, and when she opened her eyes again she could see the Sears Tower out beyond the roadway. Seeing it there made no sense. It was on the other side of town. It made even less sense that it wasn't finished. Its top half was missing, its floors exposed to the open air.

"But that's always been what this town's about. That optimism." The driver was watching her now, not watching the road, though the cab seemed to know the way forward anyway. "It's easy to forget it, though. Maybe it's because of all the things we've gone through to pay for it."

She blinked again and what had just been a parade was now a riot. Rows of police in white helmets raised their batons high as they advanced on a crowd of young people shouting and carrying signs. To her, they seemed barely older than children. The batons swung, and shouts turned to screams as the children scattered and fell with blood streaming from their foreheads. Tear gas flew, and she felt the sting of it in her nostrils as the scene faded away behind a veil of smoke. Shadows moved in the fog, resolving themselves into new images. Young bodies wrapped in plastic, pulled from beneath a brick house. White men in suits firing guns into an apartment full of black men. A room full of young women tied with bedsheets, stabbed and strangled with their own clothes. By the time she could look away, the cab was falling again.

"I want to get out," she said into the darkness, when she could speak again.

The driver's voice answered back. "You can't get out here. We're not where we're going yet."

"I want to go home," she said in a voice so small that it frightened her.

As the cab began to brighten, the driver looked back at her over the tops of his dark glasses. "If that were true, you never would have left."

Feet slipping out of shoes on a snowy balcony. A pitch forward over the rail and out into gravity.

"I want to go back."

Once again she felt the hum of pavement beneath the cab's tires, the speed of it as it hurtled onward, relentless and unstoppable.

"Can't go back," the driver said. "Can't go anywhere. Storm's got the whole city locked down."

In the gap beyond the roadway, the city was buried beneath a blanket of white. The sun shone down over empty streets, electric lines hanging limp and useless, heavy with snow. A black Model T listed sideways, half buried. This was not the city as she remembered it. The towers of glass and steel were gone. In their place were only squat buildings of brick and stone.

"Am I…?"

"Yeah. I'm afraid you are."

"Are you…?"

"Lady, I'm just a cab driver. All I know is, the only way out is down this road. Everything else is snowed under."

"But where does the road go?"

The driver said nothing as the cab trundled through a crossroads. A scratchy recording played over the radio, an almost mournful voice over the lonely twang of a guitar. *But I'm cryin' hey baby, Honey don't you want to go …*

"Will it take me out of the city?"

The driver shook his head. "You're a part of it now. Every good thing and bad. Works its way down into this place, all the way to the bones. Nothing ever leaves. Not really, anyway. After a while, it all just… is."

The cab flew by a theater where three men in fedoras chased another into an alley. They were already past when the gunfire started, but she could still hear it echoing its way up between the brick walls. On the river, a passenger ship rolled sideways, sending people overboard where the water silenced their screams. Further on, a crowd of white people threw stones at a black child drowning in the lake.

"What if I don't want to stay?"

"None of us gets a say in that," the driver said. "We already made all our choices. All our choices except one."

The road dropped away again and she felt herself leave the seat. She floated there, weightless in the dark, unsure if the cab and the driver were still there at all, unsure if she was even still herself, if she had ever been herself, and not merely something that darkness had imagined.

She landed with a jolt, and the seat and the cab and the driver were all back in their places again. The driver turned the corner of his mouth up into a wry little smile and cocked his head toward the window. "It's not all bad though," he said. "Every trip has its high points."

No longer underground, the cab hurtled down a wide lane. On either side, men in top hats strolled alongside women in wide hats and dresses with wider bustles. Beyond them stood a series of towering pavilions, all adorned with columns as if they had risen right out of ancient Rome, a white city laid out along the lakeshore and stretching out as far as her eyes could see. She stared at the buildings in wonder as she passed, and at the people who seemed plucked from an older, gentler time. They turned their heads as the cab passed by, and gave slight nods in her direction, as if in welcoming.

"I think I'd like to get out here, please."

The sky shifted and the sun dove behind the buildings to plunge the white city in darkness. All at once, the light came back, this time from the city itself. Lit by a thousand glowing bulbs, the city took on new outlines, each pavilion glowing with the safety of a welcoming fire. She'd lived with electricity all her life, but still this felt like something new, like the promise of a future that was just waiting for her to reach out and grasp.

"Yeah, I get that a lot," the driver said. "This is the city at its best, the way it always wanted to be. And look at all these people. I think they really believe it could be that way, too."

"Do you believe it?"

The driver thought for a moment, and shrugged. "It doesn't matter what I believe. What matters is out there. If you look hard enough, you'll see it's not all bright lights and cotton candy."

As the cab reached the end of the lighted causeway, she saw a man dipping his hand into a woman's pocketbook when she wasn't looking. Further on, a furtive young woman in a homespun dress stood at the steps of a boxy hotel. The man in the bowler hat with the heavy-lidded eyes beckoned her in, and beneath his mustache she caught a fleeting, sinister grin.

"Why are you so intent on showing me the bad things?" she asked. "Why would you show me something beautiful just to tear it all away?"

"Like I said, lady. I'm just the driver. You picked the trip. You picked the destination. I'm just here to get you to the end of the line."

The cab dove again, and all around them were flames. Through them she could see a line of police in civil-war uniforms advancing on a political rally, a bomb exploding, an exchange of gunfire. Through the flames, she saw bodies lining the streets, their faces covered in the raised welts of disease. Through the flames she saw children wandering the alleyways, their cheeks sunken, their bellies swollen. Through the flames she saw greed and crime and cruelty until at last there was nothing but the flames themselves, racing from intersection to intersection, burning the low wooden buildings and everything else in their path. Men in horse-drawn fire wagons worked frantically to pump water on the fire, but the conflagration barely noticed them as it jumped across the river and herded screaming people toward the lakeshore. Her ears filled with their anguished cries and the crackle of burning wood, until she too screamed, a long and terrible wail that filled the cab with the sound of her despair even as she buried her face in her hands.

All became silent then as she fought to regain her breath, wishing all the while that she could make it all go away, the cab, the driver, and everything around them, from the fire to the people, from the river to the lake and all the tunnels underground. She wished she'd never set foot in this cab. She wished she'd never stepped out onto that balcony. She wished that she could see the snow again, drifting down, covering the city with promise instead of cinders and ash.

"Take me back," she said, her voice small and trembling.

The driver shook his head. The impish malice was gone from his face now along with the glasses that had hidden his eyes. They were deep blue, and full of sympathy, topped with heavy eyebrows and set in a cherub's face. "That's the thing we can never do," he said. "There's a moment, that last moment, where we still have a choice, where we can stop what's coming. Once that moment's gone, it's gone for good."

From out of the darkness around them came a low sound, distant and faint. As it grew, it resolved into the rhythmic beating of drums, drawing closer, growing louder. Over the cab's speakers came the raised voices of hundreds of men and women, chanting in time, turning the beat into a song that rose and fell like marching footsteps, a mournful dirge punctuated with fierce ululations that shot through the thundering voices like lightning bolts.

Across the river, a line of men danced before the squat wooden houses. Stripped to the waist and clad in only loincloths, they moved in meandering circles, shifting from one foot to the other, their black hair done up in feathers, their bodies streaked with red and black. As they danced down the wide dirt road, a procession followed them. Women and old men carried heavy packs on their backs and pulled at wagons. Children huddled close, walking in their parents' footsteps, their eyes wide and fearful.

"Where are they going?" she asked.

The cab had slowed to a crawl now, a pace that matched the forward progress of the dancers. "Away," the driver said. "They'll end up somewhere in Kansas, the ones that make it."

"But why are they leaving?" she asked, even though deep in her heart she already knew.

"They don't have a choice. They lived here for hundreds of years until someone else decided they didn't. Stroke of a pen, just like that."

She closed her eyes and listened to the sound of their music, letting it fill her, letting the beat of the drum become the beating of her own heart.

"Can't they stay? It doesn't have to be this way, does it? Can't we go back just a little further and make it so they can stay?"

The cab driver shook his head. "This trip isn't for them. It's for you. All their choices were made for them. You only have one more choice to make, and it has to be for yourself."

"But what if I gave up my choice? What if I gave it to them?"

"It doesn't work like that," the driver said. "You can't change what's already happened. None of us can. And even if we could, it all would have ended up the same one way or another. Sooner or later, people take what they want, if they want it bad enough. The city might have gone up different, but the end would have been the same."

The dancers were gone now, and the street where they had marched was nothing more than brush and gravel. A wooden fort stood in the distance on a hill next to the river. Around it rode horses carrying men with bows in their hands. They loosed their arrows over the palisades where little tufts of black smoke rose into the air to be whisked away by the wind from the lake. There was no more song, only gunfire and the whooping cries of war.

"You make it sound like there's no hope," she said quietly.

"Isn't that what brought us here? Lost hope? A whole life in front of you, and you traded it in for, what? Nothing. All because you couldn't believe something better was coming down the road."

"I didn't give up hope," she said.

He turned back and stared at her, eyes penetrating, one eyebrow raised.

"All right," she said. "I did give up hope. But I shouldn't have. And I don't want to give up now."

The driver smiled at this, and as he turned back around, she could feel the cab begin to accelerate. "You made your last choice, then," he said. "And it looks like we're almost there."

The cab rolled on along the river toward the lake, and when it reached the water it jerked sideways and sent her sliding against the door. It didn't dive down this time, but merely jolted along as loose sand grabbed hold of the tires and brought them lurching to a stop. Static whistled faintly from the speakers like a distant morning breeze.

She tried the door handle, and this time it gave way with a little click and the squeal of unoiled hinges. She stepped outside and felt the sand, loose and rocky beneath her bare feet. The wind was strong and cool off the lake, full of the sounds of waves crashing against the shore and the cries of gulls circling overhead. She closed her eyes, breathed it in, and let it fill her.

"Welcome to the end of the road, I guess."

The driver stood behind her. She hadn't heard him get out of the cab. He wore a black suit with a skinny tie, and on his head was a narrow-brimmed black fedora. The fort was gone from the hill behind him, as were the wooden buildings that had once crowded the riverbanks. The wind stirred the reeds and the wild onions at the shore and played gently at her hair like the touch of a friend.

"What is this place?"

The driver smiled. "You already know the answer to that."

"All right," she said. "When is this place?"

"The beginning. After the glaciers, but before any of the people. Just a sandy spot along a brand-new lake, just sitting here, waiting to be found."

She breathed in the air, surprised that she could breathe it in, that she could smell it in her nostrils and taste it on her tongue, brisk with chill and the faint sulfur-scent of lake weeds.

"Why did you bring me here?"

"I think you know the answer to that, too."

She turned her face into the wind, to the spot where the waters of the lake met the distant reddening sky, where the sun was just beginning to rise.

"Then I can stay?"

The driver said nothing. He, too, was looking out at the lake, as if there were something out there that only he could see. And he was smiling.

"Will I be alone?" she asked.

The driver thought about this for a moment, the whole time never taking his eyes off the lake. "We'll still be around," he said. "All the ones who gave up too early, and realized it a little too late."

"Won't it change things, though? The future, I mean."

The driver turned to her, then. His glasses were gone, and his eyes were little pools of mischief beneath his storm-cloud eyebrows.

"The future's already there," he said. "It's just waiting for you and all the rest of us to make it happen. The good. The bad. All of it. Everything we've seen and everything we will see, on and on until all of it grinds back down to dust."

The thought should have frightened her. Instead, it was a spot of warmth that swelled within her and pushed away the chill wind.

"Will I still be here then?"

He turned back to the lake, but his smile told her the answer.

"How do you know?"

The driver shrugged. "How do you think I knew where to find you? How do you think I knew to be there right at the precise moment when you needed to get out of the snow?"

The waves rolled in, so close that they almost touched her toes. Sandpipers wheeled overhead, fixing their wings against the wind and letting it carry them higher.

"Magic," she said.

She wouldn't have thought it possible, but the driver's smile grew wider. "Yeah," he said. "Yeah. That it is."

She remembered then where she had seen him before. She turned her head to tell him so, but he was already off and running down the beach. The cab was gone and he was barefoot now too. He dove into a series of cartwheels, moving with a nimbleness that belied his size. His thin tie waved in the breeze, but his hat stayed firmly on his head. She turned away from him then, knowing that when she turned back he would be gone, but not for the last time. Far down the opposite end of the lakeshore, she could see the distant shapes of people wrapped in furs and taking hesitant steps closer. She ran to them, knowing that they would not see her. All around them, snow was just beginning to fall.

ALL YOU ARE IS BRIGHT AND CLEAR

Bendi Barrett

You're walking down Western Avenue, the quiet stretch that passes under the highway. It's late enough, or early enough, that there's not much foot traffic. You politely give a wide berth to the hard luck folks sleeping under the overpass as you head south. Your head feels like it's stuffed full of cotton balls and your mouth tastes like sand feels, any drier and you'd start a wildfire between tongue and front teeth. You turn your collar up against the wind and try to wrangle the drug-addled thoughts ricocheting through your brain.

Like the ones currently centered on the dagger-thin man you're approaching. He's swimming in his oversized hoodie and hiding unruly curls under a Red Sox cap. *Bold choice for Chicago*, you think. He's unlocking the front door of a tire store you've passed a million times. As you go by him on the sidewalk he glances over at you for just a half second longer than is strictly necessary for a threat assessment. You wonder if it's flirting and then he licks his lower lip, narrows his gaze ever so slightly; your pants get tighter. *He's a wolf*, you think.

Your mind tallies his lean figure, sagging jeans, the colorful tattoos across his left hand which is balled into a fist against the cold. You imagine the violence he could do to you and how you'd howl for him. The moment hangs for just another breath, then he pushes the door open and walks inside. There's a world where you follow him in and see what develops, where he puts his hands all over you and his canines into your neck, but that scenario happens to someone else. In this reality you just keep walking into the wind.

And it's fine. You didn't need to be flirted with, anyway. You're still effervescing last night's booze and more than booze, still wearing another man's underwear. A man you think you might be in love with. But it's getting harder to tell if the connection is indelible through the haze of alcohol, nicotine, and occasional MDMA—where occasional is in scare quotes.

His smell is still all over your skin, and every time you catch a whiff of it your stomach flutters a little in concern or delight; the sun is just starting to come up. Less than an hour ago, you were on top of him, dripping sweat and writhing and mumbling chaos in the base pleasure of it all. You were trying to ascend; you were trying to take him with you. But all you ended up with was a sodden pair of briefs, his come cooling on your facial hair, and the distinct urge to grind your teeth. Your aspirations for holy communion are thwarted by the hard, sharp tug of reality's leash.

A few more storefronts go by, all closed. You pass the restaurant where you sat across from him and he eviscerated your take on Sofia Coppola's filmography. He accused you of being hopelessly out of touch with modern film critique in between too-large bites of tacos al pastor. You pass the store that caters to his compulsive vape habit. You wonder, and not for the first time, about the differences between adoration and chemical dependency.

You cross the street to avoid the street corner where you had your first fight. It's not worth the psychic blowback and the cool air is just starting to help you feel human again. You usually follow the same path to his apartment and then back home, so the view from this side of the street feels slightly new. There's a cafe and a cocktail bar, both still closed. There are a handful of people out walking their dogs in the early morning gloom, but mostly it's just you and the cold gusts that the city of Chicago passes off as spring.

The neon shop sneaks up on you. It's more accurate to say that you miss it entirely. You're nearly a block down the street when something about it tickles your inattentive brain, coils a finger around your peripheral vision and yanks firmly. You've never seen it before. It could be new, or you could be so wrapped up in your own bullshit half the time that your gaze elides it from reality. The latter implication is what makes you stop, turn around, and walk back. You want to believe that you're not this fucked up over a guy that you've missed the wonders this city has to offer. You want to believe, with increasing desperation, that there is more to you than desperation. And you already called out of work, so what's stopping you?

The "Neon Shoppe" has a fairly unremarkable façade, which might be why you missed it to begin with. Yeah, that's why. Definitely.

There are three pieces arranged in the shop window with a black curtain behind them, obscuring the rest of the store. One of the neon signs reads "beer o'clock," one's an enormous Cubs logo, and then there's what looks like a vintage motor oil advertisement. And, of course, there's the bright blue open sign—which is lit. The aggregate glow of the signs casts a cool, blue-dominant aura outward onto the street. You stand in its wash and consider the open sign. It's probably just another advertisement. There's no way this shop would be open at 6:40 AM. What customer requires neon, of all things, before breakfast?

You're still coming down and you feel a chemical-derived openness that's relentlessly seeking connection and beauty, or could be that you're just really fucking lonely, but either way you decide to go in. You try the door. It opens inward and a little bell jingles above you. *Okay, I was wrong*, you think, *it is really open*. But now you're in the awkward position of being the customer that walks into a neon store before the sun has fully risen. You glance around, wondering if you should make your escape before whoever works here notices you. For some reason you think about the lean man opening the tire store and looking you over, a wolf with an appetite.

But you don't walk out, you look around and inhale sharply through your nose. The works of neon on the inside of the store are nothing like the predictable pieces in the shop window. You take in one piece in particular: an homage to *The Dream of the Fisherman's Wife* featuring a nude woman in 40s pin-up style whose pale, bare limbs of brilliant white neon are crisscrossed by long arms of pale blue belonging to a partially surfaced sea creature which feasts on her. The woman's expression is rapturous; the neon hums.

You wonder if you could experience such abandon in her stead: head back, mouth open, legs spread, only the sopping wet tendril obscuring your pleasure from full view. Your own skin grows clammy and sensitive as you imagine the slithering tendrils working their way up your body, underneath your clothes, wrapping themselves around your throat and applying enough pressure to make you see stars.

"An interesting piece," says a voice from in front of you. You look down from the wall and are a little startled to find both that you have drifted further into the store and that there is a person before you. A sallow-faced man with dark eyes wearing a beat-up leather smock over a white sleeveless button-down. His expression is neither a smile nor a frown: if pressed, you'd call it neutral. However, he does remind you of something. The unfinished comparison tickles the back of your mind.

"Oh, right, yeah. Sorry. I didn't know if you were open. I kind of assumed you wouldn't be," you say.

"I don't sleep much, so I open early. Are you in the market?" asks the sallow-faced man, gesturing to the piece you were staring at. He says, "A stunning interpretation of the Edo period painting. Scholars have debated the woman's pleasure in the ukiyo-e work, but the text in its original Japanese implies the woman is very much an active participant in the erotic scene. Perhaps it is impossible for men to truly imagine a woman experiencing pleasure."

You nod, not knowing how to respond to that, and the sallow-faced man seems to take the hint. "I'll let you browse. If you need anything, or require clarity, please come find me."

You almost laugh aloud at the offer of clarity. If it was there for the asking, you wouldn't be in therapy once a week and your thighs wouldn't be straining against the too-tight underwear of a man you're ambivalent about. But you mutter thanks and continue to browse.

The shop is a fairly small space with fairly large ceilings organized into neat, tight rows by tall metal dividers that rise at least eight feet up. Entering any given row means disappearing from the others as you become immediately cloistered by the close metal walls, washed in the glow of dozens of humming pieces of art. Some of them are more art than others. You come across two different Bart Simpsons and a rather lewd Peter Griffin, but mostly the neon depicts things and scenes you could not expect. One of them is a recreation of the Tower from the major arcana of the tarot. Lines of beige neon suggest brickwork while at the tip of the tower a bold yellow bolt of lightning blinks on and off, striking the tower in half-second increments over and over, presumably until the gas inside the artwork fails or its mechanisms do. As you stare at the neon the palm of your hand sweats, your breathing quickens ever so slightly. You have the sense, briefly, comically, that there is someone watching you from within the tower. Staring out from the structure's undepicted windows.

You remember a family vacation to Ireland, approaching a huge castle up on a big green hill. It stared down at you, threatening to crush you. You had the presentiment that all that hateful stone could stop your breath and obliterate you. They'd never even find your bones.

As that memory meets this moment, you force yourself to breathe, to blink, to look away.

You leave the row with the uncanny tower and slowly let yourself settle. You're sweating slightly, a side-effect of the drugs still coursing through your system. You wonder if you should have stayed at his place a little longer, resting on his couch until you were fully yourself. But he'd already started preparing for work in his home office and his offer to "make yourself comfortable, or whatever" seemed like a distant consolation prize. So instead, you're here freaking yourself out at imagined terrors lurking behind neon signs. A direct result of your endorphin-starved brain. You laugh, shake your head, and begin the labor of pushing the thing out of your mind.

In another row you find another piece depicting a man in a gray suit, bright red tie flapping, reaching up toward a mirror arranged horizontally above him. It's as though he's fallen out of it and is reaching for it, trying to claw his way back inside of his reflection as he falls, but his fingers don't even brush the surface of the mirror-portal, he's too far, suspended indefinitely in the moment of tumbling away.

You've always had a terror of falling. It's bad enough that you rarely fly and when you do it's with an eye-shade and headphones on for most the duration, trying not to think about the likelihood of a crash or the aftermath. You sit in darkness listening to ASMR cafe sounds trying not to let in the intrusive thoughts of burning wreckage, severed limbs, of the weak, wet moans and wracking coughs as people either bleed out or choke from smoke inhalation.

But when you look at this piece of neon you feel a relief that conflicts with the animal panic you imagine you'd be experiencing in his stead. It's as though the subject of the piece has finally escaped something, like the act of reaching for the mirror he's tumbled out of is merely animal reflex, and that once he accepts the fall, he'll be free.

You feel a presence and look over to see the sallow-faced man back at the mouth of the row you're standing in. He comes over, hands behind his back, and considers the piece you're looking at.

"It's called *Pride Goeth* and it's one from my custom collection. Looks like you have an eye for the bespoke pieces," he says.

"What's the story of it?" you ask.

"A consultant commissioned it. He wanted something to clarify his feelings about work-life balance. I think it captured the struggle, but ultimately it's not for the artist to judge."

No matter how long you look, you can't pluck anything besides relief out of the piece. Everything from the muted red illumination from the man's tie to the elaborate gold design of the mirror he's reaching up toward. The relaxed lines of his body implying an imminent cessation of pain . . .

"—of it?" You only catch the very ending of the sallow-faced man's statement.

"I'm sorry, what? I was distracted, I think."

His lips do something in the neighborhood of a smile before sliding back to their thin-lipped idling. "I was asking what you thought of it, if it invoked anything."

"It's lovely. But, why is it here? Why didn't the client pick it up?"

"He got what he needed from the creative process. He was content to leave the work here in this little gallery of mine. It's a more common practice than you might think."

"Hmm" is all you respond, and the sallow-faced man looks you over and says, "If you could commission a piece, what would it be?"

"Oh, I couldn't. I don't have that kind of money right now. I just started a new job." You can't imagine the eye-watering price of a custom piece of neon, so you try to head off whatever upsell you're about to get. You're still paying off last month's steak dinner from some absurd West Loop place with a name like Nuance or some shit. But nonetheless your gaze travels back to *Pride Goeth* and the falling man it depicts. You answer despite yourself. The words tumble out. "A man's face turned toward the viewer with a black boot on top of it. Pressing down. Hard."

A flutter of excitement goes through you. You're sweating harder now.

"Is he being punished?" the sallow-faced man asks.

"Yes," you respond immediately.

"Does he deserve it?"

"Yes."

"What is his expression?"

"He's pleased, excited, ready," you explain. Your mind is on the Red Sox cap and the lupine smile. You imagine that man's maw, dripping blood. Plane crashes and cannibalism and MDMA and the calamity of lightning striking the tower. Again and again until the end of time. Sweat drips into your eyes. You're half-hard. You're on fucking drugs. "I'm sorry," you say. "I don't know what came over me."

"For what?" asks the sallow-faced man. He looks at the neon, then back at you. This row's pieces are predominantly orange and gold; they make his sickly looking skin seem even more poisoned. Once again, he reminds you of something, but this time you know what it is: a pimple, fecund with pus, ready to pop and loose a torrent of . . . something. "May I ask you a question?"

You should go back outside where the air is plentiful. You shouldn't be standing around this tight makeshift hallway with this too-placid stranger. And you shouldn't be doing this high. But he has been nice enough to show you around his store, to talk about his work, you can answer one question *then* leave.

"Sure," you say.

"What if you were worthy of adoration? What if you were perfection itself and there was no doubt? What would you do with that knowledge?"

"I . . . I'm sorry, I don't know what you mean."

"You do," says the sallow-faced man. "You live a life of quiet degradation. You allow yourself to be taken apart piece by piece. In a year, you will be half of what you are now. In ten, completely unrecognizable. But all you are is bright and clear . . . underneath. I can remove the grime. Crystallize the perfect."

You think of the woman with the arms of a sea creature crawling all over her and her rapturous expression, a falling man with no fear, a tower with an unwelcoming figure ensconced within.

"Why didn't the client pick up the neon?" you ask again, fearing the answer.

"He was transformed. Perfected."

"And that's what you'd do to me," you say, and it's not a question. You can see his desire right there in his expression, no longer neutral, but ravenous now. Hungrier than anyone has ever been for you, practically slavering. He's discarded his disinterested mask and behind it is a void. You have to look away from him because you're afraid he will hypnotize you or swallow you up with his big, dark eyes. You see his smile out of the corner of your eye and it is many times worse than his indifference.

You look back to the falling man and consider the totality of yourself and what you'd leave behind if you let this man get his hands on you. You are a passably good violinist, a devoted brother to four siblings, a damn good kisser, a lifelong depressive, a proud slut.

You know there will be a cost; this man . . . this artisan is not offering you perfection for nothing. But the question you ask is: "Will it hurt?"

"You will feel everything that is weighing you down, tarnishing you, leaving you all at once. Yes, it will hurt, but you have never known the relief that you will feel when it's done."

There is a part of you begging you to reconsider. If you turn you can still see the door and the light coming out between the cracks. It must be daylight outside now.

And you do not know this man or his methods. You have not yet signed any pacts in blood and hellfire. You are not bound. But you consider the rest of your day: balancing your budget, eating dinner to YouTube videos, masturbating to unhinged pornography and drifting off to sleep later than you anticipated because the quiet of the late hours is the only time you feel completely yourself. You are half a man, living half a life, and the sallow-faced man knows it. Worse, it turns him on.

You wonder what the man whose underwear you are currently wearing will feel when you do not answer his texts for days then weeks. You nod gravely, consent to be changed.

And nothing happens at first.

Then a feeling tugs at your stomach, pulling upward. A hard wrench and tearing that makes your vision explode into violent stars. You retch, the room blurs, and what comes up out of your mouth is neon-colored. Your sweat drips down the side of your face and you feel like a melting candle. Maybe you are a melting candle. You groan, curl into yourself, try to flee the stabbing sensation in your stomach that spreads outward, radiating to your limbs and rendering you a twitching, weeping pile of brightly colored pain.

But then you start to feel lighter, then lighter still, rising out of your shed skin like a spirit or a gas. The sallow-faced man lets you hang in the air for some time, stares down at your abandoned body—emptied bone, sloughed-off flesh—before heading to the back of the shop. He returns with glass tubing and gently, with an artisan's eye, begins to craft the form in which you will spend the rest of your days. He is rock hard beneath his smock. And you are so excited to see the art he will make of you; you're already beginning to hum.

THE RIVER'S REVENGE

Jen Mierisch

Suki leaned against the side of the canoe and trailed a fingertip through the cold, dark water. "So, Ron," she said. "How many bodies are at the bottom of this river?"

Ron paused rowing to frown at Suki. "Bodies?"

She smiled and flipped her black hair over one shoulder. "Chicago was a gangster town, right? The bad guys must have dumped corpses in here. Cement shoes and all that. Whaddya think? A couple hundred?"

"Zero," Ron replied dryly. "The river's been dredged a few times since the 1920s."

Sandy-haired, bespectacled Ron was cute in a Clark Kent sort of way. Watching his lean arms haul the oars all afternoon had reinforced Suki's opinion. He couldn't have been more than five years older than she was. But Ron didn't seem receptive to her flirtation. He had already looked back at their trap map.

Suki was lucky to have this urban ecology internship, was delighted to be spending her spring term with Friends of the Chicago River, even if this particular Friend seemed to find her more annoying than interesting. She hadn't yet managed to get Ron to crack a smile.

The boat glided beneath the Kinzie Street Bridge as they made their way north toward Goose Island. Skyscrapers towered above the waterway, giving rivergoers the impression of traversing a steel-and-glass canyon. Bright May sunshine glittered off the windows and scattered across the calm, deep-green water. Two rowers in bright-red kayaks waved as they paddled by.

"It's great that the river has been cleaned up," said Suki. "I read about how polluted it used to be. Bet the fish had some freaky mutations then."

Ron shrugged. "We're up to seventy fish species now. I still wouldn't swim in it."

The canoe fetched up next to a cluster of rotting wood pylons draped with rusted chains. "Here." Ron handed Suki the oars, grabbed hold of a chain, and pulled the boat alongside.

"What about the beaches on the lake? I can swim there, right?" If picturing her in a swimsuit didn't faze Ron, Suki was officially giving up on flirting.

"Yeah. But I wouldn't do it until at least August if I were you. Water's too cold." He raised an eyebrow. "Where are you from again?"

"Knoxville."

Ron donned a long rubber glove, reached beneath the water, and pulled up a trap. "Here you go, Tennessee. Your turn to weigh it."

A nickname? Was that progress? Suki suppressed a smile as she put on her gloves. She hoisted the dripping trap, set it on the floor of the boat, and did a double take. "Whoa."

The semi-opaque plastic revealed a silhouette of the creature inside. It was too large to be one of the blue-spotted salamanders they were tracking. "Is this a snake?"

"Sometimes bluegills get in there," Ron said. "Just crack it open and release them."

Suki unlatched the clasp and removed the lid. "Wow!" she said. "*Anguilla rostrata*. I thought these guys were super rare in the Chicago River!"

The animal writhed and squirmed in the tight space, too small for its serpentine body. Its slimy skin was mottled olive and yellow-brown, like dead winter grass. A head with beady red eyes poked out from the tangles of flesh.

"Hang on," said Suki. "This thing's head looks too big for an eel. And check out the size of those pectoral fins."

Ron rubbed his chin thoughtfully. "With that color, it should be a juvenile. But it's at least four feet long. And they're supposed to be nocturnal."

"Whatcha doin' up early, buddy?" Suki gently poked the creature's tail.

The reaction was instantaneous. The eel's head reared up through the top of the trap. A second head appeared next to the first, attached to the same neck. Both heads faced Suki, bared their teeth, and hissed. With startling speed, the heads shot forward. Razorlike teeth closed around Suki's thumb. She shrieked and pulled her hand away.

The animal surged from the open trap and landed with a wet crash on the boat's fiberglass floor. It slithered in an arc and darted for the half-eaten hot dog left over from Suki's lunch. In seconds, the creature shredded and swallowed the pink meat.

"Holy shit," said Suki.

"Yipe!" The eel had darted for Ron's feet. He hoisted his legs into the air. The eel plowed into a paper wrapper and devoured the remains of Ron's Italian beef sandwich.

"We've got to catch it!" Suki seized the eel around its middle. It slipped out of her hands, raised its front half as if flying, and wrapped its body around the canoe's stern-side yoke.

"Open that trap and get ready to shut it!" Ron reached for the eel's neck, but its heads swayed back and forth, eluding his grasp in a game of cat and mouse. He removed one glove and wiggled his fingers a foot away from the twin heads.

Suki's stomach dropped. "Ron," she said. "What are you doing?"

Four red eyes focused on Ron's waving fingers. Finally, unable to resist, the heads shot forward. In a single swift motion, Ron pulled his fingers away and seized the eel's outstretched neck with his other hand. "Gotcha!" he said. "Tennessee, incoming!"

Suki held the trap open and braced herself to catch the animal's weight. But Ron was having trouble with the spitting, struggling eel, whose tail remained wrapped around the beam. When his poking and prodding proved futile, Ron grabbed the tail with his bare hand, wrested it free, and gathered the eel's flailing body against his own. He leaned forward over the trap and dropped the animal in. Suki stuffed the lashing tail inside, slammed down the lid, and locked it.

Wide-eyed, they looked at each other and caught their breath. Ron sat and wiped sweat from his forehead. Suki flapped the hem of her T-shirt to fan herself. The trap shook as the confined creature thrashed angrily inside.

"Did it bite you?" asked Ron.

Suki peeled off her torn glove. "No. I'm good. Hot damn, Ron. I know this town's famous for some strange critters, but Chance the Snapper has nothing on this guy."

Ron shook his head in awe. "I've never seen an eel move that fast out of water. Those jaws and teeth are at least three times the usual size. And the way it curled itself around the bar—eels don't have the musculature for that kind of grip."

"True," Suki agreed. "And then there's, you know, the extra head."

"That too."

"We've got to tell someone."

"Right." Ron brightened. "We'll show the team. It might be a new subspecies. Maybe we'll get to name it."

"No, Ron, I mean we've got to tell the authorities! This thing is dangerous. And it's obviously hungry. What if there are more of them out there and they attack someone?"

"Oh." Ron had the decency to look sheepish.

"We passed a police boat near the bridge," said Suki. "Let's turn around and flag it down."

"No," said Ron. "We should take the eel back and let the team have a look. Maybe it's something they've seen before. They'll know if we need to involve DNR or anybody else. I don't want to raise unnecessary alarms."

Suki opened her mouth to object. It seemed wrong not to tell the police, but she was the junior member of this expedition, and perhaps the boat had been rocked enough during their eel-wrestling match. She should learn the protocols, and it would make Ron happy in the process.

"We might get to name it, huh?" Suki said. "How about Wriggly Field?"

Was that a smile? "I'm thinking Muddy Waters," Ron said.

"No, wait! I've got it. Eel Capone."

Ron groaned and reached for the oars.

Heather McDowell was exhausted. It had been Noah's hare-brained idea to take the train from St. Louis to Chicago with two kids under five. The Bean! he'd said. The Aquarium! The Field Museum! Naturally, Noah had left it to his pregnant wife to make all the plans. The city's so walkable, you won't need a car, everybody said. But "everybody" was thinking of able-bodied adults, not preschoolers who got cranky when they missed their naps.

The Riverwalk was pretty, though, in the warm afternoon sun. The family strolled along the paved path and admired the state-ly Wrigley Building's white terra cotta façade, the shiny St. Regis towers that climbed the sky like vertical blue waves, and the twin corncobs of Marina Towers. Heather and Noah bought Garrett's cheddar and caramel popcorn from a cart and let the boys pet the dog-walkers' labradoodles.

They stopped to rest on wide steps leading down from street lev-el. Heather fanned herself in the shade of a tree that grew through a hole in the concrete. She'd just started to relax when four-year-old Jaden broke free of her hand and ran for the water.

How many times had she told him not to run off? Two million? Heather handed two-year-old Caden off to her husband and ran after Jaden. There was a railing next to the water, and thankfully Jaden wasn't climbing on it. He squatted next to it, peering at some-thing. "Look, Mommy," he said when her shadow fell across him. "A snake."

"A *what?*" The TripAdvisor website hadn't mentioned snakes. Heather's gaze followed her son's pointing finger to a sickly yellowish-brown heap of something. "I think that's just a pile of old clothes, honey. Don't touch it."

The heap shifted. From its depths reared a slick, wet head. The jaws opened in a sinister grin, revealing several rows of pointed teeth. And—Lord have mercy—it must have been two snakes coiled up together, because a second head appeared next to the first. Four red eyes focused on Jaden's chubby arm, and the heads lunged.

Heather screamed and scooped Jaden off the ground. The snakes' teeth missed the boy's calf by millimeters. The heads quickly refocused, this time on Heather's leg.

She barely felt the pinch, the blood trickling into her shoe. She sprinted back toward Noah. Jaden was frightened and bawling, and people were staring. Heather risked a backward glance just in time to see a scaly tail whip out and seize a small rat, which squeaked pitifully as fangs plunged into its furry body. Crimson blood spattered the concrete. The snakes appeared to be fighting over their food. With a sickening squelch, they ripped the rodent's body in half. Its head disappeared down one throat while its skinny tail vanished down the other.

Heather's stomach, already shaky from pregnancy and junk food, lurched alarmingly. She whipped a hand over Jaden's eyes and willed herself not to throw up. When she wrote her TripAdvisor review, this city was getting two stars, max.

Suki flopped onto her dorm bunk and pulled out her phone. *Ron, it's me, Suki.*

hi

About that eel. I did a paper last semester about environmental pollutants that cause DNA mutations in aquatic organisms.

ok

So today I went to the science library at U of I and did some reading.

do you have a point, tennessee? i'm running late to meet my bf

BF.

Oh.

Suki chuckled. So much for the flirtation.

I'll be quick. There's a chemical called diethyl nitrosourethane that's used in some commercial waste management systems. It's super toxic. It caused freaky genetic mutations in river catfish. Like extra fins and gills. Mizzen et al, Journal of Environmental Toxicology, July 2024. Three countries in Europe have already banned it.

you call that quick

Listen, the only way that chemical could get into the river is if some company dumped it there.

right

And the only way we can tell if it's in the river is if we collect and analyze water samples.

Suki waited for Ron to take the hint.

Nothing. She sighed and spelled it out. *What are you doing Sunday?*

Maybe he'd already gotten to his date. She made one last attempt.

Lunch is on me.

fine but doug gets to come along. he's jealous of this chick i've been spending so much time with

Suki laughed. Hopefully Ron's boyfriend didn't have expensive tastes. Her student stipend was already stretched to the max.

Chicago Boat Company had three rules for renters of its pontoon party boats: keep to the right to let tours and barges pass, don't go through the lock into Lake Michigan, and the driver stays sober. Unfortunately for Justin Carson, when he and his friends rented their boat, they followed the same rule they used at bars after last call: whoever's the least drunk drives.

That Sunday afternoon, Xavier was trying to impress Kayla by standing on the lid of the storage box and doing front flips into the driver's seat. Kayla giggled at Xavier's antics and screamed when a tour boat's wake made him teeter atop the box and nearly fall into the river. Then she resumed trying to make out with Emma, on whose lap she sat. Emma wormed her way out from underneath Kayla, fished another bottle of Corona from the cooler, and asked Justin to pour it into her mouth while she hung upside down from the canopy. Justin happily obliged, then smacked Xavier on the ass just as he was launching into a flip. Xavier tumbled side-ways, crash-landed, and knocked the radio out of its holster. Kayla laughed hysterically and slid off the cushioned bench onto the floor.

A gull dove into the water. Justin watched for it to come back up with a fish in its mouth, but it never did. Something moved through the water where the gull had been. It looked like an enormous yellow snake. Justin blinked and rubbed his eyes. It had to be a trick of the light. Come to think of it, maybe he'd chill out on the beer for a while.

Their boat, cruising westward past the House of Blues, had drifted dangerously close to the center of the river. Justin slid into the driver's seat and grabbed the wheel while Xavier got himself together. Nobody noticed the two yellow-green creatures that crept over the rudder and slipped beneath the gate.

Justin watched Xavier help Emma climb down from the canopy. He tried to wave at a group of girls on a passing cycleboat, only to find his forearm bound to the railing by a loop of what looked like a slimy greenish rope. "What the f—"

Two dinosaur-like heads with beady red eyes popped over the railing, bared their fangs, and hissed. Justin flinched. He stood, grabbed the eel by the neck, and unwound its tail. He stepped forward to throw it overboard and tripped over the second eel.

Justin toppled over the railing and into the water with a splash. Emma screamed and pointed. Xavier rushed to the rail and reached out a hand, which Justin missed by inches. Kayla freed the orange life preserver ring and tossed it out across the water. Emma grabbed the wheel, cranked it toward her friend, and hollered, "Justin! Grab the ring!"

But he didn't hear. His head kept disappearing beneath the river's surface. When it came up, he spluttered, "—got my foot!"

As Justin kicked and thrashed, the wavy motion of a yellowish creature rippled the water five feet away, then three feet, then one. Two heads breached the surface and sank their teeth into his neck.

Wet, choking gurgles cut short Justin's yell as he went under. Seeping blood dyed the river water red. The girls' screams echoed against the skyscrapers' looming flatness.

With a bright smile, Suki swung into the path of the forty-something woman exiting the Starbucks at Navy Pier. "Hi!" Suki said. "Maeve Mosley?"

"Um ... yes ..." The woman raised her to-go cup to her lips like a shield and tucked a graying blonde curl behind her ear.

"My name is Suki Lee. I've got a scoop for you. It's super important that somebody investigates this."

Maeve sighed. "Miss," she said, "please email tips@suntimes.com, and one of our editors will get back to you—"

"I thought you might say that." Suki crossed her arms. "What if I told you that your colleague's article about the pontoon boat accident was bullshit and I can prove it? Hmm, who had that byline—Steve Prince? Do you know him?"

Of course Maeve Mosley knew Steve Prince. Last night, Suki had gone to Navy Bier, the closest bar to the *Chicago Sun-Times* office and therefore its reporters' logical happy-hour spot. It was incredible how much gossip you could overhear while nursing a Scotch and scrolling Instagram. Maeve Mosley thought Steve Prince was a talentless blowhard, hired only because his uncle was the advertising director. That made her Suki's obvious choice to pitch the story.

"I spoke with Emma Aceveda," said Suki. "Emma was one of the people on that pontoon boat. The people who the police said were stoned and rambling. Your colleague didn't bother to fact-check that, by the way. Emma's been distraught since witnessing the killing. She told me everything. The police report was wrong. This was no accident."

"Oh? What was it?" Maeve frowned and sipped her latte.

"An animal attack."

"What kind of animal?"

"Eels. But not ordinary ones."

"*Eels?*"

"I have photos and video of one of these eels, which attacked me on another occasion. They have mutations consistent with industrial pollution. When you see it, you'll understand."

"Go on."

"I've collected field data that might interest you. A toxic chemical is concentrated near the outflow pipes of a building that sits right on the river."

"Which building?"

"401 North Wabash."

Maeve nodded slowly. If the opportunity to one-up Steve wasn't enough to tempt Maeve, maybe the address would be. It was part of the city's skyline, a famous building with a notorious owner.

"I'll need to speak with Emma," Maeve said, "and with anyone else who's seen this eel."

Suki brightened. "Does that mean you'll do the story?"

"We'll see." Maeve dug in her purse and handed Suki a business card. "Call me next week."

"No, no," said Suki. "Next week is too late!"

"How do you mean?"

"This weekend is Chicago River Day," said Suki. "Two thousand volunteers will be coming to remove litter and invasive plants. It's only a matter of time before these eels attack someone else!"

"All right. Email me what you've got."

"Thank you!"

Suki weaved her way between knots of tourists, found an empty bench by the water, and pulled out her phone. *Ron! I have a reporter interested in the eels!*

um

She wants to talk to us about them. Soon!

not a good idea tennessee

What? Why not?

interns aren't allowed to speak on behalf of the org and neither am i

I wouldn't be doing that. Just sharing my personal observations.

also the guy whose name is on that building might make things ugly for you

Screw him. If he's polluting the river, then he needs to be held accountable.

Suki watched the dots. Ron was typing, pausing, typing.

i can't stop you. but don't give her my name

Ron, she's a reporter. She needs multiple sources. She might not believe me otherwise. You saw what that eel did. You were with me when I analyzed those water samples. You really won't help with this?

sorry count me out

Suki jumped to her feet with an exasperated shriek and stuffed her phone into her pocket so she wouldn't chuck it into the lake. A passing family hustled their kids toward the Ferris wheel. Suki stomped off down the pier.

The water at the Ohio Street Beach was cold, but Derek Malone was hot. He was looking at Kasia in her string bikini top, her lower half hidden by the lake. Derek had met Kasia yesterday at industry night. She was a brown-eyed bartender with violet-dyed hair, and he was pretty sure he was in love.

Beach season didn't open officially for another week. The tall lifeguard chairs sat empty. But May had been warm, and several dozen people lay scattered across the beach in the noontime sun. Behind them, tall buildings gleamed against blue sky, and boats entered the river on the other side of the pier. Coconut suntan lotion scented the air. A trio of toddlers scooped sand into yellow plastic buckets near the water's edge.

Derek waded next to Kasia and looped an arm around her waist. "When do you go in tonight?"

"Four."

"Me too." Derek was a server at Pettorino's. He pressed his body against Kasia's, remembering last night's escapades at her place, hoping to remind her. He hooked a finger on her swimsuit bottom and tugged it downward.

Kasia giggled and swatted his hand away. "Derek. Stop."

"Stop what?"

"There's people right there."

"They can't see anything."

"And quit brushing my knee like that. It tickles."

"What?" Derek's hands were on Kasia's shoulders. "I'm not touching your leg, babe."

Kasia looked down. About a foot below the surface, the water rippled. A pair of yellowish, snakelike bodies moved in sinuous waves.

"Eww!" Kasia hopped sideways.

"What's the matter?"

"There's snakes in the lake!"

Derek snorted. "Snakes? It's gotta be fish, babe."

"Look!"

"I will save my lady from the nasty creatures." Derek grabbed a floating piece of driftwood and swept it through the water. A second later, he cried out. "Jesus! It bit me."

A wriggling shape darted up one leg of Derek's swim trunks. He smacked at it, but it didn't budge. Red blood bloomed across the lake's surface.

Kasia stood frozen in horror. More snakes had appeared, as if drawn like sharks to the spreading blood. She counted nine of them, ten, eleven. She turned toward shore, but all around her, the water was thick with slippery serpents. Two heads bumped against Kasia at the top of her thigh. Sharp teeth sank into flesh, finding the artery.

Hearing Kasia's screams, a gray-haired couple hurried over. The old man called, "Are you folks all right?" His wife stopped short when she saw the pooling blood. Derek, his face ghastly pale, passed out and plunged beneath the surface. His floating body twitched every few seconds with the impact of the creatures' biting jaws.

"Good Lord!" The woman reached for her husband's hand and gasped. Four eels had latched onto his arms and abdomen. He hollered and swatted at them as the blood spurted. She was vaguely aware of people screaming around them as sharp teeth pierced her legs.

In the sunny conference room overlooking the lake, Mayor Johnson stood at the podium and surveyed the crowd assembling for his press conference. There was CPD's river unit commander, folks from the Department of Natural Resources, the CDOT commissioner. The press was mostly the usual suspects. In the front row, a young woman with long black hair sat alertly, pen poised above a notebook. Probably some college reporter with an animal rights agenda.

The mayor tapped the mike. "Good afternoon. Thank you all for joining us. We're here today to discuss reports of an invasive species of eel in the Chicago River. Our multidisciplinary task force is investigating the matter now. At this time, we'd like to assure the public that there is absolutely no cause for concern. The city dealt with invasive Asian carp several years back, and we're well equipped to eradicate this new fish today. Questions."

"Mayor." It was that perky TV reporter. "Annette Ajabu, ABC7. How did eels get into the river? Did somebody's pet get loose?"

"We're looking into that possibility."

A man in a neat blue shirt and tie raised a hand. "Vijay Patel, Block Club Chicago. Do these eels pose a threat to recreational boaters?"

"No. They are merely a nuisance species. We do advise that boaters not encourage breeding by feeding the eels."

"Sir." A woman with graying blond curls stood from the third row. "Maeve Mosley, *Sun-Times*. What's the connection between these eels and the boating death reported Sunday?"

Murmurs around the room. The college reporter scribbled away.

Johnson cleared his throat. "Per the police file, that incident was an unfortunate cautionary tale. An intoxicated driver fell overboard and sustained fatal injuries from debris in the water. There is no connection to the eels."

The college girl leapt to her feet. "That's not true." Heads swiveled in her direction.

"Miss," said Johnson. "Observe proper protocol, or you'll be asked to leave."

The *Sun-Times* reporter was still standing. "An hour ago, we received a report of four deaths at the Ohio Street Beach. Multiple patrons observed eels in the water near the victims. Any comment?"

The murmurs swelled to a rumble. Johson locked eyes briefly with the police commander. "We're aware of the situation. It's too early to comment at this time."

"What about the report sent to your office yesterday?" The girl again. "The one with evidence of mutagenic chemicals in the water at 401 North Wabash? Any comment on that? Do you people ever tell the truth at these things?"

Johnson motioned for security. Two guards peeled away from the wall.

A thirtyish man with shaggy red hair raised his hand. "Mayor, I'm with Kayak Chicago. Several of our renters have reported seeing eels over the past few days. Is the river dangerous?"

The rumbles approached pandemonium. Johnson tugged at his collar. "The river is perfectly safe. There is no cause for alarm."

"Liar!" The girl pointed at Johnson. "Five people are dead! Somebody needs to do something!"

The guards hustled toward the girl and each took an arm. She was still shouting—some nonsense about two heads—when they dragged her from the room. Johnson sighed, ignored the sweat trickling down his back, and faced the sea of raised hands and rolling cameras.

Suki sat in the Cook County Jail, her head in her hands. She'd paced the cell for hours, kicking herself for how she'd handled that press conference. If only she'd gone to a print shop for a giant photo of the two-headed eel, for the TV cameras, but she'd run out of time and money. She'd made a spectacle of herself, she'd likely ruined any chance of progress on the eel situation, and Friends of the Chicago River would probably cancel her internship. Now it was almost midnight, her stomach growled, she'd have to sleep on this wooden bench, and worst of all, her parents were going to kill her.

"Miss Lee?" A chubby guard, keys jangling, unlocked the cell. "Come with me. Your bail has been posted."

Stunned, Suki followed the guard down the hall to the desk. Her jaw dropped. "*Ron?*"

Ron stood with his boyfriend, Doug, and a dark-haired woman in a pantsuit. "Tennessee," said Ron, "meet your new lawyer, Jessica Steele."

The woman extended her hand. "Pleasure to meet you, Suki. I read all about you in the *Sun-Times*. Here are the release forms for you to sign."

"You're not the first environmental activist to need legal representation," said Doug. "I've been Jessica's paralegal for six years. You're in good hands."

Ron added, "Nice job finding that Maeve Mosley to do the story. Her contacts were able to replicate your water analysis."

"The property managers don't want the optics of a lawsuit," said Doug. "We're confident they'll cave to pressure and pay to clean up the river."

"Wow." Suki grinned and fought back tears of relief. "This is so awesome, guys! So, I'm not fired?"

Ron smiled. "Are you kidding? We need you to help write our research study. I want your name on that paper when *Journal of Environmental Toxicology* publishes it."

Jessica added her signature to the forms. "You've made quite a splash, Suki. But it's not over yet. Removing those eels is going to be a tricky operation."

✶ ✶ ✶ ✶

Brent Bradford opened the door to the private dock on the river level at 401 North Wabash. He had a lady to meet, and he would pick her up in style in his 42-foot Princess V40 yacht whose name, *The Fountainhead*, was splashed across its bow.

But first, Brent would wrap up his phone call with the junior exec who he tolerated because the pup worshiped him. "Yeah, you heard right," Brent said. "The big guy put me in charge of cleanup. And I handled it." He strolled past the dockworkers who had refueled and tidied his boat and were waiting around for tips, as if his dock rental fee didn't already cover their wages, the bloodsuckers.

Brent admired his reflection in the yacht's windows, ran a hand through his blond hair. "It was easy. I hired a bunch of illegals from the Home Depot parking lot. Sent 'em out on the water with slaughterhouse scraps for bait. The buggers ate it right up. The eels liked it, too!" His laughter echoed against the cavernous walls of the dock. "I wrote off the cleanup and the new waste system as janitorial expenses. Creative accounting. Pay attention, bud. You could be me one day."

He hung up and stepped on board. The oak paneling and stainless-steel fixtures gleamed. Champagne waited on ice in the wet bar. No doubt about it, he'd be getting laid tonight, right there on the leather captain's chair, with the city glittering all around him, like the god he was.

The starting of the yacht's motor woke the creature snoozing beneath the stern. She gnashed her teeth, aware of nothing but gnawing hunger. Seven million eggs were growing inside her, and they needed feeding. It was her second brood, and she had grown to a colossal size, nine feet of slimy skin and sinewy muscle.

She whipped her tail around the exterior ladder and heaved herself onto the back of the boat. A few feet away, his back to her, stood a pale-haired man.

Her twin mouths opened, tasting the air. The man would do very nicely for her evening meal. He smelled delicious.

JUST ANOTHER FRIDAY NIGHT IN BUCKTOWN

✶ ✶ ✶ ✶

Lauren Emily Whalen

If you're reading this, you are aware that I have destroyed myself.

Red drips on the shiny wood floor of my studio apartment. First it dangles in long, languid strings, rolling down my bed frame. The drips blur into vivid raised dots, one two three four five, before merging into a thick, crimson pool.

Normally I'd curse at the latest hardening-gummy puddle that's a bitch to get out, and will undoubtedly cost me my deposit. Tonight, I just smile.

I right the bottle of nail polish and screw the cap back on. I've never been great at self-manicures, and sloppiness is now part of the persona I bring to burlesque. Bedhead hair, messily applied eyeliner, bright color smeared around the cuticles: me. Tonight, I pocket the polish in case anyone else wants red nails. A classic hot-girl shade, nothing suspicious.

After telling my cat I love her, I bounce down three flights of thinly carpeted stairs in my flowered Doc Martens and traverse half a block to the westbound 77 bus. I marvel at the twinkly lights on the streetlamps, now green from the annual citywide shitshow that is St. Patrick's Day, and the foot traffic of loud straight couples in line at the local comedy club, twenty-two-year-old zygotes popping into Walgreens and popping out with a twelve-pack, and folks like me in the lingering chill waiting for our bus. The effect is so charming that I wonder for the millionth time why the outside world associates Chicago with war zones and random acts of violence.

The violence isn't all random. And sometimes it's needed.

Traffic's clogged on Belmont as usual, but I pass the time with a new playlist our troupe collaborated on this week. Gayle's "ABCDEFU," the angry remix. The Interrupters' "She Got Arrested," which makes me want to pump my fist. And of course, Taylor Swift's "Vigilante Shit."

I am a certified piece of shit who has brought zero good to anyone around me, especially the dancers I should have kept safe.

It's when I'm transferring to the southbound 49 that I almost get myself in trouble.

He's standing just a hair too close, in the way you notice when you're a femme-presenting urbanite who's been forced to develop asshole radar with energy that could have been used to cure cancer. I shove my hands in my coat pockets, feeling for my wallet in my right hand and my keys in my left. My fingers curl around the keychain canister of pepper spray, encased in neon pink plastic.

Delilah Bon's "Dead Men Don't Rape" screams in my earbuds.

Then he grabs my ass, a little goose like he's just joking. The rage-drenaline that's built over the past seven days, the past three decades of being prey, threatens to burst a blood vessel. Nausea rises into the back of my throat. I want to growl in his face, bare my teeth around my red-lipsticked mouth, feral at last. I want to not only kick him in the balls, but shred his testicles completely.

I contemplate stomping down on his instep. Hurts like a mofo and I wouldn't even have to use my Docs' steel toes to make my point. After a lifetime of being hurt, the rush of hurting someone back, someone who truly deserves it, is not unlike orgasm.

Do straight guys get this rush or are they just used to it?

I'm raising one foot when I remember what we said last week at the Green Eye. No texts to best friends or calls to lawyer uncles, nothing *Dateline* could call receipts. Most of all, don't draw attention to yourself in public: no weird whispering, no loud sobbing, and no confrontations with jackasses someone could remember later.

I move five paces to my left, next to an older lady hugging her pocketbook. We exchange eyerolls, *just another Friday night*, and the 49 arrives.

Before I know it I'm at Western and Milwaukee, crossing the street away from the closed-down check-cashing joint and passing the brightly lit McDonald's on the corner. I nod at Caroline, our stage manager and box office maven, as I cross the threshold into the lobby of the tiny storefront theater where I've spent every Friday night for the past nine months. She has a little grin on her face as she singsongs the four words I've been waiting for all week:

"He's in the basement."

I have violated those who were already vulnerable by way of being burlesque dancers in a misogynistic society, not just in Chicago but in upstate New York, where I produced under a different name. If you want to read those stories, please look me up on Reddit. The least I can do is confess to my crimes in the most public of forums: social media.

Downstairs with forty-three minutes to curtain, I open the Producer's eyes.

"Wakey-wakey," I croon. "Just so you know, you can't move." Upstairs I hear someone cue up Lil' Kim's "The Jump Off."

He's prostrate on one of the musty faded-floral couches that populate this basement. He's not a small guy, and I imagine hauling him down here was quite the endeavor. He wheezes through pale, cracked lips. He can open his eyes, can blink, but the movement of those beady eyelids is very slow. His pupils are pinpricks. Hope he's rotting from the inside too, as the dark web promised. I deeply inhale, savoring the sweet hint of his decay mixed with my Marc Jacobs Daisy.

I pull up a chair across from him and prop my feet on his calves—I've doffed my socks and Docs in defiance. The Producer is a staunch "real burlesque dancers perform in high heels" kind of guy. I know even the sight of my sloppily painted toes is pissing him off right now.

"So here's what's going to happen," I inform him, crossing one ankle over the other. There's a hardening blob of blood red polish next to my pinky toe and basement-dust graying the bottoms of my feet. I relish how gross this all is. "Earlier today we painted poison all over your place, every surface you could touch. You're dying down here. We thought about putting you in the dressing room while we get ready for tonight's show, which by the way, is going to be the last."

I know he can't feel it, but I kick his thigh before re-crossing my ankles. "But you've already seen enough of our bodies, without our consent. Remember?"

I put my hands behind my head. "I know what you're thinking! *They'll do an autopsy, pin it on the girls*—not women, never women to you—*they'll rot in prison.*" I giggle, listening to the opening bars of Eartha Kitt's "I Want to Be Evil" kick off upstairs.

"As always, you underestimate us," I continue. "Upstairs are two lawyers, an IT superstar who also happens to be a contortionist, and best of all, a professional stage manager who has meticulously curated this run-of-show." Dramatic pause. "But of course, to you, we're just tits and ass and profit from sold-out houses that you don't share."

I reach for the phone strategically placed on the armchair catty-corner from the musty couch. I hate to touch the Producer's face again, but his eyes closed, so I gingerly prop open his eyelids with my finger and thumb and cue up his Notes app. I'm the writer of the group, so the decision of who would do this part was made before we got to the second round of tamales just seven nights ago.

Until now, I wasn't sure I was capable of murder. But feeling his body grow cold through my bare feet, listening to my friends upstairs, practically *hearing* a lightness in their collective step that wasn't there last week, I am downright fucking giddy.

"Your suicide note will go up on social media at midnight," I inform him. He's trying to groan, to protest, to move even the tiniest muscle, but all the Producer can manage is a whispery whine. "But before we start…"

I rise from the chair and look down at him. The way he used to look down at me: too curvy, too loud, too much. My eyes bore into the space where a soul should be, and I smile bright. "We found the cameras, bud."

I have underpaid my burlesque troupe, exploited their talents that far surpass my own, shamed their bodies, yelled at them so they broke out in tears. I've done worse.

If you're going to plan a murder in Chicago, go to the Green Eye Lounge.

The Green Eye is loud, it's dark and dank, and on Friday and Saturday nights it's pure energy you can reach out and touch. Shoulder to shoulder, people are practically breaking out in fistfights to snag a tiny table, and the air screams with wall-to-wall shit-talking, drunk-flirting, and "I'm just here with my friends": the latter mostly from our troupe, when some dude who'd seen the show and *already tried to get backstage* took a second shot.

Just seven nights ago, we pushed open that shattered-glass door vibrating with anger.

What do you do when a man violates you?

Most pop culture would suggest: cry on the shoulder of a Big Strong Man, go to the authorities who will immediately take you seriously (preferably with your Big Strong Man), and get the fucker locked up. Live happily ever after with the knowledge you Did Everything Right.

What you really do is go out with your friends who have also been violated, commandeer a corner table and order a shitload of alcohol. You don't cry. You don't talk. You don't have to: the horror lives in your bodies, in the now-hunched shoulders you temporarily threw back in confidence while dancing on stage but now are forced to return to; in the shadows under your eyes where the concealer has sweated off; in the knuckles gone white from gripping each other's hands and the necks cricked from looking over your shoulders, making sure he isn't following you and your friends as you make your way to a space that's hopefully safer than the one you just left.

Instead of talking through the trauma, you adopt the time-honored tradition of talking *around* it.

It started as an unrelated rant about the Producer's favorite movie, in which two young, stereotypically sexy gals seduce this middle-aged husband/father who's home alone for the weekend, and then proceed to trash his house, torture and almost-but-not-quite murder him before stealing his dog and fucking off to the next guy. Directed by a dude, naturally.

The Producer encouraged us all to watch, because "then you'll get what I'm going for in my shows," as if that made any sense. As a joke, one Friday night we got drunk and high post-show at the nearest troupe member's apartment, called in delivery from the crappy Mexican joint on Western, and screamed obscenities at the movie the whole time. And this was when we still *liked* the guy.

"It's complete crap!" Val yelled over the Green Eye din. "*Funny Games* with women, but not good. Of course he doesn't even like the *original*."

I snorted at her film-degree snobbery, which I still loved even though we'd broken up months ago. "I hate to side with the male protagonist," I said to the table, taking a slug of my second G&T. "He shouldn't have cheated on his wife." I held up a magenta-manicured finger. "But what exactly did he *do* to deserve all that? So many piece-of-shit men they could fuck up—I kept waiting for a big reveal that he's this awful person, and no, he's just stupid!"

Steph rolled her eyes. "You and you"—she pointed at Val and me, the oldest in the troupe and the de facto moms—"are giving the Producer too much credit. It's his whole fantasy: hot girls torturing him."

"Except *he* tortures *us*," Katie snorted.

The eight of us looked at each other, as Lynyrd Skynrd's "Free Bird" blared on the jukebox. Putting the pieces together. We weren't *really* talking about the movie.

We weren't violent people. It's not like we'd eradicate assault and abuse entirely by wasting one offender. But we wouldn't *not* be doing something good. Because like he'd done before, even best-case scenario if people believed us, the Producer would just move on to another city. More naive women. More chances to grab, to leer, to peep.

The night got longer. The drinks more plentiful. At one point, Tamale Guy burst in with a gust of sweet winter chill, toting his magic insulated bag of fresh and cheap goodness to fortify us. As always, his timing was impeccable.

We could have stopped with the catharsis of the hypothetical. The jokes about what exactly we'd do: shoot him right in his stupid face, aiming for the perpetual wrinkle between his eyebrows when he'd tell us our bodies weren't "athletic" enough (by "athletic" he meant "skinny"); buy a stock of baseball bats and corner him in the nearest, smelliest alley; drug him as he'd once (allegedly) drugged a dancer back where he came from. Unlike those bimbos, we wouldn't let our toyboy live.

The common threads: we'd render him powerless but not completely unconscious, so he could see our faces while we were doing it. Everyone would execute something tangible, *Julius Caesar*-style, so no one person could turn in another.

Looking back, it's amazing how fast shit got real, how easily the plan came together, how in we all were. Or maybe it's not that amazing: push a femme far enough and with the right timing, details, and group of conspirators, you could pay the price. Who's going to suspect a sweet sexy gal? Or eight? Crowded around that table at the Green Eye Lounge cluttered with empty smudged drinking glasses and the husks of the city's tastiest tamales, the individual lightbulbs went on, until we were luminescent, practically levitating off the sticky-ass floor. The air around us shifted in a way only the eight of us could sense.

Val and I reached for each other's hands and squeezed tight.

For nine months, I have spied on the dancers in my employ. Not only did I frequent their private dressing room when I knew they were fully nude, but I planted cameras in the dressing room and bathroom, so I could record their most intimate acts for my own degraded sense of pleasure.

It was bad enough when he'd walk through the dressing room.

To call it "dressing room" gives this converted garage way more credit than it deserves. The dressing room-garage alternately sweltered and froze, melted our makeup off our face and made our lips so blue that we looked like goth girls, not a bad thing but he preferred our looks "classic" (he meant fuckable, specifically to him). Our bodies "athletic" (I was "just curvy enough" he would tell me in a show of assurance that felt anything but). Our mouths painted red and open, our lingerie black and see-through ideally, our music cheesy cliché, Burlesque 101.

Now, he's the Producer, it's his troupe, he can dictate the look he wants. What felt, and was, damaging was how he saw our bodies as for his unlimited consumption, to gobble up as he strolled the perimeter of that garage of a dressing room while we were trying to stretch out, spill tea, and untangle our safety thongs from our costume thongs in a decidedly unsexy manner. He wouldn't even try to hide his ogling of our breasts, our thighs. The way he'd showily inhale us: deodorant, fragrance, our private musks. All in a space that is designated for performers to just be before offering themselves up for money and joy.

He thought we were friends—that was the excuse he gave. And besides, he reminded us, he owned the building. He owned *us* (yes, he used that word).

You could argue—and he *did*, insufferable word salad in that high reedy voice—that in burlesque, lines can and do get blurred. Most jobs don't require nudity, after all.

But in those cases, it's even *more* important there are rules in place about who can and can't touch. Who can and can't take photos that could go online and cost dancers their survival jobs (one cannot survive on burlesque tips alone). Who can and can't parade around the place where we are changing and say things like, "I wish the two of you would make out right now." (Val and I, openly sapphic and ex-girlfriends to boot, were ignored, as was our trans dancer. It was more about the dancers who were straight, or better yet, starting to question if they were into just cis guys, or cis guys at all.)

"Sexy enough to give me a lap dance after the show?" he asked me once. I glared, he threw up his hands in the universal white man *what? I'm kidding, take a joke!* The utter audacity of being a woman who was there to do her job.

Worst of all: the justifications, the lies we told ourselves because we loved each other, loved the feeling of baring it all up there for a cheering crowd. No one is above this kind of trap.

If you think the above isn't a horror story, you don't know horror.

At first we laughed off his shit: typical entitled man, only this one had the extra audacity to produce burlesque as a way to perv on femmes in their natural habitat and make money off them. It's not unheard-of in the performance world, after all. But when he asked me for the lap dance, when he acted like a jealous boyfriend around our youngest, freshest troupe member who had the *gall* to miss a show for her friend's funeral, when he just wouldn't leave the garage when we asked and asked and asked, but we were too far in it, too addicted to the lights and the choreo and each other, to take any real action, he just kept pushing and pushing and pushing.

Then we found the cameras.

Last Friday night, Val called my name. I grabbed her hand, linked her sweaty fingers in mine, when I saw the blinking red light. One by one, we gathered, looked up.

People joke about trigger warnings, how played out they are, but for us—women and nonbinary folx, three quarters of us queer or peeking their way out of the closet, *all* with our own war stories about hands that "slipped" or words that stung or people that violated, who'd found solace in each other and the beauty of our bodies that people would *pay* to see—this was the equivalent of staring down the barrel of a gun.

You might say, "why didn't they just leave? I would have!" Trust me, you don't know what you'd do. You'd likely freeze like we did, not knowing what to think, not believing anyone would go that far.

"Ladies!" That thin, reedy voice cut through our collective horror.

We broke apart, tried to carry on, business as usual. We had a show in seventeen minutes. What were we supposed to do?

The blinking red light was also in the bathroom where we'd piss or shit between acts. Change our tampons. Make faces in the mirror.

Dumbass forgot to change the batteries, and that killed him in the end.

As a cishet white man of immense privilege, I admit that I am a sicko, a pervert, a creep. I'd turn myself in, but what would that do? They'd blame the dancers as sluts who knew exactly what they were getting into. I'd be slapped on the back in congratulations. The acts I performed were disgusting transgressions that I justified for the sake of art.

You might ask, *why didn't they call the cops? Make a big stink on social media? At the very least, confront the asshole and walk out, never to return again?*

Well, we didn't call the cops because what the fuck do cops ever do, especially when it concerns people who do anything remotely adjacent to sex work? Two of us are actual sex workers. As far as cops are concerned, we ask for everything we get.

Social media posts calling him out would draw attention but wouldn't guarantee results. Who would take us seriously, anyway? The classy supper club dancers, who looked down on our ragtag crew, our dusty storefront, our smeared nails? Women don't always believe women.

Confrontation would lead to whiny word salad or worse, physical violence. He constantly referred to himself as a "nice guy." But it's the self-proclaimed "nice guys" who are capable of the worst.

Walk out? Where would we go? We hated him, but we loved burlesque. At this point, the Chicago scene wasn't what it once was. Most of us were too green for more established (safer) gigs. A few dancers *had* left months earlier, none of us blamed them. But leaving is complicated. Ask anyone in a cult, in an abusive relationship (we had members who were survivors of both).

And fear, terror, rage don't always lead to Doing Everything Right. Sometimes they crystallize. Rot you from the inside.

Besides, he'd just hire other, less experienced dancers. He'd assure them his dressing room strolls were completely and totally normal. He'd replace the batteries in his cameras.

Or he'd just pop up in another city like a goddamn whack-a-mole.

It was the night of finding the cameras that we gathered at the Green Eye and planned his murder.

The very least I can do is obliterate myself and the building I own. I am beyond saving.

"I'm sorry I got you into this," Val whispers to me. The eight of us are in the basement together, standing around the Producer's rapidly dying body. Someone brought down their phone, from which Jensen McRae's "Wolves" croons away. Our stage manager murmurs, "five minutes till curtain" and we all reply "thank you, five." A reflex, a goodbye.

I turn to her, raising my voice slightly over his breaths, increasingly rattling and growing shallower, less frequent. "Stop. You didn't know. I *wanted* to audition with you." I kiss her, feeling the sharpness of the glitter she's put on her lips.

I look down the line at my friends. A year ago I didn't even know them, except Val, and now we're co-conspirators. We'll never be together again. A few will leave town, some will audition for other gigs throughout the city. This may be the end of my glitter journey, and I'm fine with it.

"I'm proud of us," I proclaim. As we stand over a soon-to-be corpse, in a soon-to-be burned basement, a soon-to-be disbanded burlesque troupe with nothing to lose, my sick dread and anger from the last week is replaced by something surprising.

Joy.

Over the course of half an hour, we've meticulously applied wig tape to pasties, painted our lips scarlet, and sprayed on body glitter before pouring ourselves into corsets (putting on our heels and stockings first, always), snapping into push-up bras and ensuring our safety thongs are hidden but firmly in place to prevent the dreaded lip slip. We've taken turns coming downstairs to the basement, sitting in the same chair I pulled up next to the Producer, telling him just how he's hurt us because he has no choice but to lie there and take it.

After I composed his suicide note, scheduled the post to go up just after final curtain, I went upstairs to get myself ready and in the interim heard crying, screaming, the occasional slap. I notice he now has a black eye. Time for the last step.

Val hands me the pillow. We'd debated just letting him die over the course of our hourlong show, but this felt like a better end. On the playlist, the sweet sadness of "Wolves" gives way to the opening riffs of Blondie's "One Way or Another."

Smiling the whole time, I center the pillow over his face and plop my ass down, crossing my legs like the good little girl I used to be before she was suffocated by men like him. It doesn't take long for that feeble wriggle of his large body to stop, for his labored breathing to quiet, for this man who inflicted hell to go completely still.

I don't know who starts laughing first but as my ass is still on the pillow that is robbing him of his very last breaths, I hear us all giggle, then chortle, then lapse into joyful hysterics. It's witch-like, except unlike our foremothers, we're not the ones being snuffed out. We're the snuffers, the killers, the girls in sparkle who are not to be fucked with, and who are about to dazzle.

Wouldn't you laugh too?

He is our sacrifice, our effigy. Soon he will burn.

Caroline calls "places!" and we shriek "THANK YOU PLACES!", still laughing as we pound up the stairs.

I don't remember what happened after curtain call, after Caroline divvied up box office and distributed tips and locked the front door and we got into our civilian clothes and pocketed any costumes and props we wanted to take with us, knowing we'd have to leave most of it behind so it wouldn't look suspicious. I know we trooped back down to the basement. I know Steph brought a joint that we sparked up and passed around, each taking a deep inhale before setting it among the pile of discarded decades-old stage curtains.

I don't really remember being at the Green Eye, surrounded by cocktails and tamales, when we heard the first fire truck, then the second. There was a fire at the theater, from the inside, from a joint that hadn't been fully extinguished. The place was full of wooden set pieces, flammable polyester costumes, and cheap curtains. *A total fire hazard*, half-drunk folks at the Green Eye commented, shaking their heads. The bartender's world-weary tone echoed through the bar: *just another Friday night in Bucktown.*

A few looky-loos went outside to watch the flames, but we stayed put, imagined the window of the storefront gloriously blowing out and raining glass. The *whoosh* of orange and yellow and red, destroying everything that destroyed us. And him, most of all him, reduced to a pile of ash. But we stayed put. All of us, slightly stoned, kept our faces composed, reached under the table and held hands tight. Undeterred, Tamale Guy came in, made his rounds. Val ordered for the table.

What I do remember is our opening group number: "Timber" by Kesha, an oldie but goodie. The eight of us kicking high, jiggling proud, black lace and red lipstick and nails, symbolic blood gumming our fingertips. Big goofy smiles that the Producer always hated because he wanted us looking like "normal girls," whatever the fuck that meant, never mind we were grown adults and didn't all identify as female anyway.

I was joyfully barefoot. We swung our partners round and round per Pitbull's instruction, kissed one another and finally ripped off our bras, one last pastie reveal for the road, to a cheering crowd. We danced for our lives, fully ourselves, and the audience ate it up as the Producer lay dead in the basement on a smelly thrifted couch.

It remains the best night of my life.

I fucked up. I'm sorry. Goodbye.

We did take one cue from the Producer's shitty favorite movie.

We stole the dog.

Juliet was our IT goddess and contortionist royalty who earlier that day, had successfully slithered into his apartment and spread the poison, which she'd obtained from the dark web, on all touch surfaces. Also the the most devoted dog mom in the troupe, she put Oscar safely in the hallway first, before scooping him up and taking him home to her boyfriend and their bull terrier. Juliet's boyfriend had gotten a new job, and they were relocating to a different state, with their growing canine family in tow.

Of course we would have saved him regardless, but we also saw how thin Oscar was. We knew from the Producer's oversharing that he'd adopted a puppy with his ex-wife, and acquired Oscar in the split, only to borderline neglect the sweet pup who just wanted love and kibble. With the whereabouts of the ex-wife unknown, we took it upon ourselves to give Oscar the life he'd only doggy-dreamed of.

I got a postcard from Juliet last week, one line in blood-red ink:

Oscar is doing great.

LIVES MATTER

Jotham Austin II

My Bigmom told me to never play with dead things. She always said stuff like this to me. Imparting wisdom on me. Wisdom shared at eight in the morning. No sleeping in, not even on Saturdays. Cleaning day. Over the crunch of cereal, the stink of Pine-Sol, Mop & Glo, the whine of the vacuum cleaner. Bigmom preached. Respect my elders. Nothing wrong with saying Yes sir and No ma'am. Be a leader, not a follower, focus on education and not girls. I tune out, thinking about going to the park later. Charlie's house. Jessy—

Bigmom's hand slaps the table, pulling my attention to her serious face. Wiping at the worn walnut with a dishrag.

"Listen to me, Grayson," she leans in close. Cocoa butter and bleach tickle my nose. "And if you do mess around with a young lady, make sure you wear a condom. Even if she says she's on the pill."

I think about Jessy and wonder if she is on the pill. Jessy is going to be at the party tonight. Should I take a condom?

Bigmom leans in close, breath tickling my ear as she talks. "Baby boy, I don't want any great grands." Bigmom chuckles, leaning away, giving me a side eye, before wiping the table again. "I'm too young to be a great grandmamma."

She grabs my bowl, barking chores at me. I nod. Hustling out the dining room before she tells me again how periods work.

I take a break to check my phone. Billy and Jason texted me they were going to be at the Midway Plaisance Park around four to play catch and then go to Charlie's house in Kenwood to hang. Charlie has a game room in his basement. Cool parents. Jessy will be there.

I pocket the phone and get back to work. Scrub the toilet. Tub. Mop the floor. Start a load of laundry. Shower. Get dressed. Ready to go.

"See you later, Bigmom," I say, hurrying past the living room. Hand on doorknob.

Bigmom calls out, "You need a ride?"

I think about pulling up to Charlie's house in Bigmom's fifteen-year-old Ford F150. No, thank you.

"I'm going to ride my bike to the park to meet Billy and Jason. Then go to Charlie's house. Up in Kenwood. 49th and Kimbark."

Bigmom sucks her teeth, calling me into the living room. "Is Billy that big white boy that plays soccer at that expensive Lab School of yours?" Reclining in her chair. Feet up on the ottoman. She looks me up and down.

I nod. Jason and Charlie are white too, but she only mentions that when asking about Billy. She doesn't like Billy.

"My baby boy looking clean…Um, um…" Bigmom smirks. "Must be a young lady there you got eyes for."

I look away to conceal my smile. "Nah. Nothing like that, Bigmom."

"It's all right. You at that age. My baby growing up into a young man." Bigmom sits up. "You have money?"

I shake my head.

"I can give you a twenty for all your hard work today." Bigmom's eyes, head point to the coffee table. Her big black leather purse.

I hand it to Bigmom. Because you never go through a lady's purse. Another one of Bigmom's maxims. She pulls a twenty out for putting in a good day of work but holds it close to her chest. Going over my plans. She already approved my itinerary earlier. But makes me recite the plans again. She holds out the twenty. As my hand touches the crisp bill, Bigmom reminds me.

"And don't go to those white folks' house and act like I don't feed you. Or you don't have manners."

"Yes, Bigmom."

"If you need me to pick you up, call." Bigmom settles back into the chair. "Have fun."

"What time should I be home?"

Bigmom raises an eyebrow. "You're a junior in high school, close to going off to college. Living on your own soon. I trust you'll make good decisions." She pauses. Eyes close in thought. Imagining something. "I don't like you biking after dark." Bigmom's eyes open. Staring at me. Hand grabs for her glass of lemonade. She takes a sip, never taking her eyes off me.

In the quiet I want to say, "I could still be living in Munster. Safer than south side Chicago. But you didn't want to move away from your church and your friends." But bad things can happen even when you try to be safe. Like mom and dad dying in that car crash. Having to move in with Bigmom when I was ten. But I keep my mouth shut. Don't want to be accused of backtalk. Or smelling my piss. Stuck at home washing dishes and playing Scrabble watching *Double Indemnity*. Again.

Bigmom sets down her glass. "Be home by 10:30pm. Text me when you get there. When you leave. Bike down Dorchester, it's one way, the right way to 62nd and then home. And stay out of the alleys. No shortcuts. If you need me to pick you up . . . no matter how late . . . I will."

I run over, taking the twenty. Kissing Bigmom on the cheek. "Thank you," I say, waving over my shoulder. Out the door before she changes her mind.

Biking over to the park, all I can think about is having time to ask Jessy out. I slow down, hopping off my bike close to the Lab School. Locking it. Billy and Charlie aren't here. I check my messages and see Billy texted me while I was biking up here that they are closer to the ice-skating rink. I pull a pick out of my hoodie pocket. Hood down. Picking out my afro. I walk past the Ida Noyes building. Cross Wood-lawn Ave. Rockefeller Chapel. Turn south on Woodlawn. Feeling sweat trickle down my back. Should have biked closer. I hear Billy yelling at Jason playing catch, near that one statue. I pocket my pick and wave. Billy sees me. Launches the football at me. As it descends, it's going to be short. I sprint. Stretching. Grabbing it out of the air with two hands.

"You got some jets. You should be on the team. That was an amazing catch," Jason shouts.

"Thanks to my great throw," Billy yells. "If you're so good, throw it from there."

Billy is standing about 40 yards away. He waves at me. I've never thrown a football that far. I don't want them to laugh at me. At the party. Jessy hearing that I can't throw a ball across the park. I plant my feet, throwing the football as hard as I can.

I watch as it arches into that blue cloudless sky. Hovering. Like a bird caught in a breeze. As the ball descends, Billy yelps. He backpedals.

"You've got a rocket for an arm," Jason hoots.

Billy jumps. The ball slips through his outstretched arms, bouncing a few yards past him into the bushes.

"Shit. You are going in there after that," Billy yells. Hands on hips. Glaring at me.

"My bad," I say, running over.

Billy smacks me on the butt. Hard. "Show off. You got some speed, come out to soccer tryouts next week."

I step into the bushes, seeing the ball. Through the bushes I can see the statue. Reading the plaque, Carl Von Linné. I pick up the ball and see a red bird next to it. Wings spread. Motionless. I jerk back.

"Shit," I yelp. "I killed it."

"What?" Billy and Jason say, pushing through the shrubs. Looking over my shoulder. Jason kneels down to look at the bird.

"You killed it, man," Jason says, poking it with his finger.

Billy grabs a stick and pokes at it.

"Stop that," I say, pushing at his hand.

"If you poke out her eye, we can see the brain," Billy says.

"It's a male," I correct him.

"What?" Billy hovers over me.

I look up. "The males are bright red. The females have gray feathers with some red pigmentation on the wings."

Jason stands. "He's right."

"I forgot you were a country boy from Indiana." Billy messes my afro.

I smack his hand away. "Come on, man. Let's leave it."

Billy holds the stick out to me. "Do it."

"Nah."

"Do it or we'll tell Jessy that you are a chicken."

I can feel the edges of the foil wrapper in my pocket. If I don't do this, I should go home and jerk off, because I'll be the joke of the party. High school.

I snatch the stick. "Okay."

Billy and Jason lean in. I break the stick to get an angled, sharp point. I lay my hand over the bird to make sure it's dead. The bird's feathers are soft. Warm. A small twitch. Maybe just the wind. My stomach churns.

"Come on, Dr. Doolittle." Billy cackles.

My fingers tighten around the stick.

"Hurry," Billy hisses.

I swallow hard. Lower the stick closer to its black, beady eye. Billy shoves my arm—*pop*—the stick pierces the eye. A thin spurt of blood splatters across my face. I drop the stick. My heart racing. I cannot believe what I did. This isn't real. Reaching my hand out. Sorry. Stroking the bird's feathers. Sorry. Feeling the bird's body beneath my hand—still warm. Still real.

I lick my dry lips. The taste hits me. Metallic. Sickly. I jerk my hand away, gagging. My stomach clenches. My throat burns. Its blood on my lips. In my mouth.

"Shit," I say, jumping to my feet. Can I catch bird flu? Rabies? Trying to wipe, spit that metallic taste out of my mouth. "Yuck."

Billy and Jason laugh, backing away from me. "That bird spurted in your mouth." Billy slaps at Jason. "You got to swallow, Gray… don't be a spitter."

I kick the bird. "Stupid shit."

Billy shakes his head. Still laughing. Picks up the ball. "Come on. Let's go to Charlie's."

On the way over, all I can think about is Billy telling everyone about this. When we get there, everyone is in the game room. Sodas in hands. Music loud. I run into the bathroom to rinse that taste out of my mouth. Looking under the sink, I find a bottle of mouthwash. Rinse. Spit. Minty fresh.

Stepping out of the bathroom. Joining the flow of the party. I keep moving, dodging Billy and Jason's smirks. I don't want them telling people about that bird. Then I see her. Jessy. She tilts her head, a silent invitation. I nod toward the back door, and she follows. Sitting on a bench under a tree. Jessy sits next to me. Close. We talk for a while. I ask her if she wants to be my girl. She asks if I'll be her boy. We laugh. We agree. She lays her head on my shoulder. I look up. Into the tree. Eyes stare back at me. I can still taste that bird's blood. I look away. Look at Jessy. Face blurry closer. We kiss. I taste her. By nine o'clock we are walking around the party holding hands. Announcing to everyone that didn't see us making out in the yard that we are a couple. We kiss before I bicycle away at ten promising to text when I get home.

Bigmom is asleep in the living room when I walk in. And the days pass without Bigmom asking too many questions. But I'm sure she is saving them up for Saturday. Cleaning day when neither of us has any excuses to not talk with each other over soapy rags and dirty mop water.

I cannot believe Jessy and I have only been official for six days. If we pass each other in school, we make silly faces and pass notes. We hold hands any chance we get. Make out after band practice. Eat lunch together.

I get a text from Jessy that she is going to MSI after school. It's a half-day. Bigmom says it is Friday and I can go. She'll pick me up on her way home. I tell Jessy I have to meet some classmates for a group project before I can go, but I'll be there soon.

Jessy sends a winking emoji. *Hurry. Because I'm not sure how long I can wait to climb into that combine harvester.* My stomach does a stupid little flip thinking about us snuggled in that green farming equipment harvesting video corn and sneaking kisses.

I leave Lab twenty minutes after school lets out. I am walking along the Midway answering texts from Jessy when a bird's angry caw pulls me from my phone. I stop texting and look up at the telephone wire. Just a regular black bird. But another joins. Then another. Their heads tilt down at me. Watching.

Billy and Jason yell my name, running to catch up.

"Hey Gray. Mr. Lover boy," Billy says teasing. "Can't believe you snagged Jessy. Those tits. That ass…"

"Shut the fuck up. That's my girl y'all talking about."

Billy pulls my arm to go north on Blackstone. "Let's go to Trader Joe's and get some candy for the crew," he says, high-fiving Jason. "It's too expensive at that museum."

I think about what I have left of that twenty and how much to get into the museum. "I didn't bring any extra cash," I say, hopeful to get out of this diversion, wanting to get to the museum and spend as much time with Jessy as possible.

"Don't worry about it, bro. I got you," Billy says, draping his arm over my shoulder and pulling me along.

When we get to the candy aisle, Billy confesses he doesn't have any money either. He shoves a bag of candy into my hoodie pocket.

"What the fuck, man?" I snatch the candy out, flinging it at him.

"Come on man. I told the crew we'd bring snacks," Billy snaps.

I lean into his space, whisper shouting, "I'm not stealing."

Billy smirks. "Oh well. Jessy will have to find out you are just a poor boy and can't afford to take care of her." Billy smirks. "Don't worry, I can give her what she needs." He winks at Jason.

"Fuck you."

Jason tucks candy into his jacket. Billy shoves a pack of candy into his bag. He glares at me. Pulls a jumbo bag of fancy gummy bears off the rack, holding it out to me.

"These are Jessy's favorite."

Billy stares me down. My fingers brush the bag. Disappointing Bigmom again tugs at me. Her voice, sharp as the belt she only ever had to use once. Preaching as she spanked me, "Only two things…" Whack. Whack. "…I hate in this world…" Whack. Whack. "…is a liar…" Whack. Whack. "…and a thief." Whack. Whack. Whack.

My stomach twists. But Jessy's smile fills my head, soft and sweet. Bigmom's voice echoing in my head, "Be a leader, not a—"

"C'mon, man," Billy's taunting voice cuts in. "You want to impress Jessy, right?"

My stomach drops.

Then, before I can think—before I can stop myself—I snatch the bag, shoving it into my pocket.

"My man. Going to get some," Billy says, slapping my shoulder. Jason gives me a thumbs up. They run ahead laughing.

I walk after them, but Bigmom's voice echoes again in my head: "be a leader..." My stomach knots. I hear Billy shouting. Jason shouting. A man in a green smock shouting. Chasing after them like a scene out of one of those old black and white vaudeville movies Bigmom watches.

I swallow the lump in my throat and walk the opposite direction. I stand with everyone else, watching Billy and Jason run across the store and out of sight.

With everyone distracted, I sneak out the exit door. I tell myself I did nothing wrong, but my body knows otherwise. My legs and hands are shaking. I think of Bigmom, the way she caught me lying about breaking her vase when I was ten. The sting of that belt. How she made me look her in the eye and say the truth. The lingering sting of welts along my legs. The knot in my stomach standing in front of church and confessing my sins. That same feeling crawls up my spine now. But I keep walking.

Walking slow. Crossing 55th street. Down Lake Park toward MSI. Fast walking. Sirens scream in the distance. Stopping under the Metra station bridge. Stopping to catch my breath. Think.

Bigmom's maxims reciting in my head. Pull that hoodie down, so you can hear and be heard. Show respect. Yes sir. No mama. No talk back. If you can, send an SOS text.

Bigmom is going to kill me.

Sirens echo in the distance. Snapping me back to the present. I can see lights flashing down 56th street. I cross Stony and start jogging into the park. Stopping by the playground pretending to be watching the small children go up and down the slide. Sirens louder. I swallow the warm bile, trying to calm myself. Walking again through the grass away from the street.

"Don't run," Bigmom's calming voice comes to me.

Sirens screaming. I stop. Turn around. I close my eyes, expecting the squad car to pull onto the grass. Hands raising. Heart thumping against my chest. The sirens Doppler past. I open my eyes. It's just me standing in the park. Concerned parents looking at me before herding their kids away from me.

They went past. They are not after me. Bigmom will never know. Relief washes over me. A kid yells, jarring me out of my trance. Heart still pounding against my chest. But I'm safe. Legs shaky. But I start walking again. Away. Alive.

I'll stay off the street and cut through the park to the Museum. If I hurry, I can still have some quality time with Jessy. I put my hand in my pocket, pulling out my buzzing phone.

Billy: *Still going to MSI?*

Me: *What? I thought you got arrested.*

Billy: *Nah. The guy chasing us in the store was one of my dad's friends and he let us off with a warning. I've done this before, and my distraction let you get away with some premium candy.*

Me: *Yeah.*

Billy: *Jessy will be so impressed.*

I shove my phone into my pocket. My empty pockets. I ain't no thief. Just a sucker.

"Only two things I hate in this world: a liar and a thief. Can't trust either," Bigmom would always say to me.

Why the hell was I running? Could have got shot for nothing. I pat my pockets again to convince myself that I put the gummies back. Did nothing wrong. I feel stupid that I ran and got worked up.

"Don't run from cops," Bigmom always preached. "Don't give them a reason."

I can't face Billy empty handed. I'll tell him I had to go home. But what about Jessy? I cannot go to the museum. I could ask Jessy to meet me for a coffee at True North or Plein Air. Maybe hold hands sipping coffees walking through the Quad on campus. I pull my phone out to text when birds chirping pull my attention to a bench by the sidewalk. Three robins making sharp yeeps and guttural chirrs at me. I take a slow step away from the bench. Not wanting to get pecked if they have a nest in the tree above.

I turn to walk away down the path. A pair of geese honk at me. Where'd they come from? I turn. A giant heron swoops down and lands on the path in my way. It stretches to its full height. Long curved neck. Eyes daring me to pass. I look back at the bench thinking to make a run for the sidewalk and cross the street when dozens of green parakeets swoop down at me. Around me.

I turn in a slow circle looking for an escape. I'm surrounded. No way out except running back into the park. I take a step in the direction I want to go. The birds all chatter. Squeaking. Whistling. Trilling. Moving closer. I count to three in my head. One. Two. Three. Cover my face. Holler and run into the park hoping to loop around and escape to the street.

The birds all scatter. Wings flapping at me. Over me. Herding me into the park. When I try to go a different way, they swoop and peck me. I wave my hands over my head, feeling talons and beaks scratching. Pecking at my afro. Neck. Back. Pushing me along. Into the quiet of the park.

Trees and shrubs blur past through my hands protecting my face. I don't know what direction I am going. Batting away birds.

The ground shifts underfoot. A hole. Ankle twisting. Pain. Stumbling. Arms failing. Reaching. Head smacking into a tree. Ziggy lines jog across my vision.

The birds land around me. Studying me. I try to move, but pain jabs along my back. Head full of angry white noise.

Birds surrounding me. Their sounds competing with the ringing in my head. They seem to talk to each other. In code. I blink my eyes, trying to focus. Trying to make sense of the scene.

A bird perches on my stomach. I try to lift my head, but I can't. The tiny, curved claws scratch along my chest until I can see the bird. Bright red. Mohawk of feathers. It flaps its wings, making a slurred whistle followed by a slow trill.

I try to focus. On the details of the bird's face. Fading into Bigmom's smirking face. That face she makes when I don't listen to her. It whistles. Voice like Bigmom calling me.

"Bigmom, what?" I answer instinctively.

"I warned you."

"I didn't steal the candy."

"It's not that . . ." Bigmom grins, shaking her head. Morphing back into the bird making a tsk-tsk clucking sound at me, continuing, "A hard head makes a soft behind." Bigmom smiles. "You'll listen next time."

Tears blur my vision. Bigmom's face melts back into the cardinal's. I blink my eyes. Tears running down my face. The cardinal tilts its head.

My breath catches.

The right eye is missing—a dark crusty hole where it should be. My stomach flips. It's the same bird. The one I killed.

"I'm sorry," I plead. "I'm so sorry." My voice fades into a whimper. "Sorry . . . sorry . . . sorry."

The cardinal whistles at the other birds. At me. Leaning in. Beak pressing against my cheek. Soft feathers brushing my skin. It whistles—a sound almost human.

I can't move. Can't breathe.

Not real. Not real. This isn't happening. If only I could close my eyes. This would go away.

The beak edges closer, so close it's a blur. I can feel the heat of its breath. My whole body locks up in panic. I try to blink—try to move, to scream—

Pop.

White-hot agony explodes in my skull. My vision shatters. Colors bleed and kaleidoscope into each other.

Half the world collapses into darkness. Feathers brushing my skin. A cacophony of wings flapping trills, hoots, honks, and whistles.

Then silence. Then complete darkness. Then Bigmom's voice— low, knowing, final. "Everything always evens out baby boy. One way or another."

THE AVALON HAINT

Tina Jenkins Bell

Gina Farrow's new doctor had kind eyes. Soft hands. A patient, authoritative voice. She trusted him even after he told her son Karon, "Your mom's night terrors are getting worse. She could hurt herself or you if you don't act soon."

"Yeah, but y'all want me to send her to a nursing home. I can't do that to her," Karon said, massaging her back and kissing her forehead.

"Today, there's a pulsating bruise on her leg. Tomorrow it could be exponentially worse. You never know when age gets twisted up with Parkinson's," the doctor continued. "Let's not discount the forgetfulness, the hallucinations."

As Karon listened to the doctor, Gina shirked from his touch. Instantly, he stopped rubbing her back, shoving his huge hands in his pockets though his eyes slanted in her direction. Gina stopped moving.

"Got to be something you can do to help her sleep at night," Karon said, his dark, round eyes pleading.

"I hate putting older people on sleeping pills. Sometimes leads to other problems. Maybe go to the health food store. Get some melatonin. Try five milligrams to start. That might be enough to see her through," the doctor said.

"Okay, doc," Karon said, pausing. "Say, you believe in haints?"

"Haints?" the doctor asked.

"Yeah. Evil spirits, ghosts, demons, ghouls," Karon returned.

The doctor's dark face wrinkled. His full lips pooched, twisted. "I don't believe so.... Wait a minute, you're not suggesting..."

"Not suggesting. Mama believes in them. Always has since she was little girl growing up in her aunt's house.

"Listen to this," Karon said, cupping the doctor's shoulder. "When I was a kid, I had this bad fever that wouldn't quit. Ma said she saw a haint hover above my bed right before the fever came on."

The doctor angled his head away from Karon. "Did the fever break?"

"Hell yeah, it broke," Karon said, folding his arms across his chest. "Ma thumbed my forehead with holy oil. The fever broke, and I was back out there hooping with my boys not much later."

Still, seated on the exam table, Gina smiled, remembering.

The doctor turned to Gina. "So, Mrs. Farrow, do you believe you've had Parkinson's before we diagnosed it?"

Gina sniffed at the air. "Ain't got no Parkinson's," she said, turning her head toward the charts on the wall.

Even though Gina had been listening to every word, she let Karon do all the talking because she was mad at him. That morning, she'd asked him about the social security checks he claimed went missing. Then there were the real estate folks noseying around her place, asking for Karon, the homeowner interested in selling.

Above all, she'd asked Karon a bunch of times to sprinkle salt around the perimeter of the house. He said he had, but she knew differently. Otherwise, they wouldn't be here at the doctor's office prattling about night terrors.

Gina had no idea why this evil spirit, her grandmother and auntie called a haint, visited her only at night. Trenches burrowed deep folds in her forehead as she thought about other ways to get it to go away since she couldn't trust Karon to salt the place.

Maybe she'd dig up a spell her Auntie Helen used to cast out evil spirits when she was living over there on Maxwell Street, right behind the flea market where the coat sellers' stall sat next door to the joint where they got Polish sausages with grilled onions and pork chop sandwiches on white bread.

A smile pinched the edges of Gina's mouth as she remembered spending summers with her Auntie Helen who conjured up dead loved ones for her neighbors and sprinkled salt across the thresholds of her doors and windowsills to keep out evil spirits. And when the occasional relentless haint got past Auntie Helen's initial defense, there was this spell she used to chant. *What was it? Rejoice not evil spirit for. . . . Now, what's the rest of it?*

Her memory wasn't what it used to be, but her desire, to live in her house, her family's bungalow where she'd lived all her sixty years, was strong.

Her house with its colorful wildflowers, hostas, hydrangea bushes with head-sized purple blossoms that bobbed in the wind. With its pergola-covered patio and outside kitchen in the backyard. With its wide porch anchored by wide, tall columns. With its porch swing, hanging over a braided rug, covering a wooden slatted porch. With its original wood door, leading to a large living room with a wood-burning fireplace. With its four bedrooms, two on either side of the long hallway with Jack and Jill bathrooms between them.

To some, her house may not have been much, but it was everything to her. It had won the Chicago Bungalow contest, three years straight, for its beauty and adherence to its original form, and every time the City presented her with an award, she felt like a proud new mom meeting her newborn baby for the first time.

Gina and Karon shook the doctor's hand and shuffled out of the exam room into a brightly lit hallway.

As they moved along, Gina nodded at a nurse in a crisp white dress, white stockings, and white low-heeled shoes. A nurse's hat steepled atop of her head. The nurse touched Gina's arm before she could pass.. Her hand was pale blue. Her touch was icy.

"Auntie Helen wants you to know that thing in your house isn't a haint," the nurse said.

Gina grabbed her arm, rubbing. "Well, what is it then? Did she say anything about that spell she used?"

The nurse said nothing else, disappearing as Gina watched.

Karon held the door, leading outside. "Come on, Ma, before we miss the bus," he said. "Who were you talking to, anyway?"

Gina wagged her head and caught up with her son. Once outside, Gina and Karon walked toward the bus stop on 79th and King Drive. The bus arrived shortly after, and they boarded the 79th Street bus, carefully, with Karon's hand at her back, urging her to move faster. Gina ignored Karon's subtle command and mounted each step one at a time, flashing her "senior, disabled" bus pass to the driver before locating a window seat, where she watched Walgreens, a bakery, a currency exchange, Mimi's Rib Joint, Chi-town Dispensary, Lou's Flower shop, and a gas station slide by on their way back to 79th and Woodlawn. When the bus stopped at the corner of their block, they were greeted by a beautifully decorated yard sign, welcoming visitors to the Avalon community and discouraging tomfoolery. *No gangs. No loud music. No loitering,* the sign read.

Back at home, Karon went to the kitchen to make soup. He helped Gina into her favorite easy chair and turned on the flat screen, hanging just above the fireplace before going back out the door to retrieve their mail.

Karon stood before Gina searching through mail fanned out in his hand. He plucked one that looked like it carried Gina's check. He folded and pocketed it.

Gina looked at Karon with weary eyes. "Was that my check?"

"No, Ma. It's the check I get for caretaking," Karon said, plodding toward the kitchen. "I can call Social Security again though. Now, let me get back to that soup."

I can call about my own check, Gina thought. *Karon just needs to give me my cell phone.*

On the television, a news anchor stood in a clearing before a forest, reporting the discovery of the missing blonde girl with ocean blue eyes. A photo of her consumed the screen before her lifeless body stepped out of the television and hovered above Gina's waxed wood floors. Her skin was chitlin gray. Her eyes resembled eclipsed suns in darker, empty sockets. Her mouth stretched, emitting a whine.

In her mind, Gina heard the girl say, "Everyone thought Brian was perfect, too. They watched us dance across the country's landscapes. They saw him pick me up in his arms and twirl. They didn't see the times he beat me. Not the first time nor the last. They wouldn't let themselves believe it was Brian, just like you don't want to think it's Karon." The woman slurred her last words while pointing to a purplish ring around her neck and the blue-black bruises shrouding both eyes.

Gina launched from her seat, falling to the floor. She thought about the nurse's warning, the missing checks, the real estate agent visits, and her cell phone, and still she decided to give Karon the benefit of the doubt. *Hell, no child I labored 42 hours to get here would ever hurt me.*

Just then, the blonde girl spoke between ladder-stitched lips. "I loved Brian and look where it got me." She disintegrated after that, dust falling below the place she'd hovered. Her disembodied voice trailed her. "Anybody can do anything when they want what you have."

Gina began to scream, drawing Karon from the kitchen. "Mama, what now," he said, grabbing a television tray and placing the bowl on it before lifting and helping Gina back to her chair. "Damn, it's always something with you. Just eat your damn soup and go to bed," Karon said.

"Why you so mean, Karon," Gina whimpered. "You don't want to stay with me. Move. Stay with your girlfriend and all them babies y'all got."

"Why can't they come here?" he challenged. "All this space and the most you use of it is your bedroom, the bathroom, and this room right here. My lady. Our kids. They need space to grow."

"When I'm gone, it's yours. Not before then. Two queens can't run one castle," Gina retorted.

Karon balled his fists and raged forward as Gina shrank back in her chair.

"This is my house," Gina insisted. "You keep on pushing me and . . ."

"And what?" Karon challenged.

Gina pushed away her soup and watched her son walk out, slamming the door behind him.

After their spat, Karon disappeared, maybe over to his babies' Mama's house. Even though Gina had pretty much invited Karon to leave, she didn't like it when he left at night when her room became a sea of indigo ink once she locked her bedroom door and turned off the lights.

Her bedroom was the one place Karon didn't trespass as far as she knew. She was free there though not safe 'cause things move in the dark. Loom, even. Most folk don't know that. They flip on their lights or squeeze their eyes shut if they can. Anything but question their lying eyes.

The thing is, whether she turned off her lamps and ceiling lights or not, darkness consumed her. Just then, a haint materialized from grayish mounds against the blackness. Moving. Taunting. "Your time is done now. Die or move," it said. It pushed her out of her bed. Yanked the covers she pulled over her head. "Leave. You don't need all this," it hissed. "But Karon does."

Karon? Thinking about him, Gina remembered when he was a boy and told her point blank that he'd kill her between sips of root beer and licks of ice cream dripping like lava down the side of his cone.

"Love you, Mommie," the haint mimicked Karon's eight-year-old self and pinched her so hard she cried out. "But one day when I have to look out for you." Its final words rasped, drifting away. "One day, you will wish you ran away."

That day was here.

Gina was stowed away in her bedroom. Karon had taken over her home. She rolled over in her bed. Perspiration wet her sheets. The hours sauntered, finally making it to midnight. The haint hung over her. Its respiration, like a dog's pant, warmed and chilled her. "Give up this damn house or you'll be sorry," it promised, weighing her down with its malevolence, surrounding her with the putrid smell of bad beef.

Gina tried again to recall Aunt Helen's spell but couldn't remember the exact words for the life of her.

"Rejoice not evil spirit for I believe in the Lord. . . . No. . . . I believe in the Lord, not you, evil spirit. Rejoice not. . . . Yes, that's it!"

Gina reached for her cross on the nightstand. "I believe in the Lord, not you, evil spirit. . . . Rejoice not," she shouted repeatedly, spit flying with her words.

Instead of expelling the evil spirit, her words fomented more hostility. Her bed began to quake as she clung to the bedsheets. Then, something catapulted her from the bed. Still holding her cross, Gina crawled to her nightstand, grabbing her Luger from the bottom drawer, shooting at every shape and movement.

When the sun rose again, the police, called to do a wellness check by neighbors who heard gunshots, found Gina cradling Karon's bloody head in her lap. The gun tossed close to the bathroom door.

One freckled officer with a mop of red hair stood over her, frowning. She looked up at the officer. "Only a haint could walk through locked doors and solid walls. How'd this happen?"

"Ma'am, I see you locked your bedroom door, but your bathroom door leading to the other bedroom was open," the officer said. "Might be you mistook your son for an intruder?"

Gina's eyes clouded as she clutched Karon's bloodied shirt. "No, no! Karon left to go stay with his babies' Mama."

The freckled officer hunched his shoulders as Gina rocked Karon in her arms. "He left," she insisted. "Right?"

"If he left, he must have come back," the officer said, but Gina was lost in her own world. *It wasn't a haint doing all this. . . . Now what was that spell auntie used to call up the dead?*

A GOOD KID

Nick Medina

They rattled in Marco's pockets when he walked, the bricks he carried everywhere he went. He'd pull them out when he was bored, and even when he wasn't, because he loved snapping them together. He said it was a love that began before he could remember, when an aunt or his grandma gifted him a box of those extra chunky bricks, the ones toddlers couldn't choke on.

The pieces in his pockets were always random, different every day. He'd grab two fistfuls from the box beside his bed before heading to school each morning, then toss what was left of them back into the mix when he got home. The shapes and sizes didn't matter. The colors didn't either. Whether he ended up with twenty 2x2s, thirty 1x1s, an equal mix of 2x3s, 1x4s, and 1x2s, or any other of the seemingly infinite combinations he could pull from the box, he trusted his fingers to build something worth bragging about. He had the imagination. The skill. And he knew how lucky he was to have so many bricks. They weren't cheap. His family barely got by.

Bricks tumbled onto the cafeteria table from his palm, their plastic clacks pure music to Marco's ears.

Bobby swept aside the pieces that had landed next to his carton of chocolate milk, wondering what the assortment of colorful bricks would turn into today. Monday's build was an apple like the one Marco had left uneaten on the table. Tuesday's was a monstrous head with 1x1s for teeth. Yesterday's was a rainbow-striped zebra that would have been a unicorn if Marco had had an antenna to stick on its head.

Tongue between his teeth and lips, Marco, through squinted eyes, scanned the pieces before him, assessing.

"And he's off..." Bobby, watching from the corner of his eye, knew Marco had found his inspiration when his eyebrows shot high up on his forehead, which always happened a split-second before Marco's hands started snapping the bricks together.

"Duck. Turtle. Bomb," Bobby guessed. He didn't have a clue, and he knew better than to ask what Marco was building. It'd be clear in the end. It always was.

"Anyone coming?" Marco didn't look away from his bricks. Bobby slyly examined the lunchroom around them. The coast was clear. For now.

"You're good," Bobby said, prompting Marco to build faster.

"It's almost done...the big one I've been working on."

"The sky—?"

"Yep. Stayed up half the night working on it. Until my mom saw the light under my door. You're gonna come see it, right?"

Of course, Bobby would. He went to see all his best friend's builds, each bigger and better than the last. "Manny will wanna come too."

Marco nodded. He liked the attention. Most of the time. Finished, he held up his lunchtime creation.

Smirking, Bobby said, "You gotta give it to her."

"I didn't make it for her." Marco set the 3-D heart, rainbow like the zebra because he'd grabbed more than just red bricks from the box that morning, onto the table.

"You said you're gonna ask her."

"I am."

"When?"

"Next week."

"The dance is two weeks away. She'll have a date by then." He reached out and gave the heart a spin, perpetually amazed at how Marco could create curved surfaces out of bricks with hard corners.

Marco shrugged. "I can build anything."

"You can't build that. And if you do, I don't wanna know about it." The two laughed, and then Bobby hollered, "Six o'clock!" in time for Marco to scoop the heart from the table as a tray in the hands of super-senior Isaiah slammed against the tabletop, loud as a gunshot, making half the cafeteria scream.

Manny, his eyes barely over the sill, was waiting by the front window of Señora Lopez's apartment when Bobby arrived to pick him up from the sitter after school. He cried out for Señora Lopez to open the door at the sight of Bobby, then ran straight to his big brother to slap him a high-five that wasn't any higher than Bobby's waist. They walked past a skeleton and a warrior, women in swirling Jalisco dresses, and Christ on the cross on their way home, colorful murals that stood in sharp contrast to the gray of the underprivileged neighborhood around them.

Manny stopped moving his little feet outside La Casa del Pueblo. Bobby looked down at him, knowing what Manny wanted, and that the afternoon stops at the mini-mart were becoming a bad habit entirely of his making.

"What's the deal?"

The words were barely out of Bobby's mouth before Manny started his response. "Don't tell Mom."

"And?"

"Only one."

"And?"

"We brush our teeth when we get home."

Bobby jerked his head toward the door. Manny darted inside and reached for a twin-pack of Hostess chocolate cupcakes in the rack beside the register. They each ate one on the rest of the way to their apartment, enjoying grainy bites of icing between their teeth, which they brushed side-by-side in front of the narrow vanity at home, Manny standing on a chair he dragged in from the kitchen so that he could see himself in the mirror, just like he did every morning when he squeezed tight beside his big brother and rubbed wax into his hair. His quiff cut with faded sides and three shaved lines above each temple was identical to Bobby's.

He could stay out later if he didn't take Manny with him, but not after dark because that's when fights broke out on the corners and in the park, in front of bars, in alleys, and in apartment building stairwells, especially now, as the weather warmed with winter giving way to spring.

They set out after dinner, Manny's plate clean of green beans and peas. He didn't like them, but he ate a forkful each time Bobby, who ate them because he knew he'd be mimicked, brought the veggies to his mouth. Holding hands because Mom, whose eyelids had sagged during dinner, insisted on it, they crossed the street to the block that ran parallel to theirs, passing more murals—a bluesman with a guitar, a boy with a bird beak, a memorial for a girl who would stay six forever, a dark brown splotch.

"He finished it an hour ago," Marco's dad said upon opening the apartment door. The scent of warm tortillas lightly charred atop a bare stovetop burner wafted into the hall. Manny broke free from Bobby's grasp and ran into the apartment, straight to Marco's room. Bobby accepted a can of mango Jumex before chasing after his little brother.

The heart Marco had built at lunch was on the shelf above his bed alongside other miniature builds—a helicopter, a lighthouse, a fox. He had his Batman bedsheet draped over the folding table that'd become a permanent fixture in front of his bedroom window. Something big with several tall points loomed beneath the sheet.

"Ready?" Marco grabbed two corners of the bedsheet. Bobby spluttered his lips, creating a drumroll for the big reveal. Manny, hands deep in the box of bricks beside Marco's bed, looked up from where he'd knelt on the floor. "Three . . . two . . . one!" Marco quickly yet carefully whipped the sheet away, uncovering an astonishing replica of the city's grand skyline, which loomed on the horizon outside Marco's window, the buildings so far away that they appeared to be the exact same height as the models Marco had built out of his precious bricks.

"Fuck," Bobby said. The word just fell out of him. Marco's work was as stunning as the skyline itself. Glittering in the distance, the skyscrapers seemed to be made of starlight as much as steel, the most magnificent structures in the world. "Don't!" Bobby eyed Manny with a stern expression as "fuh" came from Manny's parroting mouth. "Don't tell Mom either."

"It's good?" Marco's nervous fingers fidgeted with a silver brick he must have painted to represent the Bean at the base of the skyline.

"It's art," Bobby said.

"Art!" Manny echoed.

He said it again the next day. Cupcake crème on his lips, Manny pointed up at the brick wall behind Bobby's back as they finished their secret snack around the corner from the mini-mart.

"Art!"

Bobby turned and looked up at the wall behind him. The upper third, bare the day before, was painted with the city skyline. Normally, Bobby would have dismissed the mural as no big deal; new art and territorial graffiti popped up all the time. But this one really did look like it was in homage to the incredible build in Marco's bedroom. Thin parallel and perpendicular lines were painted through the skyscrapers, as if they were built of little toy bricks.

"Weird," he muttered, aware that goosebumps had sprung up on his arms. There was something curious about the pale brown splotch painted beneath the buildings.

Marco assembled a slice of pizza complete with pepperonis at lunch on Monday. Isaiah smashed it from behind and laughed as the pieces exploded across the cafeteria.

"You were supposed to be on lookout." Marco, who still hadn't asked his crush to the dance, scrambled to recover as many pieces as he could find.

Bobby joined in on the search. "Sorry," he said. "Sometimes, you don't see them coming."

The bite of cupcake lodged in his throat when he rounded the mini-mart's corner and looked up at the building's exterior wall. The pale brown splotch had grown over the weekend, taking up the middle third of the brick wall beneath the painted skyline. There was no question what the broadened splotch was meant to be, even if the defining characteristics weren't painted in yet. It was the shape of a face, complete with ears and a ridge of black hair on top.

"What'd you want me to see?" Bricks rattled in Marco's pockets as he walked alongside Bobby, Manny between them.

Bobby struggled to swallow. He pointed. "That."

Marco cast his eyes up at the brick wall and guffawed.

"Hey!" Manny, momentarily distracted from his cupcake, cheered. "You're art!"

"Did you . . . ? How did . . . ?" Marco marveled. "What's this all about?"

Bobby took a step back, shaking his head. "I don't know. I didn't do it. I don't know who did."

Marco snorted air through his nose. He couldn't stop smiling. "You don't seem to like it."

"Do you?"

"What's not to like?"

"It's just . . . weird. Why would there be a mural of you?"

Marco shrugged. "Why any of them?" He motioned about, referring to the many murals that brightened the neighborhood on the raw brick of buildings and concrete underpasses, so everyday and ordinary that he and Bobby never stopped to ponder and appreciate the inspiration behind them—immigrants struggling to break free, pleas for peace, love, and acceptance, God almighty, liberty, celebration, political protest, anger, injustice, grief—though caricatures of President Obama, Cooky the Clown, Svengoolie, Al Capone, and Bernie Mac didn't need much pondering at all.

"Who's seen your skyline?"

"Just the two of you and my parents, but they wouldn't have . . ." Marco dug his smartphone from out of the bricks in his pocket and tossed it to Bobby. "Get a pic of me in front of it. For the 'gram."

Instead of racing home from school the next three days, Marco went to his mural. He brought other friends, his parents, even teachers from school. No one knew who had painted it. Not the mini-mart's manager or officials with the city's mural registry. There was no tag to identify the artist, just the beautiful brick skyline wrapped like a crown above the portrait of Marco's beaming face.

It made him a celebrity in the neighborhood. And it brought attention to his remarkable talent. School officials asked him to make a life-size model of the mascot, an eagle with outstretched wings. He worked on it during lunch and after school, so busy with it that he never asked his crush to the dance. He didn't even go.

Bobby and Manny stood beneath the mural for a few minutes each afternoon, licking their fingers, breaking Mom's rules. Bobby never stopped wondering where it had come from. And why. And he only grew more curious when three more splotches, blue, appeared beneath the image of Marco's face.

The splotches grew over the next three days, elongating, two of them taking on a flat side and a big round curve, the other expanding into something straight. Another depiction of one of Marco's builds, Bobby thought. Maybe. But something inside told him he wouldn't like what those splotches turned into.

Marco finished the eagle on Friday. Bobby was there when it took its place in the trophy case outside the school's main office. Marco posed for a picture with it for the school paper. The yearbook, too. "I'll probably move to Denmark one day," Marco gave the school reporter a quote. "To get my dream job at the company headquarters. I want to design brick builds of my own."

Bobby jolted upright in bed, torn from a dream of his own by three quick pops that sounded in the distance. He could be certain that he wasn't the only one in the neighborhood who'd been ripped from sleep, all with the same thoughts stabbing their brains: *Not again,* and *I hope no one got hurt.* But if it had to be someone, they'd all be glad it wasn't them. Slick with sweat, he crept to the window and slammed it shut. Still, he could hear the sirens coming closer.

Mom was pacing in the kitchen when he got up in the morning. Still in her pajamas, she said she wasn't going to work. Manny wasn't going to Señora Lopez's. Bobby wasn't going to school. She didn't know how to tell him the news. She just said Marco's name and started to sob.

Barefoot, Bobby ran from the apartment despite his mother's protests. He couldn't believe it. He wouldn't. Not without seeing for himself.

Yellow tape formed a barrier outside Marco's apartment. His bedroom window was busted.

Breathless, Bobby staggered to the mural. The blue splotches had taken shape on the lower third of the mini-mart's exterior wall. Three big letters. R.I.P.

✶ ✶ ✶ ✶

Murals with those same three letters dotted the neighborhood, the most recent from last fall, when Calvin was gunned down in the park. Until then, he'd been a problem at school. Not a bully but not academically invested. Often absent, always late. What happened to him was tragic but not inconceivable considering the crowd he ran with. When speaking of the dead, it was easier to blame the company they kept than them for their fate. He was a good kid, they said. He just got wrapped up with a bunch of bad influences.

Still, they held a vigil for him in the park. News cameras were there. His mother wailed. His sisters cried. A pastor spoke and shouted, demanding change, accountability, an end to the violence. City officials issued statements offering prayers and well wishes. And then life went on.

It wasn't supposed to happen to someone like Marco, who knew which colors not to wear, which corners to avoid, which areas of the park were off limits, and to be home before dark. It wasn't supposed to happen to the three-year-old riding in the back of her dad's car, the eleven-year-old running to the ice cream truck, or the sixteen-year-old talking with her friends on her own porch steps either. None of them had done anything wrong. They hadn't been up to no good. They hadn't gotten what they deserved. But it did happen to them. And everyone knew it would happen again.

Within hours, a memorial grew at the base of the mural. Candles, balloons, cards, stuffed animals, and bricks. So many bricks. Some formed flowers. Some spelled out messages. Some were used to create broken hearts. None were as impressive as the one Marco had built.

No one told Manny what had happened to Marco, or that he'd never get to play with all the bricks in Marco's bedroom again. He wasn't going with Bobby to say goodbye, but that didn't stop him from styling his quiff with wax as Bobby, his eyes puffy and rimmed with red, made himself look respectable in front of the bathroom mirror.

News vans sat parked outside the funeral parlor. People who never knew Marco came to pay their respects. She was there too, the one Marco never asked to the dance. Her presence made Bobby think she would have said yes, a missed opportunity with no chance for Marco to be braver next time. His was a life that would never fully form. A million moments dismissed. Thinking about how the loss would reverberate for years to come made the tragedy hurt so much more.

Marco's dad invited Bobby back to the apartment afterward. Bobby felt sick just thinking about stepping foot in there, almost afraid to go. His legs cramped along the walk leading to the apartment building's door. Marco's mom's legs appeared to be afflicted as well. She stood beside Bobby, downturned lips quivering, just staring at the door, neither of them looking in the direction of the window that had shattered. Her arm wrapped around his back and pulled him close. He felt how frail she'd become and knew that if they hadn't had each other to lean on, they'd have sunk to the sidewalk below.

Together, they made it up the walk and through the small foyer. Someone had left flowers outside the apartment door. A card jutted from between the stems. Marco's grandparents, aunts, uncles, and cousins were crammed inside. Food was too. Booze as well. It was easier to eat and drink, Bobby supposed, than talk about what had happened.

He shook his head at the colorful plate of pan dulce Marco's father offered him. The sight of it made him sicker. His stomach juddered. Saliva flooded his mouth. The close confines had him sweating and gasping for cool air. He could feel his forehead becoming slick, his shirt getting wet and heavy.

He yanked at his collar until the button holding it shut popped free. Someone passed him a glass. The cold drink dribbled down his chin. He hadn't chosen to look, but his eyes were on the closed bedroom door, closed as if Marco might be inside, too busy with a build to make an appearance.

Someone nudged him from behind. He looked up into Marco's father's face and shook his head. Marco's father nudged him again.

"Why?" he asked.

"So that you won't wonder."

The sick sensation intensified when he stopped outside the bedroom door, his hand on its knob. But Marco's father was right. If left to his imagination, the horror of the situation would only continue to swell. Better to face it as it was, no matter how painful it would be. He turned the knob and stepped inside.

Closing the door behind him, he fell against it. The downpour of his emotions saturated his face. So much inside the room was exactly as it always was—the miniatures on the shelf above the bed, the box full of bricks, the Batman bedsheet.

A thick piece of plastic covered the busted window, distorting the city skyline in the distance. The replica Marco had built upon the table in front of the window was in pieces now, as if the little buildings had been bombed, just their bases left standing, the silver brick glinting beneath them, a city in crisis, chaos, and ruins.

Bobby took a few steps forward and saw where his best friend had bled on the carpet. Mangled bricks surrounded the ugly splotch.

The bedroom door creaked open. Marco's dad, beer in hand, leaned against the doorframe. "He should have been in bed," he said, then shook his head and walked away.

Bobby wondered which part of the skyline Marco had been tweaking, trading sleep in pursuit of perfection. He scooped a handful of bricks from the floor and dropped them onto the table, wishing what was destroyed could be rebuilt.

Manny giggled in his big boy bed, innocently mistaking Bobby's worry for fun as Bobby moved the bed as far from the bedroom window as he could.

"Promise me something," he said.

Manny swung a pillow, trying to initiate a pillow fight.

"Don't wait for me by Señora Lopez's window anymore."

Manny swung again. Bobby grabbed the pillow and cast it across the room.

"Did you hear me?" Rarely was he so stern.

Manny dropped onto his butt atop the mattress. He nodded.

"Promise?"

"Promise," Manny said.

A light layer of dust had settled on the eagle's outstretched wings. Bobby had avoided looking at it in the months that followed Marco's death, but in the days leading up to graduation, more than a year having passed since the skyline shattered, Bobby found himself escaping the lonely lunchroom to eat his sandwiches in front of the trophy case, saddened by the thought that each day seemed to drag him further from his friend.

For a while, he hadn't rounded the mini-mart to look at the mural. He never knew what feeling it would rouse: anger, confusion, devastating pain. As with the eagle, however, he started visiting it again. Not every day. Only when he was sure he could handle it, often alone. Not even cupcakes could take the edge off the emotions that swelled within him there.

The memorial remained, smaller than it'd been a year ago. He could always count on the presence of a cross. And bricks, sometimes scattered, sometimes stacked in the shape of a candle, a dove, a teddy bear.

His back to the wall, Bobby slumped against it, imagining what Marco might have built in the months that had been stolen from him, and to what heights he might have soared in the many more he should have had ahead.

He heard rattling followed by hissing. Raising his eyes from the litter-strewn sidewalk at his feet, he saw a man across the street standing on a ladder propped against the building there. Paint issued from the can in his hand, turning the wall yellow.

Without waiting for the light, Bobby crossed the street and approached the ladder. A five-gallon bucket sat beside it, loaded with spray paint cans.

"What's it going to be?" Bobby called up to the man.

The hissing stopped. A narrow yellow rivulet dripped down the grout line between two bricks. The man yanked the mask he was wearing from over his mouth and nose, letting it hang against his chest. "Don't know yet," he said.

Bobby nodded, thinking, then pointed to the mural across the street. "Know anything about that one? Did you paint it?"

The man shook his head and pointed at nothing in return. "There's no tag."

That's when Bobby noticed it, a dark splotch several feet to the right of Marco's mural. His stomach sank. He prayed the splotch wouldn't grow.

It did, though. Day by day getting bigger, rounder, taking the shape of a face. For hours on end, Bobby monitored it from afar, trying to see who was doing it, if it was anyone at all. He never did spot a culprit. But he spotted something worse. A giant chocolate cupcake that had appeared overnight, next to the featureless face that now had a quiff haircut with three lines shaved above the temples. It was a haircut just like his. Just like his little brother's.

Stumbling, he gasped and then started to run, muttering, "No," and "Why?" and "Please make it stop," the same cries that rang out every time gunshots shattered the night.

He ran for home, where he'd left Manny with Mom watching something on TV. The murals in the neighborhood blurred in his peripheral vision along either side of the street as he ran, making it impossible to discern the other splotches that had appeared in the blank spaces, some of them still so small they couldn't be detected with the naked eye, but each of them growing, growing, getting bigger every day.

He was sobbing by the time he burst through the apartment door. He threw his arms around Manny. Manny threw his arms around him.

Everyone will say he was a good kid.

ENDLESS, NAMELESS

✶✶✶✶

C.J. Subko

Viktor Kowalski is a fraud. A phony. He's a charlatan who dabbles in the supernatural fringes but isn't a part of that world.

He's also the top-rated tour guide for the Ghosts After Hours walking tour covering the Loop and Near North side. On a chilly October Saturday at 8:05 at night, he fizzes a cigarette to life—gives the tourists a kind of old city charm—and stands with his back to the old Congress Plaza Hotel while people who speak five different languages stumble into a passable half circle around him.

"All right, all right, ladies, gentleman, and anybody else," he cries, in the long vowels and sharp consonants of the accent he was born with but plays up for gimmick. "Let's talk about this here hotel." Cigarette burning in one hand, in his other hand he hefts up an EMF reader. "The Congress Plaza was where Capone played poker. It's also reputed to be a place where he did in some of his victims. To this day, it remains so haunted that some guy from Maine, Mr. Stephen King, based a whole book on the hauntings of Room 1252, a book you might know as *The Shining*."

People had questions, they always did, and Jack Nicholson impressions, but Viktor could do the job in his sleep. In half an hour he was off book and in another ten he'd be home popping an Ambien, ready for a few days of spiritual monotony.

"Now, come on. We're going down Michigan Avenue north to our next stops, the old Water Tower and the site of Fort Dearborn. Come along, ducklings."

Viktor gets the itch to drag on the cigarette, but he never smokes it. It's all for show. He quit that shit years ago.

While they walk, a little Indian girl runs up next to him. "Have you ever seen a ghost?" she asks, her big brown eyes both fearful and somehow hopeful.

Hm. Has Viktor ever seen a ghost.

Most people, they don't realize how haunted Chicago is. The very bones of the city, the Potawatomi swamp paths that are now Archer and Ogden Avenue, rest on spiritual ley lines. Lincoln Park is a graveyard of 12,000 bodies. Bachelor's Grove still draws kids hoping to stumble onto a Satanic ritual. Even the Chicago River itself is a graveyard, home to some of the 844 people who died in the *Eastland* riverboat sinking.

Oh, Viktor could tell her about all this. He could tell her about the Woman in Red and the Woman in Black. He could tell her about John Dillinger and the Iroquois Theatre fire. These are only the famous stories and Viktor knows them all, has hurried excited, jittery tourists past their sites every day for three years. By night, he visits them with his EMF reader and other gadgets in search of paranormal activity.

Viktor is sick of the bullshit. Because the truth is, Viktor has never seen a ghost.

He's tired of the same false stories.

But it's a little girl and this is his job. He starts to answer at random when someone shrieks. Aw shit, not again. "With me! My group, stay close!" he says, throwing up his arm. But of course people scatter, and the woman—it was distinctly a woman—shrieks again down the block, only the shriek is of such a curdling, piercing quality that it's almost dizzying to hear.

Overriding his instincts, Viktor flings his cigarette aside and runs toward the source of the sound. Viktor's chest constricts; his lungs flatten. There is no third shriek, no woman to be found, but splayed across the wide sidewalk that fringes Grant Park is a spray-painted black circle and, within it, the bloodied, severed head of a male deer, its antlers twined with battery-powered fairy lights, its eyes scooped out and replaced with two bulbs of light. Underneath, the artist has painted two words: THE NAMELESS.

What the fuck is going on? It is stupid, obviously just a joke, and yet something about it pokes at the deepest pit of Viktor's stomach and fills his veins with icy dread.

And a single coherent thought: He should get the hell out of here, of course, but first he takes out his phone and snaps a picture of the eerie tableau. On the little screen, it looks less frightening, almost silly. It shouldn't make his skin crawl or his stomach churn with misgiving.

Yet, in the old way his grandmother taught him, he crosses his fingers behind his back as he thuds away from the display toward his tour group. Half of them are holding each other, snapping off about how this is what happens in the big city, and the other half are taking selfies. Viktor ends the tour early with a discount and heads home. He doesn't look back once, not until he's squarely in his Bucktown apartment. His sister must be out with friends. Good. He needs alone time to settle the warble of his heart.

Curled up in his bed, he posts the picture on his blog with a simple message:

Has anybody heard of THE NAMELESS? What's the deal?

Hesitantly, he hits "post" and flops into bed, and he can almost still see the ghosts of fairy lights behind his eyelids.

Viktor can't sleep.

No one has answered his blog yet, not with anything actionable, anyway, just scads of spam and a couple ardent followers asking him if he really saw that or if it's just some meme and one asking if he's okay in the head, and he's not okay, not really.

Because he can't sleep.

It's been four days.

And everywhere he looks, he sees the deer head and its fairy lights and those splashed out words, THE NAMELESS. It's random, like a flash, a memory, but in front of him. He's sure he's hallucinating but how can he be? He's never been psychotic, even at his most ill.

He's been afraid to leave his apartment, so he hasn't.

He turns to look at the clock and the deer head flashes before him, leering with its fairy light eyes for just a moment before he blinks and it's gone.

Heart thundering, he pops another Ambien, praying this one will take.

Evil, bright light slats in through the blinds, slicing into Viktor's eyes through his thin pale eyelids. "Christ, Agata!" he cries, smushing the pillow over his head. "What's that for? I'm sleeping!" Finally, finally sleeping, after so many days awake he thought his burning eyes would never have relief.

Viktor's sister, a sturdy, tall woman with straight blond hair like him, a straight nose like him, yanks the pillow out of his hands. "You're marinating. Or something, I don't know. You haven't left your room in a week."

"That's not true," Viktor whines, "I've gone to the bathroom, and the kitchen."

She throws her hands up. "And then straight back!" She brandishes the pillow at him. "Viktor, I read your silly blog. What is 'The Nameless'?" Viktor's insides squirm cold, noodles around a fork. Then Agata sighs. "No, you know what, never mind. I don't want to know. I just want my brother back. And preferably clean."

"I haven't gone anywhere. I'm right here."

"That's the problem!" she protests. "You're always right here. You aren't even going out on your little ghost missions."

"You don't understand!" he cries. "I have to be here in case—" His mouth snaps shut. Shit. He's said too much.

"In case what?"

He looks shiftily, left, right. Can he trust her? He isn't sure. He lowers his voice. They could be listening. "In case they answer my message."

Agata drops the pillow. "Your message. Your—your message. That blog post? Jesus Christ, Vitek, there's internet everywhere. Why do you need to be here?"

"Because I'm safe here," he says, yanking the blankets around him, gritting his teeth. Why won't she listen? Why won't she understand?

Her eyes droop. "Viktor, we can get you help. There's this psychiatrist—"

"I'm not crazy!"

"I never said—"

"Get out!" he shrieks, startling her backward. "Get out get out get out!"

"Okay, okay!" She holds her hands up, don't shoot the messenger, and backs out the door, closing it as she goes. Closing him into his safe hidey-hole.

Once she's gone for sure, he pulls up the blog post on his phone. Another spam comment, no answer.

But when he refreshes again, there's a video.

A close-up shot in the dark with a white night-vision filter, of a deer head seemingly floating from the ceiling in an empty basement, its antlers and eyes glittering with fairy lights. Then the image cuts briefly to a black background with a spray-painted white circle, then back to the image of the hanging deer head. Back and forth, back and forth, faster and more frenetic until a woman screams and the video cuts off.

By the time Viktor, shaking, clicks through the YouTube link to find out who posted the video, both the video and the account have been deleted. But those images stick in his brain and filter dread into his churning stomach.

That's it! It must be. That was his mistake. The Nameless isn't going to come find him.

The Nameless wants *him* to find *it*.

"Where are you going?" says Agata, when she finally sees him approaching the door. Her tone is hopeful.

"Out," says Viktor. He would be out already, but he must make sure he has everything. His camera. His EMF detector. His flashlight. His keys. He stuffs them all into the bulging pockets of a black trench coat and slicks back his blond hair.

"You look like a school shooter," Agata snaps. She does not just mean the trench coat; he knows she can see the hollows in his cheeks, the bluish bags beneath his eyes, and the raw, twitchy look in them.

Viktor narrows his eyes. "Would you let mom hear you talking that way?"

"Don't bring mom into this. Vitek. Viktor, please, stay here. You don't look well. Let's talk. I'll make haluski. We'll talk about the nice doctor I found. Viktor. Viktor!"

But he has already slammed the door shut on her final "Viktor," and she does not follow him out into the hall.

Viktor fiddles with the EMF reader in his pocket. If he were a nameless, wailing female ghost, where would he haunt? There are many choices in a city of thriving murders and three million people. The space around the YouTube video looked like a basement, or an honest-to-God Gacy crawlspace. So, his search would start underground.

He does what he always did when he started a ghost search.

He goes to the Chicago History Museum.

The volunteers at the museum are trained to deal in "fun facts" more than lurid hearsay, but if you can get them talking, most of them know the lurid hearsay anyway. They'll peel away from their script about the 1893 Columbian Exposition and the 1933 Century of Progress Fair to regale you with creepy tales of H.H. Holmes, the Lipstick killer, and the St. Valentine's Day Massacre.

Today, Viktor finds a short, mousy Indian man he's worked with before, Raj.

"Oh hey, how's the *ghost hunting*." Raj ends on a whisper.

"Got a new ghost lead," says Viktor tetchily. He isn't sure how much he should tell about The Nameless. She has come to him, after all, has found him, no one else. He'll have to play it cool. "I'm wondering if you know of any famous female ghosts that were killed or trapped in basements, or maybe their case had something to do with being locked in a basement."

"You're saying female? Because we have——"

"Gacy, I know." Everyone knows the Killer Clown. "No, this is definitely a woman."

Raj narrows his eyes and bleps out his tongue in thought. "Hm. Hm."

"Come on, Raj, you gotta give me something."

Raj looks nervous, then sidles close. "Look, I don't know any specific cases. For what you're looking for, you need a medium."

Viktor starts to roll his eyes.

"I'm serious! Not one of the ones with neon 'psychic' signs but a real practitioner."

Viktor is just desperate enough to bite onto any piece of hope he can get between his teeth. "You know of any?"

"Three Goddess Apothecary on Damen in Bucktown. Ask for Janice."

Viktor makes to leave when Raj stops him by the arm. "You be careful, dude. And come back when you're done! I want to know how it went."

Viktor says something unintelligible and noncommittal and hurries out of the museum into the chilly autumn sun. He punches in the directions for an Uber on his phone. No time to take the Blue line. He needs to get there as fast as possible. While the images of the video are still burned like acid into his eyeballs.

It isn't Viktor's first time in an occult bookstore. He's a ghost hunter; he tends to spend a great deal of time with the kind of people who burn sage and pray to pagan spirits. Three Goddess Apothecary is much the same as all the others, with its strong patchouli scent and its shelves laden with crystals, spell books, tarot decks, and candles shaped like human genitals, skulls, and pyramids.

Janice turns out to be a tall woman in a lurid purple wig who staffs the counter in back, where clients could make requests for private tarot readings or mediumship sessions.

"What'll it be, darling?" she says in an affected Southern drawl. She pops her gum and twirls her pen between her fingers.

"I need to find a spirit," he says quietly, although there is no one else in the shop except for the other staff. "A specific spirit."

Janice dabbles something down on her notepad. "That'll be—"

"I don't care how much it costs. Whatever it takes."

Janice winks at him. "Well alright, big spender. Let's get you all set up. Do you have a picture of the ghost? Something they owned?"

"No. Just—" He quickly explains the video.

Janice nods. "All right. It'll make it tricky, but we can use that. Come on."

While another staffer takes over the desk, Janice leads Viktor into a back room, dimly lit by a lone lamp with a purple scarf thrown over it. Viktor sits on one side of an ordinary wooden table while Janice walks a big circle around them, dumping something powdery and white in a line.

"Salt," she says. "To protect anything from getting out or coming in."

Viktor nods. Of course. He'd heard that ghosts couldn't cross salt lines. "What else?"

She shows him the blue and black and white glass eye charm hanging around her neck. "A nazar, to ward off evil."

"And a quartz?" He gestures to the large point of clear stone at the center of the table.

"To focus the energy."

Interesting. Other mediums he had used employed tarot cards or Ouija boards or pendulum boards to communicate with the dead. But Janice simply sits down at the other side of the table and holds out her hands.

"Hold my hands," she says. "And treat it like a rollercoaster, sweetie. Don't let go. Even if it gets bumpy."

He takes her hands with his cold, clammy ones.

In a lower voice, probably her natural accent, she says, "Now, keep that image of the video in your mind. The deer head. The lights. The screams. The circle. Picture it as clearly as though it were happening now, so that I can use it to draw our ghost onto the physical plane."

"I'm picturing it," says Viktor, letting the video's sound and images suffuse his brain.

"Good, good," says Janice. "Now, when we connect with the ghost, we may feel a chill. See a flickering light. If we're lucky, there might even be a floating orb hovering between us."

Janice continues, "Spirit, come to us. Speak with us. Show us a sign of your presence, that we may be grateful." And she repeats it again, and again.

"This isn't working," says Viktor testily.

"Be patient!" Janice clutches his hands even tighter. "Spirit, come to us. Speak with us. Show us a sign of your—oh. Oh, Viktor, I've connected with something. I've connected with your girl."

Viktor sits up in the chair, leaning in toward the quartz crystal, which has begun to strobe faintly and fuzzily white.

"She says she's waiting for you, Viktor. She's in the basement, your basement. She needs you to bring Agata. She wants to play. She wants to see."

A smile plays over Janice's lips, a toothy grin—and then suddenly her head snaps back and her eyes roll back into her skull, rolling wildly around as she begins to shake so violently that her chair shakes beneath her.

Viktor knows not to let go, squeezes her hands tighter as he yells, "Janice! Janice! What do you see!"

"No!" Janice cries. "No! No! No! Get away from me. Get away!"

"Janice, come back!" Viktor calls, yanking her forward.

And it's at that minute that, in a mix of blood and jelly, Janice's eyes explode out of her skull.

Viktor doesn't hesitate; he lets go of her hands and hightails it out the door, racing through the shop around the bemused staffers to Damen Avenue, where he runs until he finds the first available cab. By the time he's whizzing off towards his apartment, they'll have found Janice, comatose with horror, staring eyeless at the ceiling.

He can't help her now. He knows what he has to do to save The Nameless, to free the screaming ghost girl and end this madness once and for all.

He needs help. He needs Agata.

He finds her at the kitchen table, reading some Cynthia Pelayo book. She gasps and throws it down when he enters. "Viktor, what's wrong? You're white as a sheet! Come here, sit down. Sit down."

"No, I'm fine," he seethes, "I'm better, more than fine, I'm glorious. I need your help, Agata. I've got my message. I've found my ghost." Viktor shakes, shudders with the energy of a glorious purpose.

"Is this still about the ghost?" Agata moans. "Viktor, I've told you—"

He looks deep into her eyes, with those matching blue ones he knows will sway her. "Please, I need your help. One last mission. One last ghost. Then I'll hang it up for good. I'll go back to the tour company."

"You will?" She's dubious.

"I promise. Hand to God." Crossing his fingers behind his back, but she doesn't need to know that, and she smiles weakly.

"All right. What do I need to do?"

"Come with me, to the basement. That's where I can talk to her."

"Okay," says Agata nervously. "Okay, we're going to take one of your readings."

Viktor grins manically. "Yes! We're going to take a reading. And then it will all be just like it should be and this will all be behind us."

Tightening the belt around his trench coat, Viktor grabs Agata's hand and they race down the four flights of stairs to the creaky dark basement that was only used for resident storage and the water heater. The remaining available space is dark and empty, lit only by a single, buzzing bare bulb that sways from side to side as they enter.

The door suddenly slams shut behind them.

"The wind," Agata cries.

"Yes," says Viktor.

It is time.

Viktor blinks. Waiting for his ghost girl. Waiting for the scream.

The light explodes overhead, plunging the room into black.

A woman screams.

Then a glow, a white glow like from a television screen in the dark, begins to emanate from the walls, so that Viktor, trembling with dread, can see the massive shadow creature somehow encapsulated by the basement ceiling, somehow existing through and above and beyond it. It is formless at first and yet the light flares so that he can detect a long neck, clicking mandibles, many legs and many eyes and deer antlers sprawling out from either side of its head, strung with fairy lights.

So that Viktor can see its sharp white claw gouged through Agata's sternum, dark black blood glugging down like a waterfall from her quivering jaw.

Viktor cannot scream "No!" He cannot scream anything. He can only stand and watch in perfect, agonized horror as the creature sprays a white fiber out of its belly and begins spinning his sister rapidly, spraying her as she spins, whirling her up into a cotton candy whorl.

Can only stand stock-still in sheer terror and dread as with its two claws The Nameless lifts Agata toward its mouth, then unhinges its jaw like a snake and begins to suck in, not her body, not her blood and flesh, but something made of stars and dreams, until the fuzzy spiral is all sucked up and her body is a desiccated cocooned husk to be thrown aside.

At last, Viktor too, drained, thuds to his knees.

But The Nameless isn't done. In a voiceless voice that speaks through the language of stardust and brimfire, it gives it commands.

Viktor understands. It is hungry. It needs more. Viktor has awakened it, but one is not enough.

Viktor needs to get a deer head. He needs to buy fairy lights and black spray paint. He needs to help spawn a new legend in Chicago.

For the circle must be endless, and the god satisfied.

THE HOUSE WITH BLUE SHUTTERS

★ ★ ★ ★

Sahar Mustafah

From her good eye, the old woman regarded us with suspicion. The other eye was covered by a worn leather patch. Two scars ran from it, like twin streams down her wrinkled face. My father nudged me forward. "Say hello to your grandmother," Baba said in English.

She was actually my great-grandmother's cousin, a woman who had never married, had no children of her own. But it didn't matter. To me, she was an old lady I was supposed to be polite to. I leaned in and gave her a hasty kiss on each of her papery cheeks. She smelled like orange zest and mildew. My nostrils twitched.

"Salaam, Sitti," I said. My Arabic was thick, but respectable for moments like this. I was meeting a woman so ancient she seemed to have fallen out of a museum exhibit. Gray wisps escaped her white veil. She wore one of those old-fashioned, cross-stitched thawbs that my mother wore to weddings. Her back curved like a dented spoon.

The last time my family saw Sitti Marwa was a decade ago. I was only six years old and the old woman had scared me even then. There's a photograph of the two us pasted in some long-forgotten album. I was sitting in her lap, bawling, my eyes two frightened slits. She was staring at the camera, an impassive expression like the one she had on now as she studied me. I was sixteen years old, far from that mewling child, but still as scared. Only this time I could take a few safe steps away.

Sitti Marwa kept her one eye trained on me as if I were prey—or perhaps she thought I was the threat. My mother gently took her hand, which made the old woman flinch. "This way, ya Hajja," Mama said, as if guiding a small child who was ready to throw a tantrum.

Sitti Marwa allowed herself to be led into our family room. But before they reached the threshold, she yanked her hand free and darted toward a portrait on the foyer wall, leading up the staircase.

"Bayti! Bayti!" she cried, straightening up for the first time. "My house! My house!" She touched the glass protecting a framed sepia-colored photograph. I'd passed it every day, going up and down the staircase to the upper floor. I paid it no more attention than the paint itself on the wall, or the crystal chandelier above our heads.

I knew the story behind it. *This is our ancestral home*, my father had solemnly explained when I was much younger. *Three generations of our family lived here.*

Did you live there, Baba? I'd asked, unable to fathom what a generation was. Nor could I appreciate the sadness of his one-syllable response: *No*. And then he squeezed me close and said, *Inshallah one day you'll see it.*

It looked like the other relics on display around our house. The gilded rendering of the Dome of the Rock. A map of Palestine carved from olive wood. Coffee trays inlaid with mother-of-pearl. Random shrines to a native land I'd never seen. The farthest I'd ever gone was to Disney World when I was seven.

Now we all stared as Sitti Marwa traced the stone-brick house with an orchard peeking behind it. "Bayti!" she repeated, her voice dipping. Then her shoulders began to quake and she sobbed. "Bayti! When will I return to you?"

It took both Mama and Baba to unscrew the old woman from the spot in front of that portrait. I watched dumbly as they steered her toward my old playroom where Mama had set her up—a flight of stairs to the spare room was too much for Sitti Marwa. Baba assembled a daybed and added a tray table with water bottles and snack packets of mixed nuts though I doubted the old woman could chew much with her remaining teeth.

"She is fine," my mother tossed over her shoulder at me. She gave me that fake smile indicating Sitti Marwa was far from fine. She seemed hysterical as they dragged her away and shut the door.

I stood in front of the photograph. I remembered something about it being the only image of the house someone had recovered and imparted to my father before I was even born. The house was actually a backdrop to a wedding procession, which was the main focus. A single car with a groom and bride stuffed into the backseat drove along while the rest of the wedding party and its revelers clapped behind it, their mouths open in mid-verse. I imagined high-pitched ululations among the women, each taking her turn, each louder than the previous one.

According to my father, the shutters of the house were actually blue. *And you see that balcony?* he'd pointed. *It is called a barranda. That is where my father—your grandfather—played marbles on hot summer nights.* The entrance to the house was shrouded in flowering foliage, the color of their petals unreadable in monochrome.

I glanced back at the playroom. What was it like to see your home confined to a frame with no hope of returning to it? The whole thing weirded me out.

I slunk up the stairs. My cat, Olive, followed, scampering past me to my room. Even she, an orange and black tabby, was perturbed by the arrival of this stranger. She leaped onto my bed and I closed the door behind me, muffling the whimpers of the old woman.

Because of our new houseguest, my spring break had taken a rather grim turn. I would have rather gone to Wisconsin Dells than be forced to accompany them to all the tourist traps in the city. I took some quiet satisfaction in the old woman's lackluster reaction to everything my father still marveled at.

Sitti Marwa was unimpressed with the Willis Tower, which Baba kept referring to as the Sears Tower as his generation always would. Or as he, in his thick accent, called the "See-rus" as if it were some prehistoric creature piercing the sky. Mama quickly advised against the

Sky Deck. Instead, Baba drove us to Navy Pier and snapped pictures of me and Mama posed on either side of Sitti Marwa, who was unsmiling, the gray-blue waters surging behind us. She refused to ride the giant Ferris wheel—I didn't blame her. I was terrified of heights, too.

People passed us by, throwing curious glances at Sitti Marwa. Children stared longer until their parents tugged them along. She was like a carnival spectacle, her long white veil trailing behind her. Her eye patch was ominous and her black thawb needed hemming, but she seemed unperturbed.

From time to time, she pulled a linen cloth from her chest pocket and coughed into it. I felt bad for her though at the same time she creeped me out. When she caught me staring, she stared back with her one eye. It was clear and unclouded by age or sickness. I quickly looked away.

At home, she shuffled to the playroom and closed the door. I could hear her in the old rocking chair my mother couldn't bear to get rid of, the one she had sat in as I played with my blocks and baby dolls.

Now when I put my ear to the door, all I heard was creaking.

I spent the last night of my break in my darkened room. The only light came from my phone screen. And the only sounds were those annoying windchimes suspended on our neighbors' wooden deck, Olive's deep purring as I rubbed her belly with my free hand, and the bloop alert every time I sent a text or received a message.

It had gotten out that my best friend Lena had a crush on Aydin Al-Massari who drove a souped up Jeep Wrangler, and that he actually liked Maha Basheer, a sophomore. They were spotted at a boba tea café.

Times like these I was grateful no one knew how long I'd been crushing on Sameer, who was the only arrabi boy I knew who enjoyed taking AP science classes as much as me and not simply for college credit. His father owned a Middle Eastern restaurant though it was dubbed "Mediterranean" when it was featured on *Windy City Live* and *Check, Please!* But you wouldn't guess it if you met Sameer. He was a quiet kid—like me. Uninterested in teenage drama—like me. This year, he sat across from me at the lab table in AP Physics. My hands got clammy every time he walked past my desk and I pretended I was checking my phone.

"Hi, Janna," he'd say. His hair was cut close to his scalp. His eyes were honey-brown.

"Hi, Sam," I'd say, trying to play it cool, my cheeks searing beneath my long, straight-ironed bangs. And that was the extent of our pleasantries until we paired up for labs.

Everyone wanted to be Sameer's partner. He didn't complain if his group was lazy and played video games on their school-issued tablets instead of documenting evidence for the weekly lab reports we had to submit to Mr. Njoku, our physics teacher.

I loved Mr. N. On the walls of his classroom, he displayed posters of prominent African scientists I'd never heard of: Thierry Zomahoun. Noble Banadda. Wilfred Ndifon. He'd won Teacher of the Year every term since I was a freshman and I was thrilled to be in his class. With Sameer. After the bell rang, when every other kid was dashing out the door, already on their phones, Sameer lingered to talk with Mr. Njoku about the lesson that day or something he'd read on a science blog. I tried to stall, slowly slipping my textbook inside my backpack then gradually sliding off my stool as if I was in a stop-motion film. God—I was lame!

But as soon as I reached Sameer at our teacher's giant lab table where he conducted demonstrations or lectured, I lost my nerve to wait for him to finish so we could walk a stretch of hallway to the stairwell before parting ways to different classes on different floors. I trudged to Gym and Sameer, oblivious to my desire, would head to English. (I knew his entire schedule). At least he didn't have to see me sweat and look all gross.

Ayden is conceited, someone was typing in the chat.

And he only likes white girls, Zainab added, a desperate contradiction to the clear boba tea café evidence that was recorded on Snapchat.

Then came a series of crying emojis from Lena.

I was about to respond to ease my friend's agony with the blue-people-hugging emoji when I saw it.

Sparks beneath my door, like fireworks.

"What the—"

Olive hopped off my bed. She saw it, too. She was on high alert, her ears pointed and tail thwacking the carpeted floor. She pawed at the sparks like she was trying to catch the red dot of her laser toy I waved on the floor that drove her nuts.

I followed her, clutching my phone. "Shoo, Olive!"

She sprang away and I stuck my head out the door.

The hallway was empty. I could hear Baba's snoring from my parents' bedroom on the other end. A snorting sound my older sister Aya liked to imitate. *Like Mr. Snuffleupagus*, we'd joke. I peered in the direction of her room across from mine. It had been vacant for almost two years while she was away at college. Silence.

"God. I must be tired," I muttered to myself and carefully closed my door.

I settled back into my bed while Olive, her lean body taut, positioned herself like a sentry on the corner of the mattress, her attention fixated on the door.

I grabbed my phone and thumbed the screen to life again. Another romantic rant had transpired in the seconds I looked away. Lena was rage-texting and I imagined her all alone in her room, wallowing in painful adolescent tears. Poor Lena!

I sank against my pile of pillows, trying to catch up in the thread. And then it happened again!

Yellow sparks danced beneath my door and this time my stomach sank. Olive was on her feet again, but this time she seemed to sense it wasn't a game. She cowered in the corner where my hamper of dirty clothes was overflowing. It drove my mother crazy. She couldn't understand why everything in my room seemed to reach critical mass before I did something about it. Half a dozen empty water bottles gathered on my dresser like bodies at a rave party, and a handful of candy wrappers were strewn across my night stand. *Why, ya Janna, do you let things pile up?* she always admonished.

And now I wanted to call for her and didn't care if I got in trouble for being up so late. It couldn't be my imagination when Olive was also a witness.

I stared at the sparks licking the floor. If I wasn't so terrified, I would call them pretty, like flickering candles on a birthday cake. Or bursting stars.

I took a deep breath, my sweaty hand clutching the doorknob. "Just do it," I muttered.

This time I stepped out into the hallway. The sparks were gone, but there was something else shining downstairs. I glanced at my parents' door. Nothing. Olive was in my doorframe, deciding whether to accompany me on this midnight reconnaissance. She thought better of it and darted back into my room. I was on my own.

I slowly padded toward the landing, unaware I was on tip-toe like a kid about to commit a prank. Except I felt like I was the victim of some kind of weird joke. What the hell was going on?

The answer came as soon as I peered down the staircase. There was Sitti Marwa in a white linen underdress with long billowy sleeves. She was standing in front of the portrait of the house. Her gray hair was loose and flowed to the middle of her back. Something illuminated the image as if she was holding a flashlight to it. Only when she turned to look up at me did I see it.

Her empty eye socket was a swirling ball of light, sparks glinting across her face.

I stumbled backward. What the actual fuck! I must be dreaming. Or was I sleepwalking?

She reached her hand out, summoning me. I slowly edged away from her—from that brilliant eye—back to my bedroom.

I jumped under my blanket and pulled it over my head, listening. I must be dreaming. But as desperately as I wished it to be a nightmare, I was fully awake.

"What the fuck!" I whispered then clamped a hand over my mouth.

There were footsteps climbing the stairs and then a shuffling of slippers. My mouth went dry. I wanted to call for my parents, but my scream wilted inside my throat. I snatched my blanket to my chest.

It couldn't be the old woman. She couldn't climb those stairs.

I peeked over my blanket. Light glowed beneath my door. And then darkness again.

The next morning I was actually grateful for school to start again and I hurried out the door to catch my bus, avoiding the old woman. I hid behind my sunglasses, my sleep-deprived eyes shunning daylight. It would be hell today, but I would soldier through on two hours of sleep.

"Hey! Posh!" a white middle-aged security guard called sarcastically to me. "Shades off in the building."

Who the hell is Posh? I wanted to yell back, but it wasn't important. I had to figure out if I was losing my mind.

Over the drone of lecturing teachers in each class, I replayed the previous night. Maybe it was too much caffeine. Or maybe what my mother had been threatening forever—my devices would blind me if I didn't take breaks—had finally come to fruition.

But Olive had seen it, too. And animals—especially felines—were the most intuitive creatures.

So there had to be a logical reason. I racked my brain. In Physics, we'd studied Coulomb's Law about electrostatic forces. When particles attract or repulse each other, electric charges occur.

Could that crazy fireball raging in Sitti Marwa's eye be scientifically explained? But what was causing such a force? And how could she contain it inside her eye socket? Maybe I could record it and show Mr. Njoku and then he could—

"You okay, Janna?"

It was Sameer. I was so locked up in my head that I had, for the first time, missed his usual greeting. He was pointing at my face. "What's that?"

I wasn't sure what was more shocking: the fact that Sameer was actually looking closely at me or that he found my face disturbing. "What do you mean?" I managed to say. My ears burned and soon the flush of embarrassment would reach my cheeks.

"Your eye. Did you hurt it?" he said.

"What are you talking about?" I pulled out my phone, and hit the camera button. It was already in selfie mode so I saw it immediately. Two thin, jagged scratches beneath my right eye. They looked like a pair of lightning bolts except they were red. "I dunno—I mean, I must have—" I was stammering.

The bell rang and everyone shuffled to their lab stools, updates on their spring breaks cut short.

"Welcome back, scientists," Mr. Njoku announced. "Cell phones down, brains on."

I hopped off my lab stool and dashed past Mr. N., nearly knocking down a late straggler. "Watch it!" she hollered.

"Miss Taweel!" Mr. N. called after me. But I didn't stop until I made it to the girls' washroom at the end of the long corridor.

My heart thudded loudly in my ears. I stood in front of a sink and examined my face. I ran my fingers from the outer corner of my upper lid and down, just an inch-deep into my cheekbone. The twin scratches felt like dried blood. Like it had just happened. "What the fuck," I whispered, my reflection turning pale. And then I realized!

Olive! It had to be my cat! She must have been as freaked out as me. Maybe she'd climbed on top of me when I finally managed to fall asleep.

I exhaled, realizing I'd been holding my breath. I felt woozy and clutched the steel basin of the sink. Oh, God! I better not faint! I quickly turned on the faucet and splashed water in my face. The coolness helped. I blinked liquid beads away and looked at my reflection again.

The lightning-bolts were still there.

I wished I could hide in the stall. I was so embarrassed. As if on cue, a security guard entered the washroom for her daily sweep. "Get to class, please." She stood by the doorway. "Have a good day," she said as I rushed past her.

Back in class, Mr. N. was cool about my sudden exit and didn't press me. He only nodded and jerked his chin at my lab table for me to settle in.

"You okay?" Sameer whispered, his eyes flitting between me and the whiteboard where our teacher was writing the coefficient for friction: $\mu = F/N$

"Where F is the frictional force and N is the normal force, yes?" Mr. N. reminded the class.

"Yeah," I whispered back to Sameer. "I'll be fine." But even I wasn't convinced.

At the lunch table, I tried hard to concentrate on the latest developments in Lena's drama with Ayden. I could tell she was eager to move past my fake story about Olive getting feisty with me last night.

"Hope that doesn't leave a scar," she said immediately. "Anyway. Ayden texted me last period—"

A din of noise rose around me. Students laughing and talking, utensils clinking in metal bins, deans ordering us to buss our trays or else. I kept touching the scabs. Did Sitti Marwa do it? With that fireball eye?

Lena shoved my shoulder. "Are you listening, Jan?"

"Yes," I said automatically, confirming I hadn't heard a single word.

"What's up with you?"

"Nothing, nothing," I lied. "I didn't get much sleep."

"Oh," she said. "So anyway, Ayden wants to meet me at…"

I forced my attention on my friend without actually absorbing her rambling. I'd have to investigate this strange matter. I'd stay up tonight and record everything. According to a theory called cyclical recurrence, if it happened once, science dictated it was likely to happen again.

✶ ✶ ✶ ✶

On the bus ride home, I kept my glasses on and poked my finger under the frame, touching the small gashes as if expecting them to suddenly disappear as mysteriously as they'd formed. When I opened the garage door, I heard my sister's voice, loud and cheerful. Aya was home for her spring break. Maybe she'd get to see the freak show tonight if it happened again and I wouldn't feel all alone.

"Look who is home," my mother crooned in English like I'd been the one away at college. My mother was always good at making me feel included no matter what.

"What's up, Jan?" Aya said. She was wearing an oversized college sweatshirt and leggings. As much as she irked me, I had to admit how pretty my sister was. I always felt like such a runt beside her. "What happened there, Scarface?"

I glanced at Sitti Marwa who was also seated at the kitchen table, hands clasped in her lap. Her tea cup was half-empty, but her slice of a burned version of hareesa cake was untouched. Poor Mama. She was not a great cook, let alone a precise baker. If I was in the mood, I wouldn't have minded and would've scraped off the charred bottom of my slice with traces of pineapple juice, and happily eaten it.

The old woman fixed her eye on me.

My fingers darted to my face. "I dunno," I said, shrugging. "Olive." I kept my responses short and sweet, suppressing my fear.

"Let me see, habibti." My mother held my chin and examined my eye. I could smell the fresh mint leaves she dropped into the teapot before serving. "Alhamdullah, it is not deep. Go put some Neosporin on it. Or it will scar."

Grateful for the command, I sprung up the stairs to my room, Sitti Marwa's eye boring into my back.

Later that night, Aya burst into my room without knocking—typical of her. "What are you doin' hiding up here?" she said, hopping onto my bed. She reached to pet Olive, but Olive sprung from the mattress, eluding her grasp. Olive knew what was up.

"Homework," I said, though I'd been sitting cross-legged, thumbing my phone for the last hour.

"Sitti Marwa is wild, huh?" Aya said.

I sat up. "What do you mean?" Had she noticed the strange energy that surrounded the old woman like a force field?

"She's like a hundred years old," Aya chuckled. "And that eye patch!"

"Yeah," I said, forcing a smile. "How did her eye—I mean—what happened to it?"

Aya bounced off my bed and went to my dresser. She snooped through my stuff with her finger, held up a rubber wrist band then dropped it again. I hated her pawing at my things but I held my tongue. "Um, Baba said she, like, got poked in the eye," Aya said. "By a rooster or something, right?"

I shook my head, but my sister didn't see it since she was still touching my stuff. She held up a scrunchy and looped it over her wrist. "Can I have this?"

"Yeah," I said, trying not to sound annoyed. I needed information. Facts. Anything that could help me make sense of everything I'd witnessed since the arrival of our great grandmother's cousin. "But—did anything else happen to her?"

"You mean besides being disfigured and never getting married?" Aya huffed as if such tragedy had escaped my naïve sensibilities.

I would have to try a direct tack with my sister. "There's something weird about her," I began.

"What do you mean?" Aya said, hopping back onto my bed. She was scrolling Instagram, her lips curling into a small smile then straightening again when she was unamused or miffed by someone's post.

"I mean, like—" I spluttered. I realized I'd have to just come out with it. There was no way to describe something so peculiar except by telling it straight. "Her eye. Sitti Marwa's eye is—" I hesitated. "—possessed." I cringed hearing the words out loud. But then I was relieved. Now it was out there for someone else. It wasn't my secret anymore.

"What are you talking about?" Aya grinned. "You know, you should be honored she's visiting. She—wait a second!" Her eyes widened. Then she clasped my knee.

Hope surged inside my chest. She'd noticed something was completely off, too!

"OMG!" Aya cried. "I'm gonna interview her! This will be the coolest oral history project! My Poli-Sci professor will love this…"

I didn't hear the rest of Aya's plan. She didn't believe me. Which meant others were unlikely to believe me.

I was on my own. And tonight I'd get to the bottom of it.

It was funny how much you discovered in utter darkness. The objects in my room took on an eerie presence, their edges shape-shifting before turning sharp again. I silenced my phone, muted my chats, and kept guard from my bed. Olive was curled into a ring of fur in my lap, but like me, she was not asleep. By one o'clock, even Aya was finally snoozing in her bedroom across the hall from me.

I sipped Red Bull and let my mind drift to Sameer. He'd been genuinely concerned about me, as if seeing me for the first time. Something fluttered in my stomach. Maybe he and I could meet up for boba tea—actually, no way. I didn't want to be the subject of scrutiny and jokes. Maybe we could meet at the Museum of Science and Industry—I mean, if he didn't think it was lame now that we were older. I still loved it. And so did Baba who'd been taking me ever since I was six years old. My favorite exhibit was weather systems. I got to see the inner workings of a tornado and it was the coolest thing ever. The vortex of wind blew in my hair while I watched the wind tunnel change direction, then increase its speed and altitude. I squeezed Baba's hand—not in fear, but in sheer delight for this incredible force of nature. Maybe that's when I was hooked on science. Everything scary to me had an explanation, a reason for happening.

Sameer would appreciate that. I could ask him what his first science moment was and then we could—

A noise cut off my silly thoughts. Olive stood at attention before I sat up. We both cocked our ears toward the door. And then it happened. Tiny bursting stars. I fumbled my phone and it took three tries before I could unlock it. I approached the door and began recording.

"Unexplained disturbance," I whispered, then winced. I sounded so dumb. I shut up. The evidence would speak for itself.

I slowly turned the knob and stepped into the hallway. I creeped toward the landing.

And there she was. Sitti Marwa in her linen underdress. The photograph illuminated. Her craggly finger was tracing the stone house protected by the glass frame. My hand was shaking so badly I almost dropped my phone. But I kept recording and took a step closer, the floor creaking beneath my bare feet.

She turned at the sound and I saw it again. A swirling galaxy of light, like some sort of tunnel. And it beckoned me closer. Despite my terror,

I slowly padded down the stairs, still recording, gripping my phone in both hands. I was a scientist. I must not be afraid, I told myself.

When I reached her, she pulled my phone down so that I could see her face without the obstruction of a small screen. Before I could shriek, she clamped her hands on my shoulders and her fiery eye socket enthralled me. Those bursting stars became radiant ribbons of light and they were pulling me in, a magnetic force tugging at the core of my body.

Then suddenly, I was no longer standing in the foyer of my house. I felt light and heavy all at once, my limbs my own, but I had no control over them. It was like I'd been cast into outer space, without gravity to contain me. Nothing I'd ever learned or seen or heard could've prepared me for this. And before I could begin to interpret what was happening to me, I was still again.

It was night. A dry heat warmed my cold skin. My legs were wobbly, but I didn't tumble over. I was standing in front of a house. A stone house. Sitti Marwa's house. The shutters were actually turquoise in this moonlight and I could see a few windows had been shattered, shards of glass glittering on the rocky ground. I was still barefoot but felt nothing as I walked toward the entrance, a bougainvillea bush forming a half-arc above me. Crickets hummed and I heard a distant braying. The heavy fragrance of a flower wafted toward me, and I somehow knew its name: jasmine. The branches of a lemon tree swayed slightly, their shadows dancing along the front of the house.

Everything the photograph at home had not captured was alive here and I was in it. I reached out my hand to pluck a lemon—I was suddenly desperate to inhale its citrus wonder—when a series of loud cracking sounds broke the still of the night.

I startled and ran through an open door to see what was happening. Inside the stone house was a family. I didn't know them but they looked familiar. Was it Baba's father? My grandfather? He and the others were being herded outdoors by men holding automatic weapons but they weren't soldiers. Were they some kind of militia? A few women were sobbing and children were whimpering, their fingers interlaced with their mother's.

As I watched them leave, a girl appeared from nowhere and pounced on one of the men who was pointing his weapon at the children's backs. In one swift motion, he knocked her to the floor. A butcher knife fell from her small hand. He pinned her down. Another man plucked up the knife and plunged it deep into her eye socket.

Except it was my eye socket, too!

I yelped at the searing pain, white-hot like a poker. Then an awful scarlet tidal wave blinded me. I couldn't see through my right eye—it was gone, but this didn't diminish the sheer agony of my empty socket, every severed nerve throbbing with rage.

The men laughed as they dragged me across the limestone floor and out the door. My toes scraped the rocky ground and kicked up dust. Before flinging me away, the men kicked me, each vicious pummel a tiny prickle compared to the fire burning my eye. They shouted at me in a language that wasn't Arabic. They shouted as if I were the trespasser and not them with their combat boots and civilian clothes.

Through my lonely eye, I came upon other bodies outside the stone house. A few were moving, rising to their feet. A few lay as still as the night after the machine guns ripped through them. I saw and saw and saw more than a single eye should ever absorb. I saw so much that all my other senses were blunted. A man and a woman, faces blood-streaked, their chest wounds looked like an animal had mauled their flesh. A child—was it a girl or boy? I couldn't tell from the way their body was splayed across the ground.

I quickly understood that some of us survived and we were being ordered away from the stone house, that our lives were our rewards if we left immediately.

Someone lifted my body and before I could ask where he was taking me, I was back in my bedroom, gripping my phone. I jolted up. My t-shirt was drenched in sweat. My fingers shot to my eye. It was there but the scabs were gone. My body was safe. There were no bruises on my arms or thighs, no tender wounds.

"Mama!" I screamed. "Mama!" I leapt from my bedroom and ran down the hallway. But my parents weren't there. I skidded back to the landing. Dawn broke through the arched window, the crystals of the chandelier catching the light. I could hear voices on the first floor and I flew down the stairs.

The door to my old playroom was open. Baba was talking and I heard muffled crying. Was it Mama? I slowed down, a sudden dread sinking my stomach. Aya was there, too, and she was saying something comforting.

Baba emerged, his phone to his ear. "Salaam, Yaseen," he was saying to his brother. He didn't notice me yet. "I have some bad news. Hajja Marwa has passed away." And then he caught sight of me and hurried to hold me in a kind of half-hug while he still spoke into his phone.

I wriggled free and entered the playroom. It appeared strange to me now. The old woman's black shawl and threadbare thawb hanging over the old rocking chair was incongruous with the bright yellow paint.

And there she was. On the daybed. She was unmoving, her long hair framed her face. It was as impassive in death as it was in life. Someone had removed the eye patch and I saw it. The sealed space where her eye had once been. The scars began beneath her brow line and dipped into the empty socket that curved like a small bowl.

Before my mother could intercept me, I ran to the old woman's side. "I saw it!" I cried in Arabic, dropping to my knees. "I saw your house! I saw you! I saw what they did to you!"

"May the Lord keep evil far from us!" my mother said, pulling me away. "She's dead, my love. Allah yarhamha. God have mercy on her soul."

Aya tried to comfort me. "She lived a long life, Jan. She—"

But I pulled away from their hands that tried to hold me back. "I saw you," I whispered into Sitti Marwa's ear. "I saw you."

For a moment, a soft light glowed beneath the sealed skin.

The burial and ceremonial azza were a blur. I sat between my mother and sister as the faithful from our mosque bade their condolences. The women on our side of the assembly hall spoke in low voices, their conversations drifting away from the old woman to their own lives. Lena and a few of our friends came and I was sure I said something when they hugged me, but I couldn't remember.

When I finally checked my phone, there were a dozen texts, offering me condolences. One was from an unfamiliar number.

Hello, Janna. It's Saleem from school.

I'm sorry to hear about your grandmother.

I hope to see you soon.

There was no emoji and he spelled out every word. Tears welled in my eyes.

And then I remembered. The recording. I swiped my screen and pulled up the gallery. I thumbed to the most recent images and clicked.

The video was of me, in selfie mode. I checked again. There was no recording of Sitti Marwa in front of the portrait. I swiped the video in reverse. I was coming down the stairs. There was no sound, only light illuminating the terror on my face.

At home that night, everyone was exhausted from the funeral rites and fell fast asleep. Except for me. I sat in my bed, Olive in my lap, and I stroked her. She rolled onto her back, signaling her content. The house creaked as it settled. I heard the howl of a coyote in the distance. I was wide awake, waiting until I saw it.

This light was much dimmer as if the stars were imploding into a black hole. Still it glowed beneath my door. Olive scampered from me and I hurried down the stairs and stood in front of the portrait of Sitti Marwa's house. But it was no longer day in the photo and the wedding procession had disappeared. A crescent moon hung above the roof. I could still make out everything in full bloom at the entrance—the bougainvillea, the lemon tree. They were now dipped in nighttime shadows.

My eyes roved over the stone house. Everything was peaceful. The windows were unbroken. On the second floor beside the balcony, the turquoise-blue shutters were thrown open.

In one of the windows, there was a light, softly framing a young girl.

BODY CAM

TJ Cimfel

ampos leans in close. Squints. In the shadows, he can see the reflection of his eyes looking back at him. There's a faint hum of electricity coming off the screen, the scene. He's been feeling it in the back of his head for the last few months. He has tinnitus from a botched job down in Calumet City. This is like that, only much lower in pitch.

He's viewed this footage countless times, memorized every detail down to the thinnest slice. By now the timecode has burnt a loop in his brain.

2025-07-27 02:14:13

Hillard and Jackson throw their doors open in near-perfect synchronicity. This one's from one of the impound lot's surveillance cameras. Getting ahold of it was a minor coup as it filled in some of the early blanks before Hillard activated his body-worn camera. It's the one that shows Jackson's relative distance coming up from Hillard's six.

2025-07-27 02:14:27

Hillard begins recording. He was a little slow to double-press the EVENT button on the Axon, as the audio doesn't come on until after he has his firearm drawn. His flashlight cuts across concrete redwoods. Bright ivory slicing through the umber and maroon and chocolate stains of shadows. He trains it on the second dumpster from the left. His breathing is heavy and quick, epinephrine flooding his system.

2025-07-27 02:15:08

Get on the ground!
Don't shoot! Please!
I said get on the fucking ground!

Campos mouths the words along with them, not even aware he's doing it. He can recite every line, nail every inflection, the change in pitch. The dialogue lessens in the later acts. Don't mistake it for Shakespeare though. There are only three acts. Suspect gets spotted. Suspect becomes Vic. And then.

2025-07-27 02:15:59

The Vic bounces off the dumpster, knocking a cardboard box to the ground, which he quickly follows. He tried to squirt past Hillard, but Hillard has real mass to him and though he doesn't move fast, he moves hard. A cop got gunned down near Clark and Lake two weeks ago and everyone's running hot.

It's at this point the impound lot camera footage jellies, smears to gray. A nebulous conspiracy has naturally formed around this. The CPD got ahold of the impound lot's drive, wiped out Jackson's involvement. Like there isn't enough incriminating footage as it is. Besides, Campos had nothing to do with that. Not that he's above such moves. Hell, those moves are why they hire him.

He could only stonewall for so long. The prying journalists and their relentless FOIA requests. The family, crying on the news every other day. Woke mobs spitting vitriol outside City Hall, shutting down traffic in the Loop. All of it so tiresomely predictable, so tiresomely effective.

And so, on October 25, 2025, after one successful and one unsuccessful request for delayed release from the city, 90 days after the incident on Lower Lower Wacker, the Civilian Office of Police Accountability released the damning footage involving sixteen-year-old Reginald Jalen Dumar, Lieutenant Jeffrey Thaddeus Hillard, and Officer Quentin Tanner Jackson.

Some of it, at least.

Campos's breath comes out in great foggy cones that partially obscure the screen. Heat is just one of the creature comforts forbidden in the Closet, along with basic plumbing and electricity. Campos is forced to watch on his laptop. The CPD tries to keep this particular facility's utility usage to a bare minimum lest an enterprising journalist discover what that Ackerman fellow who worked for the Guardian would have found had he kept digging beyond Homan Square. Homan was just the tip of the black iceberg. As if the CPD would only keep a single site off the books. It's quite clever actually, a magic trick Campos supposes, that the city became an early pioneer of transparency tools. Keep your eye on the bouncing ball of this huffing puffing cop's BWC footage, people, but pay no mind to the empty warehouse only a few thousand feet away where far more unspeakable acts occur on a daily basis. Campos admires the maneuver. As a fixer, it's good to know your client has some moves of its own.

2025-07-27 02:16:13

Stop moving! Let me see your hands—
Fucking get off me!

By now, every grunt has imprinted itself on the loop burned in Campos's brain. Hillard's breathing is heavy in the mic. The man surely qualifies as obese, if not morbidly so, and it's a marvel he doesn't keel over.

It used to bother Campos that it was impossible to see Hillard's relative angle in relation to the Vic, where his right knee landed when he first came down. But Hillard's camera was angled a little too high, glinting off the "Solid Waste" sticker on the nearby dumpster. As for Jackson, he never started his BWC, a fact that had the public howling like wolves outside the Mayor's office. To slake the beasts' thirst, Jackson surely would have faced strict disciplinary action.

If only he hadn't gone missing during the incident itself.

2025-07-27 02:16:43

Hillard is bent over now, affording a good look at the Vic's face, his white eyes flashing with fear.

C'mon man!

STOP MOVING!

I didn't do—

Right here. This image has been shared more than six million times on social media. The Vic can't finish his sentence. He's trying to save his breath, literally.

2025-07-27 02:16:48

The Vic looks over Hillard's right shoulder. Conventional wisdom is that he's looking at Jackson standing watch. There is no second beam of light cast from behind though. Internet sleuths have posited that Jackson chose not to employ his Streamlight in an attempt to, if not obfuscate any potential wrongdoing by his partner, avoid further clarifying details that could land them both in hot water.

Campos has information the Internet does not. The unimaginative might assume his job involves nothing more than a comprehensive grasp of the corrosive power of sodium hydroxide, but more and more these days it's about information. Who holds it. Who thinks they hold it. Who's willing to pay for it.

The information: Roughly thirty feet from where Hillard engaged the Vic, not ten feet from the Interceptor, a parallel set of faint, uninterrupted scuff marks was discovered on the Lower Lower Wacker asphalt, the kind that might be recreated by dragging the heel of a black Chukka boot with no small degree of force across the ground. Forensics was able to locate the terminus of the marks. The base of a massive concrete pillar.

2025-07-27 02:16:53

The Vic's eyes roll upward from Hillard's right shoulder to a spot directly above them. His pupils shrink to a pinprick. And then for a single frame, a frame that Campos removed and replaced with a hybrid clone of the previous and following frames—a feat of subterfuge involving social engineering, palm greasing, breaking and entering, and a pirated copy of Final Cut Pro—something unexplainable happens. BWCs are built for high quality video, but the image breaks down quickly upon zooming. Brightening the image confirms it though. For a millisecond, on the night of his death, Reginald Jalen Dumar's eyeballs went away.

Not the 1000-yard stare of someone peering into his maker's face. His eyeballs literally are not there, the lids sagged around the hollow space, two glistening pink pockets that almost look like mouths. Eyelips.

Years ago before Campos switched his allegiance to the good guys, he was called in for a job by an unsavory man with deep pockets. The guy had killed his girlfriend in a meth-fueled mania. Afterward, he removed her eyes with a melon baller. That's exactly what this looks like. Like someone scooped the eyes right out from the Vic's head.

2025-07-27 02:17:54

After one minute and one second of diminishing struggle, the Vic smiles like he knows what's coming, like he welcomes it. Hillard crushes his windpipe with his knee. For the next twelve minutes and thirty-three seconds, Hillard does not move his knee from the Vic's throat. He does not move at all.

This is peculiar behavior, to say the least. But the peculiarity of it has been of far less interest to the public than the damning fact that the Vic doesn't die for an additional five minutes and three seconds. Hypoxia sets in quickly and he isn't conscious for long. His lips go grayish-white. He can be heard gurgling. Until he can't.

During this time, and for a significant period after, Hillard remains completely still. He can be heard whimpering under his breath. Audio forensics and armchair audiologists the world over have tried every noise reduction, filtering, equalization, compression, spectral analysis trick imaginable to isolate syllables and stitch them together. So has Campos. It is a fool's errand. Hillard is not speaking any language known to man. One popular theory is that Hillard, who grew up in Memphis, attended a Pentecostal church. The Pentecostals being well known for speaking in tongues. Hillard is gibbering a beseechment to God for forgiveness, the forums say. He has gone insane from guilt, the forums say, has reverted to the religion he believes will save his soul from eternal damnation. But Hillard attended St. Peter. He's a devout Catholic.

2025-07-27 02:31:28

Hillard turns off his camera.

Hillard did not turn off his camera.

What was captured in the next 13 seconds was deemed far too distressing for the public eye. In the early stages, Campos had to take immediate and regrettable measures against two City employees who got their eyes on the footage. Frankly, they got out easy. In the early weeks, before Campos decided to reduce the circle of trust to himself, he shared the footage with a small handful of high-ranking city officials. Some took their own lives in imaginative ways. Others are now in the care of behavioral health specialists in Winfield, Des Plaines, Libertyville. The CPD Superintendent is currently on medical leave, though no one has seen or heard from him in two weeks. The Mayor leaves voicemails for Campos every night. If Campos listened to them, he would hear senseless sounds not dissimilar to Hillard's.

Since then, only Campos has viewed the footage. He watches in the Closet, a space so covert that only Campos and a few others know about it. Knew about it.

2025-07-27 02:31:29

A shadow swallows the beam of light cast from Hillard's shoulder. The camera tilts back, as though he were lying down on his back. His knee is still bearing down on the Vic's neck. Hillard is bending back, back.

A dark thing descends.

2025-07-27 02:31:30

The tilting continues, yaws upward and over, the dark thing disappearing from view. There is a series of staccato cracking sounds that seem to correlate with the vertebral trauma found in Hillard's autopsy. The camera shows an upside-down view of the Interceptor.

It is at this point that the humming begins. At first it is low and subtle, easy to dismiss as noise from the video. It is low and subtle like the hum that has taken residence in Campos's head.

2025-07-27 02:31:31

The camera lurches upward suddenly, once again catching a glimpse of the dark thing, which moves closer as the camera's frame tilts past it. The staccato cracks are tighter together, a paradiddle. The coroner said the spinal cord was severed in several places, consistent with injuries sustained during falls from great heights. Yet Hillard remains upright. The camera sways slightly, as though he were a cobra, charmed.

2025-07-27 02:31:32

Trained on the dumpster. A second voice joins the first, humming. Hillard leans over. Takes his knee off the throat of the Vic. The Vic's ruined throat pulsates, his lips vibrate slightly. His is one of the two voices humming.

2025-07-27 02:31:33

The dark thing drops into view, blocking the dumpster. It is an oil spill, iridescent hues swimming on its surface. A face births itself from the inky black, slick with translucent clots of jelly. Like the stuff they smear on an expectant mother's belly to reveal the being living inside of her.

The face is Jackson's.

2025-07-27 02:31:34

Jackson hums with his mouth closed. A third voice. It is not harmony. It is not dissonance. It is something in between. Jackson parts his lips, but the mmm continues unchanged.

2025-07-27 02:31:35

Jackson's lips peel back in a rictus of pain. He peers into the frame. If you were to pause the film, as Campos did many times before he started watching this on a loop, Jackson appears cognizant of what is happening, though he may not be able to name the what. A father, a husband, a son, an officer of the law, conscious, awake, keenly aware that something is happening, something wretched and hideous, a suffering, a spoilage, a profanity, he has plunged into the abyss. His mouth widens in agony and yet still he hums. Hillard's BWC peers down Jackson's throat, a makeshift endoscopy revealing a glistening pink pocket, like the Vic's eyes from the excised frame of film.

2025-07-27 02:31:36

A wad of grayish sputum, a bubblegum bolus, pushes up from Jackson's throat into his mouth, out of his mouth, forcing his lips so far open they curl back on themselves and continue pulling outward, like flame singeing a hole in paper, a circle consuming the sphere of his head, the strained coils of his neck, turning his face inside out as the bubblegum rises, expands, becomes another face framed within the oily black cocoon.

Campos sees his eyes in the reflection of the dark thing. Watches himself watching himself.

2025-07-27 02:31:37

It is Hillard's face now. He suffers, too. He hums, too, from his opening mouth. Three voices. This Hillard-thing, the Vic, and the spine-shattered Hillard himself, presumably.

Campos leans forward in anticipation, his nose practically touching the screen, his mouth slightly open, saliva pooling on his lower lip.

2025-07-27 02:31:38

The Hillard-thing undergoes the same abhorrent unmaking that Jackson did, the grayish wad consuming his face from the inside out, a new head crowning from within the outward peeling throat.

In the oily black margins of the screen, Campos watches as his reflection's eyes go away.

2025-07-27 02:31:39

The head cocks back, features forming from the soup. It is anguished, a filling-in-blank, it is Campos.

The battery on Campos's laptop died forty-seven days ago.

2025-07-27 02:31:40

The Campos-thing looks directly at the camera, out of the screen.

pos watching Campos watc

2025-07-27 02:31:41

The audio cuts out a second before the screen goes black.

There is no one left alive, no one whose brain has not been scrambled in some unrecoverable way, who has even heard of the Closet.

With a wide open mouth, Campos hums in solitude, in the quiet cold, close, so close to the monitor. His cheeks are sunken, face sallow and flaky. Skin sags off his bones. His belly is bloated atop his empty lap, the pencil sticks of his thighs. Bedsores bloom on his ass.

He gazes into the black screen that gazes into him. There is something above, below.

2025-07-27 02:14:13

Hillard and Jackson throw their doors open in near-perfect synchronicity.

FEED THE MONSTER EVIL

K. Saab

They say my school is cursed, but right now, I'm the one who feels cursed.

"Shit, shit, shit," I chant, taking the stairs from the L platform two at a time. I slip on the last one—no matter how much sand they drop on it, it's still wet metal—and my wrist wrenches as I catch the railing. *"Fuck!"*

My open coat flaps. The weather feels too hot for it, but that's cuz I'm rushing; it's definitely still 33° outside, which is the worst temperature, because it's *barely* above freezing, so the snow is barely starting to melt, but it's still chilly and you can't just wear a sweater without your mother who grew up in a tropical climate fussing like hell.

Or maybe that's just me.

It's ten minutes from here to my school, but I can make it in eight if I really haul ass. Today, I've got a gut feeling telling me it's important, so I haul ass.

I'm not about to tell you what school I go to, because Mama ain't raise no fool (even if she says the word "ain't" makes me *sound* like a fool, but I always rebut that the real foolishness is buying into the kyriarchal devaluation of African American Vernacular English, at which point she rolls her eyes and walks away, which means I win). But with some hints—school is cursed, ten minutes off the L—you can probably figure it out, especially as I tell more of the story. After all, there are only like 220 high schools in Chicago Public Schools.

My Computer Science teacher made me learn that. They were cool, a new teacher with cherry-red curls straight out of a bottle and a gap between their front teeth that made their smile even better. Jamel—my best friend—had the *worst* crush on them, and he failed Comp Sci on purpose. But they left the next year, so that backfired.

We were all sad to see them go, especially Principal Jones, who wrote them a glowing letter of rec. She *never* does that. Lowkey, whenever I help out in her office, it seems like she kind of hates half her staff. Weird cuz she hired them, but I know she has her reasons. And all the really terrible teachers either leave, disappear, or kill themselves.

Yeah, that definitely narrows it down.

A big part of the so-called curse is how many teachers we lose, both good and bad alike. The *real* part, actually—everything else, the two kids who got shot like three blocks away, the boy who got expelled for "accidentally" (yeah, right) dosing half the freshman class with marijuana—all that shit is just normal Chicago Poverty facts of life. The "curse" is about the adults.

Of course, the students know the truth, and there's no curse: we have a Monster.

If teachers who leave say the school is broke, admin is overbearing, the students are unruly and unwilling to learn, then people will nod their heads sympathetically and say some patronizing, virtue-signalling bullshit about "those inner-city kids." Same old story, from Howard to 134th. We get a lot of those White-Savior types who wanna give us poor kids "the education we deserve," only to be disgusted when it turns out that we're actually "horribly behaved" and "willingly gang-affiliated."

(We don't have time to unpack that last one, but boy, could I. Jamel is in a gang and to call it "willing" when he was born into that life is a stretch, but they take care of him better than his Mama ever did. And those gangbangers are the reason he's in AP Calculus while I'm taking Transitional Math.)

All of that crap is totally reasonable to other adults. But if those teachers say they left because of a monster, they'll be—at best—

laughed out of any room. Even though the students all know it's true.

And besides the ones that leave, three teachers (so far) have "committed suicide." No one ever acted like it was anything other than normal, but we know none were the type to kill themselves, not even the one with pending felony charges.

It was the middle suicide three years ago—the felony—that really caught everyone's attention. He was a respected lawyer turned Social Studies teacher, and his knowledge of the law kept him from getting in trouble even when it turned out he'd dated a former student. What got him in the end was Dr. Jones catching him in a classroom taking pictures of a half-naked student. Obviously she called the cops, but he killed himself rather than go to prison. (So the story goes.)

They found the teacher's hard drive full of child pornography, including several of that freshman girl he'd gotten caught with. Unfortunately a lot of it—including her—had already been posted online, but at least the FBI seized it.

That girl was me, by the way. My identity was protected since I was a minor, but I'm nearly eighteen; I figure I'm allowed to control my own story. It ain't like the anonymity actually protected me at school—everyone knew it was me, anyway, and by now so many of them have seen most (if not all) of my body. Boys talk about searching me up online.

It's why I dress how I dress. What do I have that they haven't already seen? So sure, I'll wear my crop tops and show off my belly button ring. It's got a garnet fox, it's cute. I like my fishnets and push-up bras; why shouldn't I wear them?

The thing about me is I'm one of those girls they call "fast-tailed," a.k.a. I hit puberty at about ten years old and men ain't been normal around me ever since. My dad once punched a guy's tooth out for some comment I didn't hear and he wouldn't tell me. In spite of this, my parents never forced me to dress a certain way or blamed me. Mama grew up with a government that told girls what to wear, and she said no way was she doing that to her own daughter.

Daddy said he was getting out of shape and this was just motivation to make sure he could still fight.

I shiver as I take off my coat and shove it in my narrow red locker. There's a book on string theory at the bottom, underneath Stephen Hawking's *A Brief History of Time* and some volume of *Naruto*. I roll my eyes, because it means Jamel beat me here and wants me to know it. Those sure as hell ain't mine.

An obnoxious brassy sound startles me into shoving a couple books in my bag. If I make it close enough to the bell, Mr. Bose shouldn't make me go grab a tardy pass (ugh), especially if I lean forward a little bit and give him a view. I know exactly what he's thinking, what he wants; I feel the echoes of three years ago every time he looks at me a bit too intensely.

I've been debating *giving* him what he wants. I think that gut feeling means today is the day.

With my music theory notebook clutched to my chest—tight enough to emphasize my cleavage—I hurry down the hallway, turning the corner and finding myself in front of the shadowy music room. The lights are always half burnt by this door; nothing the building engineer does ever seems to work.

Mr. Bose is closing the door when I approach, and his eyes light up when he sees me.

"Ah, Nevaeh!" He grins, showing too many teeth. He always does, has every day since the first day of school. His teeth are a bit too straight and a bit too white, like his family had more money for orthodontics than they knew what to do with.

Which, maybe they did. He said he grew up in Evanston.

"I was worried you'd be absent today," he adds, not sounding worried at all.

I shake my head, bounce a little, cutesy. I watch his eyes drift down, down, snap back up. "No, I just missed the train," I tell him. It's even the truth.

Fuck the CTA. Like, I love it, but fuck them.

"All good," Mr. Bose says, still grinning unnervingly. He ushers me in, hand between my shoulder blades.

I suppress a shudder. I hate being touched, but I ain't about to let anyone but Jamel know that; it's a weakness. Because of how I look, nobody expects it, which is dumb but unsurprising.

I throw myself down onto the chair beside Jamel, dodging his judgmental look. He only knows part of the story: he knows everything from freshman year, held me through the aftermath, but he doesn't know why I act like this now, why I revel in the attention from men and boys I have no interest in. To be fair, I don't completely understand either, but . . . it feels good to be desired.

My therapist says the fact I won't fuck the guys is part of the appeal. That I like the control it gives me after being in a situation I had no control over, and I'm trying to take back my agency in my sexuality. She doesn't quite believe me that I'm asexual, says the lack of attraction and general disinterest in sex is a trauma response, but hey, there's no such thing as a perfect therapist. I was this way before Fuckface (my abuser doesn't get the dignity of a name), and I'll be this way till I die.

I'm barely even messed up about what happened anymore. I could have sex just fine—could probably have any guy I wanted in this school—I just don't want to. I've got better things to do. There's only so many minutes in a day, and I refuse to waste 'em on something stupid. (Even if it'd only last five minutes with some of these assholes.)

Jamel's got a book open on the music stand—a book about economics, not our Music Theory textbook. Neither of us wants to be here, but this was the only class that fit the graduation requirement. And goddammit, we *will* be graduating, the both of us, even if I have to drag that boy across the stage by his ear.

At least we have each other. Besides us, there's a group of five boys that want to fuck me (though only two have said it), a couple who're perpetually stoned in the back row, and a sophomore with a stupidly obvious crush on Mr. Bose. She's also stupidly obvious in her jealousy of me.

Sometimes I consider pulling her aside and explaining that actually, it's a *bad* thing when an adult shows interest in you like that, even if he's fresh out of college and you think you're grown. (These girls always think they're grown, right up until someone makes them realize they're not.) That yeah, it feels nice to be treated special, but really it's predatory.

Except I don't try that anymore. A couple weeks after the incident, this girl loftily proclaimed Fuckface should have chosen her, and I tried to explain it. That went about as badly as you expect, maybe worse.

"Nevaeh," Mr. Bose calls—seemingly not for the first time—with his eyes glued inarguably lower than my face. A few of the boys chuckle, the sophomore looks somehow even more upset, and Jamel tenses like he's gonna spring up and fight.

I catch his wrist, tugging twice on the woven friendship bracelet. It used to be a rainbow, but now it's kind of grimy and hard to see the colors because teenage boys are gross and he never takes it off. Still, that's part of why I always sit on his right—the bracelet is in tugging distance. One short for yes, two short for no.

One long for "Don't you fucking dare," and a twist around my fingers for "Are you out of your fucking mind?" Those get used more than I wish.

At my "no," he settles back, still frowning. There's bad blood there, including Bose trying to get him suspended for no damn reason. I dunno why he hates Jamel, besides maybe racism. Jamel thinks it's jealousy, that Bose thinks we're dating, which is laughable—Jamel ever liking a woman. Me, ever liking anyone. But heteronormativity is a hell of a drug.

"What?" I ask after a stretch of silence where we've made eye contact for way too long—or rather, I've looked at his eyes and he's looked at my tits.

"Are you with us?" he finally asks, frowning slightly.

Digging in myself for a bit of energy to play, I give a flirty giggle. "Are you?"

His face goes red and his eyes snap upward. I wink, a little "don't worry about it," and he relaxes. "Of course," he replies, still a bit awkward. "Would you mind answering the question?"

Before I can ask him to repeat it, Jamel's reached over to my Music Theory notebook and tapped the number we're on. I don't know how to answer, because I'm truly shit at music—give me Social Studies any day, even if that was what got me in trouble in the first place—but I give it my level best, and Bose doesn't tell me

I'm wrong even though I am and we all know it, and the sophomore glares at me harder.

I again consider talking to her, but I still don't think it'll work.

The class drags on as we discuss minor scales and my fingers twitch with the urge to play one, which is the only way any of this ever makes any goddamn sense to me, but unfortunately, the ever-familiar brassy tone of the bell tells me I'm not destined to touch a piano today.

Or so I think, until Mr. Bose motions for me to stay behind. Jamel hovers by the door, but at the insistent look from our teacher, I hurry him along, promising to meet up again third period. Jamel's off to Computer Science—actually trying this time, and passing easily—while I'll be in AP Gov as soon as I leave this class. We have a test tomorrow, so today's probably a review—she's been on a Kahoot kick lately...

"Nevaeh?" Mr. Bose asks. I've spaced—again—so I laugh the little ditzy laugh that makes everyone forgive me about it.

"Sorry." I duck my head bashfully; the gold rings around my twists click against each other softly. "What's up?"

"I've noticed your grade has been slipping," he begins, and I know it's a lie. For one, I check my grades daily—Northwestern doesn't accept just anyone—but even if I didn't, Dr. Jones taught me to detect lies with near-supernatural accuracy. It's hard to explain; still, I feel that viscous desperation now, like someone quietly chanting *"Believe me"* right up against my ear.

But why lie?

"I was wondering if you wanted to stay after today for some practice," he offers, and it clicks. I get a wave of déjà vu so strong it almost knocks me over. "I've noticed you benefit from instruction that's a little more...hands-on." He winks conspiratorially.

My heart beats faster. I debate asking if Jamel can come, but I know if I do, it's over. This is what I've been waiting for all year, isn't it? Hell, maybe what I've been waiting for since my freshman year.

I shrug my shoulder delicately, at just the right angle for my sleeve to fall and reveal my red lace bra strap. "Debate Team is cancelled this week," I reply with a smile, watching his eyes track to my shoulder. Watching him imagine what the rest might look like. "So I've got the afternoon free. I'll be here."

That's *also* not true, but I figure if he's allowed to lie, so am I. There's no way he'll go through with this if I say another teacher will know where I am. Especially since Mr. Alvarez would actually care—he's one of the good ones, and the other teachers know it.

Bose smiles that too-sharp smile, a predator not realizing he has become prey, and touches my bare shoulder to send me off to second period. I actually let myself shudder this time, once he's out of sight, and promise myself it will be over soon.

I should go straight to AP Gov. Maybe part of me even intends to go straight there, because I do start out in that direction, but when I hit a stairwell, I head up to the third floor. I don't even really think about it, just climb, and then I walk a little faster than necessary to room 300 at the very end of the hall until I enter the Shrine.

I spent a lot of time on my back in this room. I'm intimately familiar with the cracks in the ceiling, all seventeen of them that splinter out from atop the corner window. His desk used to be right in front of that window, and sometimes I'd watch the football team practice while ignoring what was happening to the other half of my body.

I always did like the photoshoots and the attention; not so much the rest of it.

The desk is gone now, because even though our school is strapped for funding, Principal Jones let me burn it. Said my healing was worth more than a few hundred dollars, and besides, she made enough money to replace one teacher desk for her school. I suspect she buys a lot more than that with her own salary, but I have no proof, and she'll never admit it. She doesn't do it for praise.

In the place where the desk used to sit is a mismatched set of garden furniture from the Village Discount down the street, positioned strategically to hide the bloodstains and claw marks on the floorboards. She said the custodians couldn't fix it, but I think Dr. Jones left it as a reminder.

There's a trellis, too, covered in fake flowers made of tissue paper and fabric because nothing green stays alive in a CPS building;

that was the first offering, by a girl named Samantha Park who graduated top of her class and used to be as close to Dr. Jones as I am now. (She was a senior when I was a freshman, and although we never talked about it, I think I sort of took over for her when she graduated.) I added some tea lights that matched the colors of her flowers. Battery-powered, because I don't trust teenagers for shit.

There are other things in the Shrine, most of which scream "high school" and are decidedly less nice than our art project: a pair of broken Beats, two empty bags of Flamin' Hot Cheetos that definitely were full when someone placed them here, a couple pictures of teachers with frowny faces or their eyes x'ed out. Every teacher who ends up on the Shrine is gone by the end of the year, but only if they really deserve it; if they don't, the photo disappears immediately and the kid who put it there gets detention.

We all know the Monster watches the Shrine, because that's who it's dedicated to, but there's debate over whether the Monster snitches to Dr. Jones or if there's some other way she always catches the students. I think it's a stupid debate.

I've never put a picture on the Shrine; I've never needed to.

I sit there, cross-legged on the floor, and I stare at the blinking plastic candle, and really ask myself what I'm doing. Who do I think I am, trying to Jezebel Mr. Bose to his doom? I'm just a girl a couple months out from her eighteenth birthday, with far more boobs than are good for my back and the kind of hubris found in Greek myth.

But then I think about the sophomore, with her unpleasant little scowl and the braids she still has those baby-ass plastic clips on the end of, and what if she's next? What if I turn him down and he decides to go for someone easier? Someone who doesn't know better?

Shit, I don't want another girl to end up like me. Like yeah, I'm fine, I'm over it, but I had to fucking *claw* my way here, fight for every tiny scrap of mental stability I have. And aren't I still dressing like a slut and teasing, thinking of seducing a grown man? Because I'm already tainted, so better me than anyone else? I'm not naive; I'm aware I'm not the poster child for mental health.

That reaffirms my conviction.

The bell rings. Apparently I accidentally dissociated for fifty minutes staring at the Shrine and debating my life choices. When I unfold, my knees crack and I wince. Then I shoulder my bag and hurry to third period because I didn't even mean to skip one class—I'm not about to skip two.

The rest of the day goes by in a flurry of anticipation, now that I'm committed and sure of myself. I'm so distracted that Jamel notices—of course he does—but I brush him off when he asks what's up. I love him, but this is my secret. This is something I have to handle by myself.

For all that Dr. Jones is magical, there'll be nothing she can do if Jamel decides to bring his gun and fucking shoots Bose. Even if she agreed with the choice wholeheartedly.

Finally, I make it to the last period. My English teacher also tells me I seem particularly distracted today, but I remind her my IEP is mostly for ADHD which is literally just "Can't Fucking Focus" disease. For all my parents are cool and progressive, they've got a massive fear of Big Pharma, so ya girl is out here with no Adderall, just iced coffee and a prayer.

It's got mixed results.

She rolls her eyes at me, because she also has ADHD and she knows damn well that's not what's up, but she also drops the subject, without even scolding me for cussing. So double win, really. I'm supposed to be writing an essay making an argument that Jordan Baker is a lesbian, and normally I'd be all over that shit, but today I'm just blinking at the cursor, which blinks back, and then I blink, and so on, and then the bell rings and I'm up like a shot, shouting goodbyes to my teachers.

I make one stop in the girl's bathroom—a place I normally avoid if I can help it, because Hell No public bathrooms, and also those supposedly-inclusive "Women +" signs just piss me off—to fix my makeup and my hair, and to unfix my clothes, slipping the neckline off my shoulder again and tugging my jeans down just enough to expose my tattoo. It's a stupid butterfly stick-n-poke Jamel did while high one day: maybe not the sexiest thing in the world, but I love it.

I'm nearly breathless when I make it to the music room, but hopefully in an alluring way. I dash off one final text, hit "record" in my voice notes app, then square my shoulders—pushing my tits forward—and knock.

Mr. Bose answers and immediately looks straight down my shirt. He smiles that unnerving smile, close enough for me to feel his hot breath, and I use my ironclad control over my body not to flinch.

I'm more uncomfortable than I expected. My therapist would probably tell me "No shit"—after, of course, chewing me out for being a reckless idiot—but I genuinely thought I was over it. Yet despite there being no danger, despite me being the one with all the power in this situation, I *still* feel like prey.

I don't like it.

I'm not the kind of person that regrets things, and I don't regret this, but I do regret that I put myself in a situation to feel these things again. They were ugly the first go round and they're uglier now that I'm not an innocent kid who doesn't know better. Now that the curtain's been pulled back. This man is supposed to guide me and protect me, and here he is, eyeing me like a conquest and practically drooling over the concept of assaulting me.

(And it is assault. I may be seventeen and legally able to consent, but I'm still his student, which puts him in a position of power over me. I'm not saying no, but if I wanted to, could I? Without him failing me, without anyone ostracizing and blaming me? Dr. Jones is cool, but she's not the only person around me, and there are a million students—not just girls—who don't even have a person like her.)

"Mr. Bose—" I begin, but he cuts me off.

"Please, call me Alexander."

"Alex?" I try with a vapid smile. Men always buy it, which astounds me every time, but I guess it's easy to believe someone who looks like me is stupid to match. Even with the AP classes, the boobs make people forget.

He laughs indulgently. "Alex works just fine." All of his earlier awkwardness is gone, now that he's away from other students—other eyes. He runs a hand absently from my bare shoulder down my arm, stopping to twist my bra strap. I stay still.

Prey. But while all he sees is the lure, I remind myself, I'm actually the anglerfish.

Well. No. I am the lure. But the anglerfish is nearby, ready.

"So would you rather use your hands, or do you want something to blow?" he asks, and I giggle to cover how startled I am at the blatant innuendo. Fuckface did not go zero to a hundred like this; he had finesse. Maybe it's cuz Mr. Bose—Alex—is younger.

"Hands," I reply, seeing him grin. "I'm thinking . . . piano?"

"That works just fine," he says, putting a hand on the small of my back—bare, not covered by my crop top—and guiding me to the piano bench.

He gestures to his lap but I pretend not to understand and instead sit beside him, still pressed close. I think I'd die if I tried sitting in his lap. I don't want to feel his excitement any more than I already do.

He shrugs, takes it in stride, and leans around me so his chest is pressed against my back. He took off his tie at some point before I got here and his sleeves are rolled up, letting his bare forearms press against mine as he takes my hands and guides them to the keys.

I feel sick.

We play like that for a little while, him making music-based innuendos the whole time with his face drifting closer and closer to mine. Then, out of nowhere—and I mean really nowhere, he didn't telegraph his intent or anything—he sinks his teeth into the meat of my shoulder.

I squeal. It's not a noise I'm proud of, but better than a squeak, I guess. He just laughs breathily and laves his tongue across it.

"Wouldn't want to leave a mark where anyone can see, hmm?" he asks. I've learned these kinds of questions are rhetorical; they just like to hear themselves talk, like to make you listen. "It can be our little secret. I wonder where else I could leave a mark for no one to see? It's not like you cover up much skin of yours. It's like you were just begging for a private lesson."

He slips his hands under my shirt and rips it off fluidly, tossing it somewhere toward his desk. I shiver, as much at the cold as in surprise, while he runs his hands up and down my sides, over my breasts.

"And with the whorish little bra, too, like you knew today would be the day I couldn't help myself any longer." He grins—I feel it against my skin—before he bites down again, harder than before.

I can't. I can't do this. This has to be enough.

Mouth clamped shut, I scream my desperation as loud as I can into the universe. Instantly, there are keys jingling outside. Bose stops, frozen like a deer in the headlights, and for some stupid fucking reasons, doesn't take his hands off my breasts, so I help him with that step while Dr. Jones comes through the door.

"Alexander Bose, what is the meaning of this?" she demands. Shadows dance around her, and for a moment I can see the ancient entity everyone thinks she is, can imagine she really has been here since before the school was founded.

The gears stutter in his brain as I push myself away, hurrying to grab my shirt from behind his desk. I scamper over to Dr. Jones's side and she hands me a hoodie—one of Jamel's, probably plucked from the lost-and-found—that I gratefully zip over my crop top. Involuntarily, I shiver.

The gears turn, click. "You little bitch, you set me up!" he shouts, outraged. "Dr. Jones, it's not like that, she seduced me—"

"Oh, the white man blames the little black girl temptress?" Dr. Jones snorts. "Like I've never heard that one before. Neveah, darling, turn away, please."

I do as she asks and end the recording on my phone. I'll only have to edit it a little bit before we give it to the police as evidence. I ignore the sound of screams, of wetly rending flesh, of crunching bones; I'd rather keep it to my imagination when I think about Dr. Jones being a decades-old Eldritch being.

Because the thing is, all the students know our school has a monster. But she's the one that keeps us safe from the *real* evils in this city.

All she asks in return is that someone help feed the monster.

LI'L FLUBBER

★ ★ ★ ★

Theodore C. Van Alst Jr.

Tiny screams squeaked out of the tentacles writhing on the sidewalk, flailing green and bright.

Razor white lights flashed from overhead, down the alley, in his eyes. Everything had happened all at once, kinda. Ralph'd decided on a quick trip to the White Hen for some Twinkies and an RC, along with a peek at the girlie magazines behind the counter. While his eyes strained to take in as much as he could of the dozen or so titles with brown paper hiding most of the covers, hot silver flashes burst everywhere followed by a huge plopping sound, like when his ma turned a dough out onto the kitchen counter, getting ready to make bread, or whatever she did in her kingdom. He thought he should be scared of all the wriggly masses out there, but he really just wanted to go out and touch one. Hooked tips beckoned and obscene suckers pulsed, glistening and writhing, high-pitched squeals and gurgles leaking out onto the concrete of Clark Street down from the Broadway bus turnaround. He opened his Twinkies and ate half of one in a single bite, pushed the glass doors open. Standing in the dirty tiled doorway, he smiled, glowing in the opera of their shrieks—gruesome choruses from blobby clumps, gleaming divas offering hideous arias.

He slammed the rest of his Twinkies, chugged the pop, and just couldn't help himself. Picking up and swallowing a tentacle resting up for another solo, he closed his eyes as it slid down deep inside him, suddenly alive, racing for his stomach. He kept them shut tight, waited. His gut churned, a gut he longed to be free of, his addictions to sugar keeping him chubby and lonely. We'll see what happens next, he told himself, and smiled as one tentacle became dozens, reached up and popped through his arms, neck, shoulder, legs. He sprung high above the street, twisting with new freedom, thinking the only thing he needed to feed on now were souls, like he'd seen in monster movies late at night on Channel 32. Coming down in front of the convenience store doors, he burbled back inside, hungry to find out what the clerk behind the counter tasted like.

That was only a few weeks ago now, but it seemed like decades had passed since that night. His ma and sisters were gone, just as traceless as his dad so many years back. He stayed in the top-floor apartment of the six flat they'd all once shared, now by himself.

And that was okay by him. He didn't feel lonely or even alone. Spent his time figuring out who he was, what he'd become. Guess his drama that night wasn't the only one. Pop a tentacle here, or there, anywhere on his body, and his brain would start to hum with the feelings of other tentacles like his, no matter who they were attached to or where they were in this new world. Together they swallowed lots of souls. He learned a lot. Even gave himself a new name.

One thing Johnny Dynamite learned that was extra handy? Turned out souls weren't enough for him. There was booze, too. Neither of the two to survive, but both to enjoy. Okay, maybe to survive better, even if he didn't understand quite why. And yeah, he could eat if he wanted, but glances at his new rugged body told him he didn't want to. However, unless he was tentacled out, he required regular-type food. The key to cure that was going full jelly boy, but along the way he learned that he could drink all he wanted, get fucked up, have some fun, then just go back to his springy, squishy self and the hunger would pass. Like a reset button or something.

As time went on, the urge for souls came and went and his need for sugar vanished— well, mostly. At first he'd gone back to the deserted White Hen pretty regularly, barely giving the dried-up clerk behind the counter a second glance while picking through all the Good Humor bars in the freezer. His choices were down to pop-sicles when the electricity went out for the last time, and when he returned a couple days later the case held a rainbowed gooey mess that was starting to stink in ways that made him pretty much give up on food for good. He flipped the bird at the Hostess display and oozed into full tentacles, squished his way out the door.

Johnny D. also found he liked Moscato, of all things. And he hat-ed brownies. But here at the end of the world, no one gave a fuck what he liked, or didn't. No TVs, dish towels, newscasters, none of those everyday things existed to give a sense of what might be considered normal anymore.

And maybe normal was overrated. That birds could now talk seemed great, until they spent all their time complaining to humans what dumbfucks they'd been all this time. And since they already passed down stories from previous generations, people had to hear what their greatgreatgrandparents on back had done to fuck things up. Still, Johnny liked stories like this best of all. 'Cause those peo-ple had fucked up a lot. He never closed his windows anymore, left plenty of peanuts and jerky and sunflower seeds from the White Hen all over the sills. Crows and pigeons, robins and bluejays, even a little falcon one time came to visit. But never his favorite, the nighthawks.

If he thought about it long enough, he'd find himself glad to be alive in these times rather than hysterical and horrified like ev-eryone else. After all, life was pretty shit before, and after years of struggling to level up and living at home, he was delighted to see ev-eryone else level down. Sure, food was scarce, but that didn't really matter anymore, and he hadn't had a smoke in a day or two, but if you were wily, and used to being poor, things weren't too bad. And when he found four cases of screw-top Stella Rosa in the back of his local liquor store, he grabbed them up, didn't stop to judge the taste (or lack thereof, he smiled) of the looters who'd been through before him. Shiiiit. Who needed evening newscasts when you could drink as much as you wanted and not have to worry about going to some stupid job in the morning. That night, the more he drank, the more he hoped his landlord would come around wheedling for his nonexistent rent money. Johnny Dynamite had something for him, all right.

Third bottle cracked, Johnny leaned back on the couch in his apparently rent-free apartment and sent his mind back to Sunday at church with his fellow survivors. Because of course it had all started at St. Michael's. The Baptists had the Lord's fiery vengeance, but the Catholics had whole armies of pissed-off angels and hordes of unruly demons just waiting to get at each other over the long millennia since their last war. That's what he chalked this apocalypse up to. Without rich-boy and -girl "news" to tell folks what they thought had happened, or what they were paid to tell you happened, folks were left free to make up their own minds about things. And Johnny thought maybe that was the problem with the last world, the one they'd just left—folks were told what to think, what to do. And though it seemed like maybe they liked it, maybe they didn't after all. So, when the altar split wide open in a flash of fierce gold light and the guy whose name was on the door outside stepped into the breach and started with the big sword and the flames and all that, well shiiiit. That was the most honest and refreshing thing Johnny (and probably everyone else in the Lord's House that day) had seen in his entire life. And this badass with the big white wings didn't proclaim jack, didn't offer God's word or Jesus's love, just said to go CLEANSE THE WORLD. And yup. That's what folks did. Most of the assholes were gone now, and all of their money no longer meant a thing. Yeah, he thought, life was pretty good right now. He tipped the bottle all the way back, walked over to the window and sailed the empty through the back glass of an abandoned Buick three stories below. Bottle number four gave him a come hither stare from her perch on the kitchen table and he obliged.

He had to wonder though about the others who'd survived the Rain of Tentacles or whatever it would be called if anyone in the media had lived to make up a name for that beautiful night. They'd never talked to him all that much, and since he never really talked to anyone before, solitude was fine by him. Didn't stop him from wondering though, and to make sense of it all, he told himself they were just like him—brave enough to swallow a tentacle or two on their own.

Turned out he was mostly right; those who made it through had largely succumbed to their lust or gluttony, sucked down a tentacle, but the rest had prayed to St. Michael, which probably explained why he was still here: he had a double insurance policy. Well, at least they still prayed on Sundays, he figured, taking a final peek in the doors of the church he'd stopped going to after that big dramatic afternoon, deciding to do his praying at home. That's what Mrs. Louvris, the old Greek lady from down the street had told him, anyway, when she stopped him to chat the other day when he was taking a stroll around his mostly deserted neighborhood, finally deciding to end it with a trip to the 24th District cop shop to see if they'd left any guns around. While he could pretty much end the life of anyone who wasn't a jelly, it didn't hurt to have some backup if he ran into a whole gang of stiffies. Besides, all the post-apocalypse shit he'd read and watched in the movies said that guns were handy.

The 24th was abandoned. Wild to think they'd built it only a couple years ago and now look at it. Holy shit. He walked right through the front doors like he owned the place. It was a regular morgue in here, but fluorescent lights snapped overhead, their low hum already giving him a headache. Maybe there was a lonely backup generator somewhere. There were definitely a couple of dead cops splayed out on the floor with no pants on. One of them had a cheap chrome .22 drop in his sock. They still had shoes on. Johnny raised an eyebrow wondering what they'd been doing, made his way past the front desk.

More dead cops sat behind office desks, mummied out over their electric typewriters. A vending machine flickered on and off. Johnny peeked in at a row of Hot Stuff potato chips that had expired six months ago. Seven months ago, and he would've smashed the fire extinguisher on the wall over there right through the glass and eaten every bag, but today he just kept on moving, backing away from the chips and mice-chewed Baby Ruth bars on the bottom rack. He jumped as he bumped into an outstretched hand. His hair caught in the overlong fingernails of some poor sucker trapped in the holding cell who had glooped into the bars when he died, then dried out in upright eternal agony. His lips were pulled back enough that Johnny could make out a couple of fillings and a tooth that needed one. A bored fly perched on the guy's eye socket quick-buzzed its wings at him. Johnny winked back.

There were only a couple more offices until he found himself at the armory. It'd been raided and most of the good stuff was gone. He tracked back to the locker room and found the pants of the pair up front thrown on the floor by the showers. There was a .45 service pistol on one belt and a 9mm on the other. He grabbed them both and found a couple partial boxes of shells back in the armory. Good enough, he told himself. He considered taking the holsters but figured the .45 in his waistband and the 9 in his pocket would be fine, way less dorky and conspicuous. He stretched his White Sox SouthSide Hitmen t-shirt over both and headed up front, stepped out onto Clark Street.

It was quiet enough he could hear the El go by a half mile to the east. It rattled down the tracks a couple three times a week, never on a schedule, but at any rate reassuring that some things still worked, he guessed, imagining tentacled buddies manning electrical controls and train cars, keeping the lights on.

Johnny loved trains, missed taking the El. Maybe a walk down that way would be good. It was magic light time, starting to get dark, his favorite time of the day. A quick trip down to Addison if a train came by after a while, see what Wrigley Field was up to? He hadn't left the neighborhood since it all went down, so why not? Stop by the crib, pick up a bottle and go for a walk. Yeah. That was a good plan for the night.

His mind drifted as he walked the empty streets home. It occurred to him that speaking in tongues, handling snakes, and the laying on of hands appeared in neighboring passages in the Bible. Johnny hadn't been all that religious in his life, but he did go to CCD on Saturdays even if he had to attend public school during the week. He knew his ma wished he could go to St. Gregory's, but they didn't have the money for that, so Johnny's knowledge of the Bible was mostly self-directed. He liked the weird Malachi passages, sure, but Revelations were his jam. He read a thing one time in a magazine that talked about who are the three people you'd like to have dinner with or something. He didn't need a beat to say Crazy Horse, Bob Marley, and St. John the Divine. That last dude was on something, sounded like a real blast. But since it was never gonna happen, he read his stuff over and over. Good times. Johnny hit the crib, grabbed a bottle of Stella Rosa, and headed back out.

It was prime golden hour, the dreamy time when everywhere the light touched looked like faeries and elves brushed leaves and bricks with dust that would let you live forever. Every leaf on every tree tilted magic in the dying sunlight, warming even the hardest soul. Johnny loved it, because he knew, too, that right after dusk hushed the streets, the deep purpleblue of night would fall all around him, bringing his absolute favorite time of the day.

His reverie was interrupted by undeniable thoughts crowding his brain. Even though he was walking stiffy, the tentacle network told him they were going to take out all the non-jellies, including St. Michael.

Tonight.

What the fuck, that's crazy.

It's time, the network said. *We can do this.*

He wasn't too sure about that. He turned left onto Loyola from Glenwood, headed for the station. *Do we have enough people for this?* he sent into the network.

We do. You know we do, came the response.

And then what?

You'll see. We have it all worked out.

Hmmm. That seemed . . . what was the fancy word . . . debatable. And he wasn't too sure he wanted some kind of new world with new rules. The last one sucked pretty hard. He picked his way down Loyola, visions of stupid paperwork and offices pissing him off. Tuned out the network, listened for nighthawks on the hunt for mosquitoes and those jeezusfriggin flies that were everywhere here once night fell, but the birds didn't come this early anymore.

Johnny walked through the big double glass door entrance on Sheridan. All the lights were out. Maybe they came on whenever a train was running its route. The ticket booths were empty, and the little newsstand was deserted, so he hopped the turnstiles, headed upstairs.

It was him and some other guy on the dark platform. Johnny kept his distance, checked him out from the corner of his eye. He was bigger than him, at least six and a half feet. Johnny thought of himself as pretty tall, like 5'10", but this dude was way taller. He seemed to be chillin' though, just hanging out. Maybe a little lost, even. Looked around like he'd never been here before. Johnny relaxed.

Bad idea, 'cause that dude turned out to be St. Michael. At least that's what he told Johnny when he walked over to him, stuck out his hand, said, "Hey man, I'm St. Michael. How's it going?"

Johnny hesitated, of course. What the fuck was this? And sure, dude looked a little like St. Michael from what he could see of the guy's face with the blinding armor and big wings back in the church that day, but not all that much. Besides, Michael wasn't a saint, really. He didn't need to be, was born and raised upstairs. Johnny had paid attention to the interesting stuff in Catechism, looked for discrepancies.

"You all right?" this supposed Archangel said, still offering his hand.

"Yeah, I'm fine," Johnny said, taking it.

"Good, good. I'm glad you're here."

"Not sure I am," Johnny said.

"Relax, son."

"Why would I do that?" he said, checking him out. This guy was pretty casual, Levi's with combat boots and a black t-shirt. Johnny smirked at his cheesy jacket. Then he took a closer look at the silky black bomber writhing with an elaborate embroidered dragon over his left chest; green, copper, and gold scales rippled as he clenched his sky-blue taloned feet, bloody red jaws holding the head of Lucifer by the hair in its teeth. The Morning Star's right eye winked at him.

"Because you got nothing to worry about."

"I ain't so sure about that," Johnny said, reached in the pocket of his leather for the Stella Rosa. He slapped his heel on the butt of the bottle, twisted off the cap and took a big swig. His eyes watered and he offered it to this guy who said his name was St. Michael.

"Want some?" he said.

"What is it?"

"Wine, Your Eminence, or whatever I'm supposed to call you?"

"Michael is fine," the Archangel said, took the bottle and a drink.

"Why are you here?" Johnny said, watching his throat jump up and down.

"For you, I guess," St. Michael said, handing him the bottle. Johnny popped out a couple tentacles, took it with the nearest one.

"How come?"

"Because we're ending this tonight."

"Ending what?"

"All of it. You, your network. Your squiggly friends."

Johnny pulsed all this out, felt a million frantic replies. "That's bullshit," he said. "Not fair."

"I know, but that's how it's going down."

"But we've been doing what you told us to."

"Have you? Or have you been doing some … extra things?" He leaned in with those judgy eyes just like the Jesus pics in everyone's windows, the little radiant heart up top and the blessing fingers and all that.

"So, all this, the tentacles and whatnot, you, what, made a deal with some Old God or something? Isn't that blasphemy?" He waved one at him.

"It's all the Lord's work. If I had to give you a modern reference point, I'd say look at the Society of St. Edmund." The Archangel smirked. "Their charism reads, 'Unity is the sole basis of life, strength, development, and endurance for any institution.' Did you not feel the blessings and sensations of your fellow, what do you call yourselves, *jellies?*"

Wow. Kind of a dick.

"It continues. They say, 'to be open to the call and the needs of the Church, both universal and local' and what am I, *Ralph*, but the Guardian of the Church?

"Uh, my na—"

"That's right. I know your true appellation. You're named for a saint. He was from Maynooth, if you know anything about your mother's old country."

"*Saint Ralph?*"

"That's right. St. Ralph Corby. We've actually had drinks a couple of times."

"You're shitting me."

"I shit you not, as they say." Johnny D. watched him visibly relax with that usage. "Had a terrible time down here back in the day. At the hands of the Anglicans, of course."

The former Ralph Connolly could've guessed. "So, what happened?"

"He got the full English, as it were." St. Michael twitched his heavenly mouth at that. This contemporary language held interesting opportunities for humor. "Hanged half dead, drawn and quartered alive."

"Jesus Chr—"

"Don't you say it."

"Sorry. For what?"

"Doing the Lord's Work, of course."

"That's it?"

"That's it."

Johnny had a pack of Reds in his pocket. He didn't smoke much anymore but still liked one every now and again. He pulled them out, along with a baby blue Bic.

"Oh yes, and I'm bound to cast into Hell the evil who would corrupt and devour souls. Is this ringing a bell for you?"

Man, he was sooo uptight. Johnny D. tentacled an arm. "You want one of these?" he said, suckering a smoke, waving it at the archangel.

"*And*, I do the Justice thing, so, here we are," St. Michael said, looking him up and down.

"But we were doing *your* work," he burbled. "You told us to do this stuff yourself."

"You were just my instruments."

"But . . . faithful ones. Yes or no on the smoke."

"War is a long game, my son. Not to worry, though. I'm also the Angel of Death, so I can give you a lift to where you're going. No charge." The archangel looked at the smoke stuck on the end of Johnny's tentacle, popped it off, stuck it in his mouth.

"And where would that be?" Johnny asked, lighting it for him.

"We'll know when we get there, I guess. It goes up or down. That depends on you." He took a drag, blew it out long and slow. "This cigarette thing is amazing. I've seen mortals using them but never tried it before. I get it now."

Johnny's head crackled with pulses from the network. A jelly holed up in the Granada Theater down the street who'd been watching them confirmed his drinking and smoking buddy was in fact, the Archangel Michael. Waves of panic and anxiety tsunamied to either side of his mind as a clear voice cut down the middle, said *Kill him, now. Before it's too late.*

That's not possible, Johnny sent back. *If he is who you say he is, then nope.*

He's in human form. It's our only chance.

If I had a paycheck I'd bet it he don't stay that way.

Strike quick!

How the fuck was he going to do this? Michael was relaxed, full on enjoying his cigarette. He blew smoke rings that warped into cherubim and Levantine coasts, market scenes and beings he'd never explain in ten thousand lifetimes. But that didn't mean he wasn't his ever-vigilant self. Johnny knew the Archangel's eyes were watching his every move, no matter what the rest of his face said.

"You'll never win, son," his mouth confirmed Johnny's fears.

"What do you mean?"

"I'm the Archangel, man. I'm not omnipotent like You know who, but I know plenty."

"Shit," Johnny said.

"Pretty much."

NOW.

Fuck it. Figuring his pistols were useless, Johnny full jellied, went for it. He managed a moment of surprise, and they wrestled on the platform, dozens of his tentacles covering the Archangel's body, squeezing his mouth and throat.

The dragon on St. Michael's jacket roared to life, spit out Satan's head, rippled around Johnny, threw him off the wooden platform and onto the tracks. Michael burst into his true angelic form, matching eyes for tentacles, crashed down on top of him. Johnny knew he'd look like this, but was horrified nonetheless, both by the angel's form as well as his own actions. That guilt they'd always talked about was a real thing after all.

Lights down the platform fuzzed to life as Johnny tried his best to strangle the Archangel, yank out his immortal soul. He could see the lead train car, a deep crimson sign flashing to life with an "A" in the portal over the driver's window. It signaled this was an Englewood train, if that still mattered. Loyola was an A-stop, at least in the time before.

Johnny's tentacles tangled up in the tracks and the third rail as they struggled, and since the Archangel had a heavenly death grip on his throat, he quickly lost control of them altogether. The heat of a thousand burning churches arced through his flailing body as the station and the tracks snapped to life. The El never dies. The train thundered closer, and Michael rode the lightning high and fast through the acrid smoke, twisting away into night over Chicago, a thousand more Johnnys awaiting his vengeance.

Nighthawks swooped in overhead, finally coming to visit Ralph, Saint of a Dead New Order.

THE BATTLE OF FORGOTTEN PRAIRIE

★ ★ ★ ★

Priya Chand

Mindset: grindset. I have to be a winner before winter sets in. Not in here, unplaces will/do/not/have time; but there, where I was born, thin umbilicus that refuses to separate entirely, even though I've sawed and bitten and repudiated. It's pulling on me, and if it pulls too hard—if *there* and *here* are no longer linked by season, no longer share bright leaves and long, hot sunlight—I'll lose.

Here: sweet summer smell, sunwarmed straw, body shape amid the tall prairie grasses. Distant smoke rising. Too distant: controlled burns were how the Indigenous people managed this place, ensured it renewed itself, and among the voices (talking backward; even if I knew the languages I wouldn't understand them) is the occasional bark of a musket. Reality is trickling in. Wait much longer and the swathes of tall grass will be trampled beneath cows and crops, rising fences of thorns from across an ocean that doesn't exist here, overgrowth of sugar maples, *only useful things allowed*. It's like erosion, events happen on a geological scale, but still insist on happening in progression, and so the change begins its consumption of all that this prairie once was.

As a sentient, the nothing places are outside time, hard to hold on to my memories of lived events as everything/nothing happens at once/in sequence/out of order like falling leaves, but I'd studied the prairie. *Was* the prairie when my power first came in, for days at a time forgetting how to be anything smaller than an ecosystem, until the Dragon of Undoing came for me and I had to remind it that, outside time, it was not only undoing but already undone.

The Red Line still bears those scars, permanent smell and screechy rails. Those who loved it were not willing to be its next guard.

Here: fingers into dirt. Burrow through the straw and reach. Bury soil under my nails, deep-deeper to mingle-be (in the future, I remember, the future inside the world. I need to seal it there). All the sounds are setting not event. I take advantage. I fix the image of this place as it was when I first stumbled in a decade ago, loved and abundant in its loving back. Prepare to cement it once and for all time, no short-rooted invaders in the dirt, spread by trampling ignorant feet.

I linger because I don't want to return to that warm mouth of a place, roaring pollution of gas, noise, minds. Lower Wacker, Chicago, doesn't show right on the GPS. This is because it is a paper layer over a great gash in the world.

My fingers and toes are as heavy with dirt as they'll ever be. Can't grow overlong nails, that's cheating. I ease up slowly. I live in time, am a creature of time: I have aged. Back stiff, knees pop from squat to standing. I remember when it wasn't like this, but the memory isn't visceral enough to make it so here.

Foolish/not a problem/real-body's a distraction. There's/will/ always has been buzzing by my ear. Event-noise not place-noise, which means I have to pay attention because it's not a memory of how it was before the *is*, and so I clap my hands to my ears.

More than a deed: power.

The lesser angels whining by my ears spin away. Warning shot. Carefully aimed beside them, as they are aiming beside me. They're tempting me to be the aggressor. I show my hand: *I know your game.*

The beings who swoop in next on gossamer and silence snap up one, two, the whining buzz of the lesser angels' extended proboscises, six crooked legs, and in moments (except there aren't really moments, just sequences of events) the mosquito-beings scatter and it is only me and the greater angels with their luminescent bodies.

"Leave," one/all of them say/s.

"This place is mine," I snarl, I am, I extend. Raise encrusted fingernails that shade into dirty palms: this place is me. The angels don't fully grasp the distinctions of flesh, the shapes they wear now are little more than optical illusion.

They have no answer. They swoop at me. Try to intimidate me into batting at them, scattering the dirt from under my nails, but we were allied against the Dragon, and because they have no time they are still allied, still mine, as long as I don't cave in and counter-attack.

I force myself past the edge of the prairie into the nothing space where lost ideas go (don't tell me the pre-Columbian prairie is lost, too; I found it) and back and back and the crowbar in my jacket comes out, gripped in tight pale fingers, and runes I close my eyes against glow and twist, and—

The warm mouth of Lower Wacker Drive is on me and a car skates by honk-honk—but there's no personality in the sound, just mechanics, and I force myself to the riverfront and it's all just people inside their own skin, and I think:

It isn't fair.

It isn't fair I have to be one of them.

I have to play by the rules of this world where I had no choice but to be born, find what little soil remains of my prairie *here* so that I can connect to it *there*,

and, physical senses buffeted by a summer evening on a human-chaotic riverfront, my thoughts aren't disjointed enough for the magic to work right but at last I remember how to fold myself outside of logic and spend the night safe, sleeping in a drifting balloon loosed from the hand of a child who doesn't yet know what birthdays are.

And I wake up and I'm human, except humans can't be inside balloons and so I fall out with a pop and go screaming toward the earth until I remind gravity that I'm better than it, better than this stiffened body with all its demands for material comfort,

and land on two feet whose shape I can see winding all the way back through protein scaffolding into DNA, and resent the millennia of physicality weighing me down, and, having followed me into time, a swarm of angels rushes at me, except they look like mosquitoes and so here I am, on a warm summer morning in the heart of the city of Chicago, just outside the sacred electric loop, swatting at myself slap-slap-slap, twisting and writhing but it's not enough, they've really anchored themselves *here*, my purpose begins crumbling as my mind turns to resisting them, but inspiration flashes and I jump forward and dive into the filthy shallow water with a great SPLASH (broadcasting to the onlookers this is impossible, and therefore there is nothing to remember), and the mosquitoes/lesser angels drown because they let the shape of their bodies anchor themselves and for a moment I am free.

And a moment in time is all I need to skate across the city streets, find the ones which connect to the broken-souled suburbs, and with my senses extended I feel the lesser angels wander lost and, once I'm sure they're too far to pick up my trail easily, I withdraw my awareness of them (magic has no one-way streets) and go go go to where the, my, mine, prairie remnant is waiting, fly over the dead dull highways and the living lines of trains and—

The greater angels have set up a cordon. Of course they have, it's not like there is much prairie to search among, here in the 21st century. A whole line of not-dragonflies, a couple of onlookers— parent-child pair—taking photos, oohing and aahing, no questions as to if this is really how dragonflies behave, and so in that moment of wonder the greater angels have an in to the world, and I—

I fight. Because we are in the world, and I can/need/want to.

I ripple my hands through air, remind myself nitrogen-oxygen-trace elements and throw handfuls at them, remember ozone and throw that too, the burning crackle of half-remembered news articles in my mind.

Eat reality, you fuckers.

But they've brought the full strength of their kind to bear, and borrowed more besides, and I feel my feet slipping on the asphalt, and remember friction and $F = MA$ and Newton and physics, my god I hated that subject, only took what was required for an environmental sciences major, put the force of my hate and the weight of unmet expectations (*why aren't you doing something more profitable*) at my back and—yes—they can't budge me. They can't budge me enough.

They are keening. The watching parent-child fade away, parent suddenly remembers not to leave child standing around in the presence of an ambiguously clothed stranger. Sweet suburban fear of the unknown. The line of dragonflies is easily dismissed as animal behavior, and besides, everyone knows they don't harm people.

Good.

The angels scream impotence as I dig my fingers into the dirt, real soil mixing with the so/i/u/l wedged under my nails, and they're too late. And they know it, and they can beat all they like against my eardrums, and I don't care

but I am not done.

There is one more piece left.

The dirt, precious, under my nails as I walk out of the bare patch of nature preserve, this minuscule fragment of the mighty prairie that once defined this region, I cannot let it unwedge. I ignore the angels beating at my unprotected face, sucking my veins with all the instinct of their mosquito forms, fine-veined wings of the greater angels darting back and forth across my vision, I am purpose I am slipping across the city-veins to the long lit tunnel of Lower Wacker where there lies the greatest crack in all this world's reality, and ever so softly with my fingers held flat I draw out my rune-engraved crowbar and pry it into this gap, and against the pressure of the will of angels I work it back and forth until it is just enough for me to slip through and

the space is nothing, from the perspective of reality. It's a gap between spaces. It's filled with concepts that have fallen through the cracks, a landfill for the collective memory of humanity (and, as always, I wonder if there's pathways that lead to things forgotten by other living beings, if they're even capable of forgetting like we are, or if it's all instinct wound in their DNA like the scientists used to believe). I turn right at the *use-all-parts* and wind through a narrow corridor of *nothing-is-disposable* and then there is one last membrane to get through, filmy wings and iridescent and translucent whining bodies all together. We stood together against the dragon. I turn my heels and they turn, too, unable to resist facing the same direction as me. Unable to resist me, outside time.

"Don't," they echo, a reminder of thoughts I will/had/haven't. We're still in the unformed not-space. Things are more conceptual here:

I remember reluctance, shame-clutch around my heart; if I take the prairie for myself it will be eternal/isolated/untouchable. And then what's the point/benefit/good (here a vague twinge of English class, the ancient philosophical version like the briefest flare of magnesium light)? If I am the only one who gets to see it?

The soil packed under my nails starts loosening. Once it escapes, the prairie is free to others—to change.

"No," I growl, assert the first moment I realized this was the best thing I could do with the rest of my life, starting to unspool as it is, body increasing its physical demands year by year, asserting reality over magic—reality is killing the/my prairie, settler-shadow falling across the landscape that, later, will be blotted out by roads and buildings and carelessness. There won't be a prairie for anyone at all, eventually. The best thing I can do is clutch it tight.

The dirt recedes into me, pries open space between the soft beds and my nails. It is excruciating/right/power/lancing red-bright jets at the angels, a hose I only have to aim that blasts them away, and sideways I turn, in this place without direction, and—

Mine.

Sink my still-spurting fingers into the earth.

Mine.

Nails grow/crack/change. The angels have followed me in, buffeted now by rising wind, sweet straw-smell I batter them with, waves of gold and hints of green and twenty shades of flower.

The sky is not their friend. The sky is closer to me, my jaw reaching long to drink in the infinite blue, wrap my tail around the whole of it as the first pinpricks stab my stretching skin. They can hurt me now. They're sworn to fight dragons.

Greed, they hiss at me, circling around so I pivot and pivot my body after them, snapping up one, another, quickly replaced by more. Greed,

I snag this title with my teeth, shake it over myself, expanding armor, scales everywhere (I think there's a spot on my head too reflective to absorb it, but no matter, my ear is long and spiny and hides it well), claws penetrating the earth's secret core, entwined in the deep deep roots of grasses that have held the soil together for millennia, all *mine*, for/by/of me,

and the angels rush at me, and we fight.

CONTENT WARNINGS

Lucky Charms: racist violence and language

Notes from the Dunning Asylum: mental illness neglect

The Papergirl: Violence. Story based on an infamous murder spree. References to murder, suicide, drug use, real and fictional killers.

Pedal to the Floor into Darkness: references to suicide

Lowest Wacker: impliction of suicide

Just Another Friday Night in Bucktown: sexual harassment

Lives Matter: eye trauma, animal death

The Avalon Haint: elder abuse

A Good Kid: child death

Endless, Nameless: eye trauma, gore, violence, death, dead animal

Body Cam: police brutality

Feed the Monster Evil: references to past child abuse and child pornography by a teacher, semi-graphic depictions of current abuse by a teacher, and a mild moment of gore near the end

BIOS

Authors

Jotham Austin II has a PhD in Botany and specializes in electron microscopy as a research associate professor at The University of Chicago. He is the author of the sci-fi psychological thriller *Will You Still Love Me, If I Become Someone Else?* and is represented by Kat Kerr at DMLA. As a board member of the Chicago Writers Association, he directs the Book Of The Year contest. Jotham also co-hosts the Rabbit Hole of Research podcast, exploring the science in fiction and separating real science from Handwavium in sci-fi, fantasy, and pop culture.

Bendi Barrett (he/him) is a Black speculative fiction writer, game designer, and definitely-alive person living precariously close to Graceland Cemetery in Chicago. He's published interactive novels through Choice of Games, and his debut novella *Empire of the Feast* was a 2023 Ignyte Best Novella finalist. He also writes queer erotic fiction as Benji Bright and runs a Patreon for the thirsty masses. He can be found at benmakesstuff.com and occasionally on bluesky as @bendibarrett.bsky.social.

Tina Jenkins Bell, a published speculative fiction writer, playwright, and literary activist, recently won Definition Theater's Amplify competition for her play *Death of a Marriage*. Her short stories have appeared in numerous journals/anthologies, including *The Overturning*, featuring her short story, "Kaiko." She is finishing her novel manuscript, *Down and Dirty in Kosciusko, Mississippi*, is a co-founder of FLOW (For Love of Writing), and collaborates with other authors/literary groups to offer literary programming on Chicago's southside.

Tara Betts is the author of *Refuse to Disappear*, *Break the Habit*, and *Arc & Hue*. In addition to her published essays, poems, interviews, and book reviews, Betts's short stories have appeared in *Octavia's Brood*, *Midnight & Indigo: Twenty-Two Speculative Stories by Black Women Writers*, *Between the Covers: A Bookstore Erotica Anthology*, *Best Women's Erotica Vol. 1*, and *Best Black Women's Erotica 2*.

Priya Chand has ridden approximately 95% of the Chicago El train lines, which she can confirm are a great way to bear witness to 3am eldritch horrors. She has previously been published in the *Death in the Mouth* anthologies and *Nightmare Magazine*, and can be found online at priyachandwrites.wordpress.com.

TJ Cimfel is an award-winning screenwriter, author, and creative director based in Chicago. His latest film, *Don't Move*, was one of Netflix's biggest hits of 2024. His other films include *There's Something Wrong with the Children*, *Intruders*, and *V/H/S: Viral*. His fiction has appeared in *The Dark Magazine*, Crystal Lake Publishing's *Never Wake* anthology, and Kangas Kahn's *October Screams* anthology. You can find him @tj_cimfel on Insta or IRL at The Brewed.

RL Gehringer grew up on the north side of Chicago and attended Chicago Public Schools. After high school, he drove delivery vans and Yellow Cabs. RL has two grown children and resides with his wife in Northern California, where he likes to catch fish and snakes. He eats the fish and releases the snakes. Being a boomer, RL's only social media is Facebook. Feel free to contact him there.

Christopher Hawkins is the multi-award-winning author of *Downpour* and *Suburban Monsters*. He is the former editor of the *One Buck Horror* anthology series and the co-chair of the Chicagoland chapter of the Horror Writers Association. When he's not writing, he spends his time exploring old cemeteries, lurking in museums, and searching for a decent cup of tea. For more information about his upcoming projects, visit his website, christopher-hawkins.com, or follow him on Bluesky @christopherhawkins.bsky.social and

Instagram/Threads @hawkinswrites.

Sandra Jackson-Opoku is author of the novels *The River Where Blood Is Born* and *Hot Johnny and the Women Who Loved Him*. Her debut mystery *Savvy Summers and the Sweet Potato Crimes* was published in July 2025. Jackson-Opoku's fiction, nonfiction, and dramatic works are widely published and produced. Professional recognition includes a National Endowment for the Arts Fellowship, the American Library Association Black Caucus Award, a Chicago Esteemed Artist Award, an Iceland Writers Retreat Alumni Award, the Globe Soup Story Award, a Pushcart Prize nomination, and others. She presents literary programs and writing workshops across the country and worldwide.

Aleco Julius is the author of *Weird Tales of the Great Lakes* and *Endless Depths: Cosmic Themes, Weird Lore, & Hidden Knowledge*. His fiction has appeared in publications such as *Dark Matter Magazine, Dolls in the Attic, Always Night, Writers Retreat*, and *Anterior Skies*. Look for his essays in *Hellebore, Vastarien, Myth & Lore, Cold Signal Magazine, Seeds of Ares*, and more. He lives beneath the busy skies of Midway Airport.

Born in Chicago, Illinois, **Nick Medina** is the author of *Sisters of the Lost Nation* and *Indian Burial Ground*. His third novel, *The Whistler*, will be available from Berkley on September 16, 2025. Connect with him on nickmedina.net, Instagram (@nickmedinawrites), and X (@MedinaNick).

Jen Mierisch's dream job is to write *Twilight Zone* episodes, but until then, she's a website administrator by day and a writer of odd stories by night. Jen's work can be found in the *Arcanist, NoSleep Podcast, Scare Street*, and numerous anthologies. Jen can be found haunting her local library near Chicago. She is an active member of the Horror Writers Association.

Sahar Mustafah's first novel *The Beauty of Your Face* was named a 2020 Notable Book and Editor's Choice by *New York Times Book Review*, and one of *Marie Claire Magazine*'s 2020 Best Fiction by Women. It was long-listed for the Center for Fiction 2020 First Novel Prize, and was a finalist for the Palestine Book Awards. Most recently, her short story "Star of Bethlehem" was awarded the Lawrence Prize for Best Fiction in 2022 by *Prairie Schooner*, and her short story "Tree of Life" won the 2023 Robert J. DeMott Prize, selected by author Kirstin Valdez Quade. Her latest story "The Peacock" is featured in *Stories from the Center of the World: New Middle East Fiction* (City Light Books, May 2024). Mustafah was awarded a 2023 Jack Hazard Fellowship from New Literary Project, and a 2023 Illinois Arts Council Agency grant. She writes and teaches outside of Chicago.

Cynthia Pelayo is a Bram Stoker Award–winning author. Her novels include *Vanishing Daughters*, *Forgotten Sisters*, *Children of Chicago*, and *The Shoemaker's Magician*. She is also the editor of *Ghosts of Where We Are From*, a Latinx Horror anthology featuring today's bestselling Latin American authors. In addition to writing genre-blending novels that incorporate elements of fairy tales, mystery, detective, crime, and horror, Pelayo has written numerous short stories and the poetry collection *Crime Scene*. The recipient of the 2021 International Latino Book Award, she holds a Master of Fine Arts in writing from the School of the Art Institute of Chicago. She lives in Chicago with her family. For more information, visit cinapelayo.com.

K.A. Roy (she/her) haunts the suburbs of Chicago alongside her family and three cats. Her work has been featured at *Shotgun Honey*, *Creepy Podcast*, *Malarkey Books*, *Spindle House*, and more. Find her at kayleighroywrites.com

K. Saab (they/them) has wanted to be an author since they were eight years old, rewriting their favorite novels to feature their stuffed animals. Nowadays, their characters and stories are a little more original and a little less cotton-stuffed, frequently exploring the queer, disabled, Arab-diaspora experience in weird and fantastical situations. When not writing, Saab can be found reading, playing video games, sewing, cross-stitching, lesson-planning and grading, or snuggling with their two cats. (To be fair, they can also be found snuggling the cats when they are writing. Cats are demanding.) They live in Chicago with those two cats and a pretty cool fiancé.

C.J. Subko is a dreamer and a dabbler. She has a Ph.D. in Clinical Psychology from Michigan State University and a B.A. in Psychology and English from the University of Notre Dame, which makes her highly qualified to think too much. Her short fiction publications include *Die Laughing* (October 2024), *Small Wonders* (November 2024), *Morgana le Fay* (Flame Tree Press; March 2025), *The Deadlands* (April 2025), and an upcoming issue of *Penumbric Speculative Fiction*. She is a member of the HWA and SFWA. Her novels are represented by Maria Brannan at Greyhound Literary Agency. She can be found at www.cjsubko.com.

Theodore C. Van Alst Jr. is the author of Chicago-set award-winning story collections *Sacred Smokes* and *Sacred City* as well as the editor of *The Faster Redder Road: The Best UnAmerican Stories of Stephen Graham Jones*. His co-edited (with Shane Hawk) *Never Whistle at Night: An Indigenous Dark Fiction Anthology* was published in September 2023 by Vintage/Penguin Random House and has been a finalist for the Bram Stoker, British Fantasy, Locus, and Shirley Jackson Awards. His Southern Gothic novella *Pour One for the Devil* was released by Lanternfish Press in March 2024 and his third collection of linked stories, *Sacred Folks*, was published Fall 2024 by the University of New Mexico Press. His debut novel, *The El*, was published by Vintage/Penguin Random House in 2025. His work has appeared in *Southwest Review*, *Chicago Review*, *The Journal of Working-Class Studies*, *Massachusetts Review*, *Red Earth Review*, *Indian Country Today*, and elsewhere.

Lauren Emily Whalen's sapphic horror story "We Did It" is free to read on Chain Letter, a platform of short-form horror produced by Electric Postcard Entertainment (weeklychainletter.substack.

com). Her latest novel *Tomorrow and Tomorrow* (Sword & Silk, 2023) is a "cozy horror" reimagining of Shakespeare's Macbeth through the perspective of an all-female Southern rock band, co-authored with Lillah Lawson. Lauren has published novels, nonfiction books, short stories, articles, and essays about everything from Catholic school to Dutch cartoon rabbits to circus erotica to queer-coded Taylor Swift albums. Her book *I Heart Jennifer Coolidge: A Celebration of Your Favorite Pop Culture Icon* (Running Press/Hachette, 2024) paid off her student loans. You may have seen her performing in Chicago storefront theaters on Friday nights in the 2010s. Instagram, BlueSky, and LinkTree @laurenemilywrites.

Editor

Michael W. Phillips Jr. (he/him) is the publisher of From Beyond Press. His fiction has appeared in various now-defunct magazines and is forthcoming (someday) in the *Magazine of Fantasy and Science Fiction*. He is the editor of *This World Belongs to Us: An Anthology of Horror Stories about Bugs* and *Fettered and Other Tales of Terror* by Greye La Spina, and the co-editor of *Escalators to Hell: Shopping Mall Horrors* (with Jennifer Jeanne McArdle) and *Xanax Hamster* (with Ende Mac). He worked for twenty years in Chicago's film exhibition industry, and he makes found-footage music videos and short documentaries for and about Chicago musicians. He lives in Hyde Park.

Cover Artist

Daimon Hampton is a comic book artist in Chicago. He has been self-publishing comics since 2012, and was selected to be in DC Comics' Milestone Initiative in 2022. He is well known by like dozens of people for the comics *Microphone Misfits: Escape From Babylon, Become, The Rose Society, Stellar Remnant, The Archon Experiment,* and *Story of Solace*. People have said he's a good artist; he knows all those people personally but why would they lie?